OTHER RANKS

OTHER RANKS

W. V. TILSLEY

WITH AN INTRODUCTION BY
EDMUND BLUNDEN

UNIFORM

Published by Uniform
An imprint of Unicorn Publishing Group
5 Newburgh Street London W1F 7RG

www.unicornpublishing.org

A catalogue record for this book is available from
the British Library

5 4 3 2 1

ISBN 978-1-912690-18-3

Cover design Unicorn Publishing Group
Typeset by Vivian@Bookscribe

Printed and bound in the UK

CONTENTS

ACKNOWLEDGEMENTS

For their military knowledge I would like to give thanks to Jane Davies (Curator) and her team at the Lancashire Infantry Museum, Preston; the Great War historian Jonathan D'Hooghe; the military historian Paul McCormick (www.loyalregiment.com); and Ian Verrinder, author of *Tank Action in the Great War*. And special thanks to my editor, Emily Lane, for her unwavering help and support.

PREFACE

The first time I read *Other Ranks* it would have been a near impossibility to find much information on the characters and events mentioned in the book. Nearly thirty years on, with the availability of records on the internet, WWI became well-worn keys on my computer. *Other Ranks* has also been singled out for mention in various websites as having literary merit, and enquiries followed in regard to possible republication.

I first took a serious interest in the book when I came across a handwritten letter sent to my husband John's uncle, Ernest Magnall, dated December 1931 (see below, pp. 243–4). This was from the book's author, Bill Tilsley – William Vincent Tilsley, known to his family as Vincent, and in my mind as WVT – who I now know to be 'Bradshaw' in *Other Ranks*. The tone of the letter is very warm, and talks of WVT being pleased that the book has elicited a response from Ernest. As well as referring to how they have both fared post-war, the letter acknowledges that Ernest is Bagnall, and that proper names could not be used in the book 'without running the risk of hurting certain people'. The wish of the author was 'to be truthful without being spiteful'.

What I found poignant when I researched WVT was that his 'small boy of two years', John, who was mentioned in the letter, died suddenly aged ten. This tragic event was followed two and a half years later by his own untimely death. WVT left his widow, Bessena (Bessie), but no direct descendants. By chance and through his membership of a bowling club (many years ago!) I was able to trace Bessie's nephew Don Wild, who miraculously had WVT's copy of *Other Ranks*. The book had been dedicated to his son John, and it contained a photograph of him in uniform dated 1918.

I was able to find more about WVT through his great-niece and nephews. WVT's younger brother Frank had become a celebrated novelist and broadcaster. It was Frank's granddaughter who directed me to his great-nephew, David Tilsley, who is the Lancashire Archives Collection Manager, and David was able to provide me with some very interesting information (see below, pp. 230–7). The Tilsleys, though from a modest background, were a very talented lot.

Having had confirmation from WVT's letter that *Other Ranks* was based on real events and that the characters had existed, I reread the book (several times) and started to look for the names behind the pseudonyms. The author and dedicatees were easy enough: Tilsley = Bradshaw, Magnall = Bagnall, O'Neill = Driver.

Ernest Magnall's family has a reputation for not throwing anything away. His service records no longer exist, but every piece of paper they were given from his time in the war survives, including documentation issued after he was taken as a wounded prisoner of war at Passchendaele.

The search for Charles O'Neill wasn't quite so straight-forward. Despite many clerical errors and misspellings of his surname I eventually discovered his records. It would have been a tall order looking for an O'Neill descendant in the Manchester area – with or without the right spelling. Fortunately while looking at a post for Charles on the Loyal North Lancashire Regiment website I found a comment left by his nephew Francis. The site owners enabled contact, and I was keen to tell Francis about *Other Ranks*; in turn he gave me a copy of a photograph of Charles as a boy and a rich account of his discoveries (see below, pp. 248ff).

Many resources have been available online. None was completely accurate, but I would have been unable to find information about the soldiers without them. I cross-referenced the Loyal North Lancashire Regimental Book and diaries, the records of the Commonwealth War Graves Commission (CWGC, originally the Imperial War Graves Commission) and the British Army, and checked with the volunteers at the Lancashire Infantry Museum in Preston. They were able to give me the service numbers of the Manchester and East Lancashire drafts who joined the 1/4th Loyal North Lancashire Regiment in August 1916, and with familiarity I found that the numerals gave information as to whether the men were 'Festubert' (veterans of an attack at Festubert on 15 June 1915), Regular, Derby (recruited under a voluntary scheme instituted by Lord Derby), or conscripts.

The pattern that emerged from the British Army records was that, in the main, soldiers in the 1/4th Loyal North Lancashire Regiment who had been killed in action (or otherwise died) had their service records removed and filed in a different section. The War Office repository was bombed in September 1940; these records, classed WO363, survived, and became known as the 'burnt documents'. The casualty form which is part of the service records gives details of postings, illness, death, and quite often handwritten at the top of the page the company that the soldier had served with.

I restricted my search to the men of C Company between 16 August 1916 and 20 September 1917, with two exceptions: Lt Agostini in B Company (whose daughter I made contact

with in Florida), and Jem Fletcher, medical orderly, in D
Company.

As one finds information or sees photographs of the
characters mentioned in *Other Ranks* there is a real feeling
of having known them. For some of his fellow soldiers his
modus operandi to disguise their names was to change the
odd letter here and there: Hogg/Fogg, Hore/Gore, Isles/
Wiles. But if they had died, or he was going to be a little too
candid in his account, he would alter the name completely.
That would also happen with the dates of death. In a letter
to Thomas Hope Floyd (also a former soldier and author)
WVT makes the point that in some published works a little
more care could have been taken in the spelling of place
names, etc., so clearly his changes in chronology were not
just mistakes! In the Floyd correspondence there is reference
to the 'binge' and 'march' of 15 and 16 June 1917, which are
also spoken of in the Regimental Book.

Two features stood out when I looked at the records of the
soldiers – their height and build, and their religion. Ernest is
described in *Other Ranks* as tall compared to his companions.
We know him to have been 5 ft 7½ in. That would not be
regarded as tall now; but after viewing the medical forms in
the surviving records I found that the average height of these
men from the cities was about 5 ft 5 in., and that they had
a slight build. The second was religion. I learned from my
mother, who grew up in 1920s Manchester, that Catholics
and Protestants did not mix. But in the war men from all
religions were thrown together. In *Other Ranks* the religion
of the three main characters is not mentioned, except for
Bradshaw's late baptism on the front. We now know it is

unlikely that WVT came from a religious family: his sisters did not get christened until the outbreak of war, and his brother stated 'atheist/C of E' on his enlistment papers. But this didn't appear to be a barrier to him becoming close friends with Charles O'Neill, a practising Roman Catholic, and Ernest Magnall, a Methodist.

WVT states at the beginning of *Other Ranks* that 'None of the characters in this chronicle is fictitious.' It had not been my intention to discover the identities of so many soldiers, but with each reread and search of the internet another name and lead would turn up, often in an unexpected way. One of the characters is Downes. There was a Lowndes listed in the Regimental Book as a casualty with B Company, but some time later when looking through another soldier's record I came across Lowndes' casualty record: it had been misfiled, and clearly showed he had served with C Company. This happy find also recorded that from 22 September to 10 October 1916 he had been in a working party attached to XV Corp Salvage Company, possibly as stated in *Other Ranks* alongside Bradshaw/WVT.

More than fifty characters are identified to date (see below, pp. 263–4), and there are still men I would like to put a real name to: Lt Gray (Uncle), Lt Stanbridge, Slater, Birtles, Stansfield – and more. From the new year of 1917 it became more difficult to ascertain which regiment a soldier had belonged to, as more men were sent via Base Depot to strengthen the depleted companies. I have found that on CWGC records some soldiers are listed as serving with the 1/4th although they had been attached from other regiments. It was also difficult to trace a soldier if he had been transferred to or from another regiment and chosen this as his preferred medal choice.

Initially I had some misgivings about revealing the true identity of the men who were held in low regard by WVT. Presumably any soldier of C Company who read *Other Ranks* when it was published would have recognised those officers and men. With the passage of a hundred years I don't feel the concealment to be as necessary.

WVT describes Bradshaw landing in France in August 1916 as an innocent nineteen-year-old, with little comprehension of what he was about to encounter. Over the next fourteen months he vividly encounters the horrors and 'fed-upness' of daily life, and through the chronicle of *Other Ranks* we see the change in him from month to month. By Christmas 1916 he has become one of the 'old hands' who had so awed him when he first arrived.

In addition to the interest of the book itself, I think that anyone who found that their relative had served with the 1/4th Loyal North Lancashire Regiment on the Somme and at Ypres would find a good account of their time and conditions in Vincent Tilsley's *Other Ranks*.

Gaye Magnall

OTHER RANKS

INTRODUCTION

'THE strength of the raiding party will be 2 Officers and 30 Other Ranks.' The ancient operation order was lying on my table – had the raid been finally enforced, it would probably not have been – at the time when Mr. Tilsley's book was brought to me, so that I might have the privilege of an early perusal. I was trying to pierce the obscuration of fourteen years, and to shape again the figures and the characteristics, the business and the condition, of the 30 Other Ranks. The other officer named, for many reasons, was at once clear and animated in my memory; I heard him dryly commenting, as he looked up from lacing his tall boots, on the paper warfare which accompanied all our enterprise. As I scanned the list of the other raiders – the bombing and blocking parties, the mopping-up party, liaison party, and covering parties, I found that many names had gone from my mind, and not many faces looked out from the shadow of the sanded steel hats. It was not all the fault of time and the blessings of peace. The Battle of the Somme had beaten the life out of our battalion; reinforcements had come and many of them had gone; we had been almost hourly changing, and I had scarcely set eyes on a large number of the men now about to be under my direction.

What their daily and nightly experience was, and against what background, it was easier to revive, although in general terms. I saw them as Fate's prisoners, under a winter sky, sometimes darkly twining more wire on the eastern extremity of our snow-grey prison yard, sometimes moving westward – a few hundred paces – along the concealing wall of clay and metal, with burdens that sometimes moaned. I saw them in erratic processions, desperately 'keeping touch' as they met with puzzles of the trench system and traffic, or new obstacles where shells had turned the ditches into clammy mounds; and I saw them in isolated groups, eyeing the opposite parapet, nodding in anxious short sleep, dishing out the tea and cheese and bacon, and waiting for the retaliation which would fall on them in return for our gunners' work on the German sentry-groups. Then there they were in the town behind the line, marching to the baths in some brewery, organising little estaminet suppers, laying out rows of kit for inspection in their loft, and on parade with every button and buckle and badge polished as though, after all, that art gave as rich a satisfaction as any in the world. I was only at the beginning of my thought of these men. Had I pursued it, I knew that I could never completely reconstruct their war. Between the ordinary infantry officer and them there were wonderful bonds; bombardment, mud, attack, sleeplessness, exposure, over-strain, fear, humour, home, affected all in the prison of the front line; we often shared the same mug of tea, and the same smother of clods and cordite. Intense friendships were formed that defeated the barriers of military rank.

But tradition, routine, and management, together with the impossibility of being in more than one place at one time, did prevent the Officers from being entirely in the intimacies of the Other Ranks; each type, indeed, respected the other's right to a world of its own; and that is why, from the first, Mr. Tilsley's account, with all its openness and its circumstantial nicety, was a great discovery. For me, in particular, it had also the fascination, which I have almost given up trying to analyse, of showing me a period and a number of places and episodes which I had passed through; Mr. Tilsley's Potijze is the sub-sector in which the raiding party mentioned above was intended to 'capture prisoners, secure identifications, and kill as many of the enemy as possible'. Probably I saw Bradshaw, and he saw me, when my Division was relieving his; I remember the agonising wet cold in which I first followed his battalion doctor round those dejected breastworks, behind which the lively expressions of some of his Other Ranks seemed as actual light and heat in the livid dusk. When Mr. Tilsley says Haymarket, I know which Haymarket he means; indeed, I have never quite recognised the other one. All this is personal, but war-books are largely so. I have met innumerable strangers with whom the introduction of a name like Harley Street – not everybody's Harley Street! – or Kemmel was a sudden means of hearty and natural conversation. It may be that the recollections aroused are wholly terrible in themselves; but the names, now meaningless to the majority, are talismans of mutual approach to those who have moved on from Cuinchy and Dickebusch to Oldham and Market Deeping.

There must be, in Mr. Tilsley's resourceful and beautiful narrative, a number of terms of several kinds which, to the survivors, are everything, and to the rest are little or nothing. The title itself, which in its use during the war obtained such a complexity of significance, cannot now be instantaneous in its effect on a new generation, any more than the sight of a solid street reveals the Ypres of this book to the tourist. The map of Flanders in its war arrangement, which underlies all narratives of this kind, is no longer familiar to the public. In a way, Mr. Tilsley's war will be less bewildering in its topography than others, for, once his characters had been moved north to the salient, they (like my own Division) had the bad luck to stay there, month after month, as if for ever. Whatever these technical difficulties may be, they are in sum no important disadvantage; the humanity of the work presses on, the nervous exaltation and the tragic action are such as to bear the reader over all the momentary intrusions of a forgotten terminology.

It would be a bold man who could assure himself that even the most poignant statements of the nature of the war 1914–1918 have the power of restraining the race from future confusion of the same sort, and perhaps deadlier. If Regan and Goneril had been persuaded to borrow from their libraries the latest work on the atrocious behaviour of an earlier Regan and Goneril to the King their father, would they have refrained from proceeding with their own intrigues against Lear? Were I of the new generation, should I have the imaginative sympathy to turn away from present delights and perplexities and to bind my thoughts to the monotonous emplacements of an obviously absurd and long-finished war? Should I connect the past with the future so curiously as to suppose that by knowing the past I might have some influence on the future? Probably not. Yet it is to be wished, and remembered in our prayers, that the new generation shall have time and matter for clear reflection before the next challenge arises, before the spirit of adventure

and ambition of 'glorious life' are again made to serve a cause
which ought not to have their help.

I should call Mr. Tilsley's book one of the most valuable
warnings that have been written; in the first place, it is written
with natural strength and decision, and its words and their
movements convey, almost physically, an eager picture of
the strange multitudinous original. Then it has the voice of
the men (some hardly more than youths) who truly bore the
burden of the war, the sort of men who on March 21st, 1918,
especially were the loneliest of their race, and were destroyed
in their places on the parapet. They were the 'willing horses',
like and more numerous than the tired but unconquerable
subalterns in Mr. Sherriff's play; their experiences were
extreme, and the few of them whose excellence did not lead
to their extinction are rarely ready writers. Mr. Tilsley is of the
few, and has written in a masterly style a specimen of their
terribly multiplied experiences. His reader has not to wait
long for a record of what they encountered in the Battle of the
Somme on a September afternoon. 'Where was everybody?'
There were degrees of misery in the prison, and these men
accepted the worst. What was the worst? They never seemed
to touch bottom; for some passed with scarcely a break from
the Somme of 1916 to the Passchendaele battle of 1917; from
that to the storms of 1918. The newspapers reported that
'Sliding is Tommy's Chief Recreation on the Western Front'
when these men were being blown out of frozen shell-holes
by torrents of shattering flame.

Weariness was their principal protest, if it can be called
such; and in this I feel the fidelity of Mr. Tilsley's retrospect.
He does not advance arguments in frenzying effects. His

scenes (he missed nothing) are completed without an eye to his own personality. The ground is incidentally reported in its hideousness; its immediate interest is that it is to be crossed by the battalion, and it will only be crossed by superhuman exertions and resolution. The forces of death, even, seem subordinated to this tired but onward soldiering; Bradshaw, doing what is demanded of him, scrutinises the latest sacrificial arena coolly. The colours of gun-flashes impress him as the sign of a barrage of unprecedented concentration – and very extravagant. A huge shell dropping just behind him only makes him think of the *Arabian Nights*. When he is hit, he accepts the opportunity as the only one which could relieve him from the line moving on to the concrete forts; but he finds his way out of the battle with the method of one who has learned all that can be learned of the ways of the artillery, and even as he passes through he criticises a roaring area bombardment as expensive and wasteful. Such were the men who usually remained as Other Ranks until death or wounds transferred them, the closest witnesses of war, the men we trusted to be the same in the next attack as they had been in the last, and to go on leave once to our own three times. They have a candid historian and a survivor in Mr. Tilsley.

EDMUND BLUNDEN

None of the characters in this chronicle is fictitious.

NOT until he saw those seven peculiar-looking kite balloons, steel-grey and still against the evening sky, did Dick Bradshaw realise he was actually near the front. Even then, with those sentinels marking the line of the trenches, he believed some power would impose itself, single him out, expose his deficiencies, and send him back on some duty where he might help only from behind. All the way from Étaples he had been expecting an inspection, when some great general would stand before him and say: 'Fight for England – you? Run away, boy, and come back when you're a man!'

But his draft, and another from an East Lancashire battalion – all of them Derby men – had reinforced a depleted West Lancashire battalion without any such interruption. Now he tried to analyse his feelings, for the hundredth time, towards fighting.

He walked thoughtfully along the river-bank – the Somme, he supposed – towards those balloons, on his way to a B.E.F. canteen. The centre one appeared much higher than the three on either side, and, as he looked, a number of small dark puffs sprang around it, like bees about a hive. He walked up quickly behind a group of soldiers whose divisional mark – a square red patch under the collar – proclaimed them as old stagers. He learnt that the bees were German anti-aircraft shells, aimed at some British aeroplane in the same line of vision as the sausage balloon.

In the canteen, he shyly bought several bars of chocolate, then moved quickly away from the sophisticated groups at the counter towards the door, where he met Driver, of their draft. Driver was round-eyed. He motioned Bradshaw outside and cocked up his brow, ears intent.

'Hear anything?'

From where the balloons were came a rippling vibration, with louder sounds like a distant shaking of blankets. Neither of them could believe that each of the separate explosions making up that quivering of the air was the discharge of a gun. Driver entered the canteen, reappearing in a short time with a steel shaving-mirror. Bradshaw wondered whether he had purchased it for the same reason that he himself had done so at Étaples – to push in his breast pocket because everybody said they were bullet-proof.

Back at the billets a sergeant was calling from house to house: 'Fall in, the new draft!' and they arrived barely in time to line up in the roadway before a pale, moustached, irritable sergeant-major jostled them into position with repeated warnings to 'Get fell in!'

He marched them to an adjacent piece of ground, and presently a lieutenant with a clipped sandy moustache appeared, motioned them to squat on the grass and smoke, and delivered himself of a short homily. He was Mr. Armstrong, temporarily in command of the company.

'You fellows have come to a good battalion, and a good company. You have a good C.O., good officers, and good N.C.O.s. If you make as good soldiers as the men you join, you'll do nicely.'

He tapped a neatly puttee'd leg with a yellow cane,

and Bradshaw wondered why he continually looked down at it. Suddenly he looked up, staring amongst them with fixed gaze.

'It's a bloody business, this war is, as you chaps will discover before long. Old Fritz isn't cracking up, as you might have heard. He's fighting tooth and nail, and all the ground we take is dearly paid for. We are winning all right, but there's a lot to be done first – the Boche isn't beaten yet. The division you have joined attacked at Guillemont on August the 8th – luckily I was on the B Team and so missed it – but we hadn't much success. The artillery failed to destroy the Boche wire, which didn't matter a great deal at first because there was a heavy mist that morning. But the mist lifted too soon, and the Boche machine-guns got busy. In the confusion that followed, an unauthorised order was passed along to retreat, so we had over two hundred casualties without gaining anything. I am ordered to tell you that under no circumstances whatever must there be a repetition of that unordered retreat. The word retreat must be cut out entirely. Two companies of one of our sister battalions managed to get into Guillemont village, but were sacrificed because of lack of support, largely as a result of that order. The village is still in enemy hands.'

Still rapping his leg, he concluded with a few words on the discipline of the 55th Division – the 'Cast Iron Division', it was known as – and Bradshaw came away wondering at the officer's seeming pessimism. It recalled the atmosphere of Étaples, where base details gloated over the human toll taken by the Battle of the Somme. Only twenty-one of the Koylies came back yesterday, they would tell the timid Derby

men; or, the King's Own lost three hundred in two days. Yet
the wounded in Camier and Étaples spoke confidently of
Jerry being back practically on open ground, so it might be
over by Christmas after all.

Anyway, for the first time Bradshaw had heard a first-
hand opinion that carried more conviction even than the
colonel's quiet welcome earlier in the afternoon.

T HE horizon had assumed a burnished coppery
yellowness before they turned in at the billet, but
the murmuring had ceased. From grumbling at there
being no pay, the old hands had taken to ragging each other
for the benefit of the newcomers, who, glad there was no
display of acrimony because they were Derby men, grinned
their appreciation. One man, whom the others referred to as
'Legs Eleven' because his legs were so thin, grinned across
at Driver and asked:

'Arter lousy yet, chum?'

Driver looked horrified.

'No!'

'Well, tha soon will be.'

Bradshaw also looked startled. Surely there was no need
to get lousy if you took a little care? He looked across at
the sprawling figures, features indistinct in the low yellow
candlelight. Two of them had tunics over their knees, poring
over the seams and neck. Every few seconds there was an
audible 'Tchk' as thumb-nails met, followed occasionally by
a grunt of satisfaction.

'That was a big bee!'

Another, and obviously a favourite of the rest, was a boy they all called 'Chick', extremely youthful and precocious. He came from Preston, and was proud of it. Pausing in the act of pushing his feet into the sleeves of his tunic – there were no blankets – he looked across at the equally boyish Bradshaw and asked:

'Wheer's *ta* coom fra'?'

Bradshaw still resented the fact that he had done all his training with the Manchesters and then had been parted from his friends when being drafted to the Lancashires. He said shortly:

'Manchester.'

Chick grimaced, and winked noticeably at Legs Eleven.

'Manchester? Pooh, that's the spot wi' two teams at the bottom of the First Division, howdin' aw' t'others up!'

The others laughed. They knew that Manchester City and Manchester United had been in low water; that Preston had been going great guns, and had a championship team. Bradshaw grinned with the others, then asked quietly.

'Where do you come from?'

Chick had wanted this moment, and, bucked with the prowess of his team, replied:

'A coom fra' Preston, chum. Proud Preston!'

Bradshaw hesitated a few seconds; cocked his left eyebrow and rubbed his chin, as if pondering.

'Preston? Ummmmm – Preston? Let me see – they have a football team, haven't they?'

Chick nearly exploded. For a moment Bradshaw expected trouble, but Robinson burst out laughing again and soon they were all joining in, even the discomfited Chick. The atmosphere cleared.

Bradshaw settled himself for kip between Driver and Anderton, eyeing doubtfully the thin layer of dirty straw that littered the floor. Before he turned over to sleep he reviewed the happenings of the last two days.

No need now to take pains to hide surprise at the things you saw or heard. You could feel amazed at the incredibility of it all without exciting comment. Here he was, lying peacefully, whilst the great battle tossed and turned so near. He laughed to himself as he thought of preconceived notions of what to-day was to bring. When they left Étaples yesterday morning the battle seemed imminent. A few hours' grace perhaps, and he had expected being caught up in a whirlwind of yelling, hacking, hair-raising confusion; a ceaseless battle that encompassed the whole line and would end only with death or exhaustion. And always he had tried to imagine what would happen when he met one of those big Germans in a hand-to-hand encounter.

Well, they had reached farther up the line than many a thousand volunteers who had been in France a year and more. Everything calm, if uncomfortable, and the others talking as though they expected going on rest! It wasn't quite the thing to ask questions about such moves at this juncture, but surely the others wouldn't jump on Robinson so (for suggesting that the new draft meant a return to the trenches) if they hadn't all been taking a rest for granted? Funny that he knew as little about Driver and Anderton as these Lancashire lads. Rotten that he, Platt, and Wilson should have been parted and sent to three different units after being so long together at Codford and Witley; and all three afraid to approach that big bull-necked sergeant-major to see if he could arrange for them to go up together. Were all drafts split up indiscriminately now, all nominal rolls so strictly adhered to? Well, it was perhaps better that they should have been split up; couldn't expect a trio to remain long unbroken out here . . . the other two might be in action now.

He marvelled at the calm acceptance of the war by these Lancashire men. No fuss or flurry; nothing at all to suggest they had been in action. You'd to question them directly about the battle to get any information at all; even then you weren't sure whether they were joking. And the way they referred to the Germans – almost affectionately. Old Fritz, or Old Jerry! Might be an ally!

He drew comfort from the knowledge that the new draft wasn't to be hurried at once into action. That proved some sort of order; the situation was in hand.

He looked up at the low roof. Somebody blew out a candle. Strange he should come to France on August the 4th, exactly two years after the war commenced. In 1914 – and early 1915 – his mother had repeatedly told him how thankful she felt that the war would be over long before he was old enough to join. All the time he was in that remote warehouse, going to bed at night thinking what a superhuman being he could become by acquiring some of the strength that was being wasted every day in France, these men had been here in the trenches!

Yet the awe he felt when listening to them was tempered with a certain disappointment. British they might be, but none of them spoke enthusiastically of their battles; he had detected definite relief in their appreciative acceptance of the coming rest. Comforting to know there was still a respite. Might enable one to get the hang of things first.

The last candle went out. A whispering reached his ears from opposite.

'I don't like the look of things, anyway, Jem. Don't be surprised if we go up again in the morning instead of down.'

'Well, they'll come in handy for fatigues.'

'Aye, but it'll be four to a loaf again to-morrow.' He turned on his side; sniffed at the musty straw. A funny day it had been. Scuffling with fellows to get a place at the open door of a cattle truck so you could sit comfortably and dangle your legs. Buying canned fruit so you could use the tin as a receptacle for char. (Perhaps they'd issue mess tins to-morrow?) Being separated from your friends without warning and feeling a vague distrust for new acquaintances. (Ten to one they'd borrow things.)

Anyway, they were clear of Étaples and that sand. What a place! Tents and marquees, wired-in I.B.D.s; Y.M.C.A. huts and canteens, with men leaning on them all round, or sprawling in the sand. Fancy the Jocks not wearing anything under their kilts!

He wakened with a start. A pale blue-green haze hovered round the doorless entrance to the little billet. Somebody cursed, then a silhouette outlined itself in the doorway, stood for a few moments, and returned. About four o'clock, thought Bradshaw. How quiet and chilly. A match spluttered opposite, flamed, and went out. A cigarette glowed. He made no sign. He disliked men who rose in the night to indulge in insanitary practices.

A faint tremor quivered on the air. Over the top; whilst he, untried and unblooded, lay scatheless, with the prospect of further unlooked-for freedom before him. He tried to imagine the attack, but after the snippets of conversation he had picked up he knew that all his notions were far from reality. If these people were to be believed, hand-to-hand encounters were rare. You didn't run or charge across No Man's Land, but simply walked. Also, you saved your breath, and went silently! No attempt made to intimidate the enemy with blood-curdling yells as at Witley Camp; you offered yourself as a target. If you came out all right, you grinned, and agreed that Old Fritz had put up a good show. If you got a Blighty wound – *très bon*!

You had to learn not to talk shop, either. Only the boy called Chick had volunteered any information, and he could be excused, being so young. All the same, Bradshaw doubted some of the things he said. Piled on! What was it he'd said when Bradshaw asked him if they still kicked footballs across like they did at Loos?

'That's all my eye and Peggy Martin. No Man's Land is tough going – all oop and down wi' t'shell 'oils and tangled wi' barbed wire and things. They blow a whistle to let 'em know we're coming, too. Tha's no time for lakin' at football when tha's goin' ower – tha'art fagged too quick. They on'y feed us like rabbits. We'd a' give Fritz hell at Guillemont but th'artillery hadn't cut t'wire proper . . . and later it got so hot that watter-bottles was soon empty. Men were drinking their own afoort' day were ower. Wettin' their lips, onnyway. And take a tip from me. Next time we go ower, fasten thi' trenchin'-tool heead in front so it covers thi' privates. Jimmy

Blount got a short burst there – near on twenty bullets . . .'

The guns again. Their first faint mutterings had disappointed him in much the same way as did his first view of the Forth Bridge. He expected something mightier. But as he listened, lying, their power grew on him; almost dismayed him. Only stout hearts could stick that out.

Sergeant Whiteside burst in on them first thing next morning. A strong-jawed, fresh-faced man of twenty-five with the reddest hair Bradshaw had ever seen. He bubbled over with good spirits; spreadeagled Robinson and Armour, a deft movement hidden under a cloud of khaki and straw-dust; threw a bundled greatcoat at Chick; all the time roaring gleefully:

'Show a leg, you lazy bees. D'you know we're going down the line? Up, you stinkers! What d'you think you're on? Abbeville, me lads. Abbeville, hundreds of miles out of this, and a pay parade to-morrow. Vin blong and egg and chips till you bust. Get out of it, you nobbuts!'

Whilst the rudely-wakened rubbed sleep and straw from their eyes, he turned to the newcomers.

'Lucky sods, getting this far and then going back. After breakfast parade get packed up, and leave the place tidy. See these lazy bees do their share of straightening up, too. Chick, you ——, going off again! Out of it!'

Breakfast was haphazard and rather dismal without mess-tins, but several were passed across and they all mucked in. Bradshaw had left most of his fastidiousness on the filthy tables of the Étaples dining-huts, so drank from a stranger's mess-tin without recoiling.

But no orders to fall in came. Instead there was a rifle inspection, and doubt entered exuberant minds. Would they go up after all? In the afternoon the old hands had a pay, and everything connected with war was forgotten. Four men left the artillery canteen hopelessly drunk, and at midnight a disturbed reveller – Legs Eleven again – tripped over somebody's feet and fell heavily across Bradshaw, who squatted with his knees up whilst the belching man laid everything before him. The smell of beer and vomit nauseated Bradshaw; he didn't go to sleep again. Next morning Legs Eleven wakened unaware how he had managed to get back to billet. Robinson pointed to Bradshaw's greatcoat.

'Look at that! All covered wi' nast. Make him clean it, chum. Great clumsy ha'porth.'

THEY went out, the three new men, next evening, again along the river-bank. Everything around looked worn and tired, as if a peaceful countryside, resenting this intrusion, were withholding its beauty. At nine o'clock they returned to a farmhouse, where a cinematograph picture of the Somme Battle was being shown in the yard on a white sheet hanging down one side of a barn. Men crowded the yard on either side under the deepening sky, and Bradshaw saw little propaganda in the picture. It shocked him. Thin lines of strung-out infantry, yards between each man, crouching forward in the haze-laden air. Were those the waves of advancing infantry he heard of? Several attackers toppled over backwards into the trench. One lay athwart the parados like a dirty bolster – too white and natural to be faked. The most unreal and outrageous attack that could be imagined, yet the picture bore an official stamp. Enough to completely dam any flow of recruits, if shown at home.

The little daylight left scarce sufficed to show them the way back. Méricourt, village though it might be, became a maze. They walked timidly into three billets before they found their own, and Bradshaw, fully expecting to hear a violent denunciation of the film, hardly heard it mentioned. A trifling argument over whether the white-faced corpse lying across the parados was genuine or not, that was all.

Candles, spilling themselves on tin-helmet crowns, added some warmth to the dingy room. A set of hanging equipment cast a fantastic shadow on the dirty wall, and pools of darkness linked the recumbent figures. Chick again searched for lice inside his trousers, running a light along the seams. A smell of scorched khaki hung around as he hunted.

'Breadcrumbs wi' legs on', he called them, and claimed to house the biggest, squashiest specimens in the battalion, any colour.

''Ast a getten a diary, theer, chum?' he asked across the floor to Bradshaw, occupied in making notes. 'Tha'll be for it if they find out. Ah! got thee, tha' fat bee. Tchk! Hear him splash!'

Bradshaw felt already that in Driver he would find a companion more suited to his taste than in the other lads, either Lancashire or Manchester. He had a natural fastidiousness that shrank from many little habits and tendencies so common in the others: yet laughed at them rather than condemned them. He knew himself to be

superior in education, speech, and upbringing, but looked
upon these doubtful assets as things to hide and keep back
from the others whenever possible. He wasn't going to
refuse drinking from somebody's dirty mess-tin if such an
act would foster the impression that he was priggish. He
wanted to be one of them.

The others, however, were far too interested in the
coming rest to bother about a very ordinary boy of nineteen
who had only just come out. The prospect of a few drinks
was far more alluring than any number of aspirates.

Driver spoke the King's English, and besides a nice
mind had nice manners. Both he and Bradshaw recognised
very clearly what poor belongings these were to bring to a
war. Nothing but the power of making oneself invisible or
indestructible was of any value. But Driver also had other
virtues. He neither drank nor smoked, and there weren't
many companies in France that boasted two non-smokers
and non-drinkers. That was the trouble with Anderton.
Always a fag in his mouth, and always game for a drink.
Weakness of will-power, Bradshaw called it chidingly; not
without the suggestion of a sneer.

Having found in Driver such an equable companion, it
was natural that a mutual understanding sprang up between
them. They kipped together and ate together, one drawing
rations for both when the other happened to be absent.
Though there was six inches difference in their heights, they
contrived always to get next to each other on parade, and
found some comfort in doing so. Both felt that the others
were too free and easy in their ways, airily borrowing
tackle that didn't belong to them and assuming that no

remonstrance would be forthcoming from the owner.

Neither mentioned that the suspicions each began to entertain at Étaples – that the war wasn't going as well as it might have done – had received some confirmation during their short stay near the scenes of operation; both hoped they would deport themselves with the same degree of optimism, or resigned acceptance, shown by the old hands under conditions that were, to say the least, unfavourable (and, as far as the actual fighting was concerned, distinctly hazy).

In a simple way, Bradshaw had tried to jot down his impressions in a small diary, in staccato fashion. He wondered idly what use it would be keeping a record that might at any time come to an abrupt end, but each day brought some fresh incident that either shocked, surprised, or intrigued him, and, incredible as they seemed to him at the time, he meant to chronicle them. He was collecting quite a store of these surprises, but would anybody believe in their authenticity afterwards?

Those children at Boulogne who canvassed their sisters' bodies . . . The men who, too lazy to get up properly at night, used their boots and claimed that it softened the leather. . . .

He turned to Driver.

'Coming for a stroll? You, Anderton?'

They went out into the darkened streets, under a solemn sky, low and heavy. Without being aware of it, they approached the cage of German prisoners. They stared curiously but kept walking.

'I'll never be taken prisoner, if that's what it means', said Anderton emphatically.

Bradshaw looked with some fear at the dark, silent figures hovering against the barbed wire. These were the type they were matched against. Had he smoked he would have flung all the cigarettes he possessed over that wire barrier. Half starved, bearded, miserable-looking lot. He couldn't imagine meeting one like them in No Man's Land without feeling hollow. You'd get no quarter from fellows like those, unhappy as they now appeared. Good job that wire was pretty hefty.

'I'd rather be taken prisoner than lose a limb', ventured Driver. 'Rotten to lose your right arm.'

'Some of the old hands don't seem to worry about an arm or a leg', put in Bradshaw. 'Getting blinded's worst of all', he added.

They met Brettle and Bates, two aggressive-voiced older men whom the sorting out at Étaples had thrown together. They had travelled up in the same compartment as Bradshaw, who had been forced to listen to a eulogy of Brettle's wife and a summary of that man's intentions when they charged the Germans. 'I'll be among 'em red hot' (only he didn't say *red* hot). 'I'll make the bleeders squeal. They'll not have the same heart now we've got 'em on the run. Mucking swine! Got my young brother. I'll make 'em pay for that. Them or me. An' if I cop a packet, well, I'll see as half a dozen o' them swine go west with me. Just let me get among 'em!'

'Well, you'll get the chance soon', Anderton had shot out from the corner, whilst Driver maintained his timid silence. Before they arrived at Romecamps Brettle and Bates had exchanged home addresses, maudlin sentimental, 'in case they didn't come back'. When the train stopped, everybody had tumbled out into the canteen for refreshment. They had no mess-tins, but bought tins of fruit merely to use as receptacles for tea. The train stayed there for nearly three hours, during which Brettle, Bates, and several others made good use of the wet section of the canteen. They came out drunk. Bradshaw discovered that Brettle's wife was not of such a loving disposition as before. In fact, during his stay in the canteen she had been unfaithful with a greengrocer named Pettitt, whose shop was merely a cloak for a 'bookie' business. Brettle hinted darkly that that shop would also receive from his hand a due measure of violence next time he got leave. Then Anderton had put in pungently: 'Didn't you have a draft leave?' and Brettle, finding some difficulty in holding himself in rein, vomited through the window.

These things passed through Bradshaw's mind as the trio paused at Brettle's question: ''V'y'eard we're going down? Bloody muck-up. Let's get stuck into the swine.' He glowered at the prisoners' cage. 'Aren't they an awful mucking bunch? Lousy bastards. Should shoot 'em all; eatin' good rations.'

'Lucky, not having that blighter in our billet', said Anderton as they passed on. 'You know that quiet little bloke in the corner opposite me – the one they call Jem? He had a court martial for being asleep on sentry duty, but they let him off. He'd been ill, I think, beforehand.'

When they got back, boisterous sing-songs were in progress throughout the company. Brettle sounded to be the only one sorry – if he were really sorry – to be going down the line. A few short days ago Bradshaw would never have believed that soldiers could hang about singing and joking whilst on the edge of a big battle. He thought that every man in the area would be taking an active part in the offensive all the time. Now he found the war so big that men could go on rest during the battle. He couldn't grasp things. Instead of the great yelling charge he had depicted – where thousands attacked in a sweeping mass and you gained courage by being amongst it, carried along with it; where everybody fought till they dropped from exhaustion, wounds, or death – were these thin waves of extended single lines that moved at walking pace; where everybody was in front and nobody lagged. And so big was our army that you weren't in front all the time. You came out on rest after a stunt, whilst a battalion that had been resting took your place. Quite a business. Not long ago he imagined that anyone at the front in an attack could look on either flank and see thousands upon thousands of men, stretching farther than the eye could reach, packed solid; that a backward glance would also be filled with the same limitless sea of faces; and that keen eyes would be able to discern an outstanding figure on horseback, surrounded by flags and staff; Sir Douglas Haig surrounded by his mighty army.

The songs also were an illumination to Bradshaw. Instead of 'The Long, Long Trail', 'Pack up your troubles', and 'Tipperary', they started with innocent ditties like 'She wore a tulip', and 'Somebody's waiting for me'; but the interest really began with 'I wish I was single again', the last verse of which Bradshaw heard as he moved through the hazy candlelight to his place. Then they had the Amours of a young lady from Armentières, which lasted for about seventeen verses; the exploits of a licentious monk of great renown, 'Old Riley's Daughter' (for some time a puzzle to

the Manchester men because the Lancashires pronounced
it 'dowter'); and a rather disgusting verse about a man who
loved his wife very, very dearly. The new men listened and
laughed, and Bradshaw went to sleep wondering how much
of it he dared record.

After breakfast some overdue mail arrived from Étaples,
but, whilst they were in the midst of reading letters and
sorting out the contents of parcels, a sharp order came to
fall in quickly on the road. The entire company assembled,
and were told to be ready to march off by two o'clock,
everything packed and billets tidy. Back at their mail,
Anderton discovered that somebody had won two of the
four tins of cigarettes he had just received.

SAIGNVILLE might have been in Cheshire. A village smaller
than Méricourt, and infinitely cleaner and fresher. Always
for Bradshaw it remained the one and only place he saw
that bore any resemblance to a Fair France. It lay snug in a
shallow depression ringed by trees, untouched by the war till
these, the first, Tommies came.

No. 9 Platoon had a good-sized barn for its billet, with
fresh clean straw thickly cushioning the floor. They tumbled
amongst it gleefully, old and new alike, good-naturedly
wrestling like schoolboys. The war was over, for a time.

They were happy days, those at Saignville, the war an
outcast; never mentioned save during some explanation
of tactics on parade. Bradshaw liked the training – mild
when contrasted with the 'I'll-make-you-sweat' variety of

the Bull Ring, and far more instructive. After tea, except for an occasional picket or guard, everybody was free to follow his own pleasures. Most of the men flocked to one of the two little estaminets, squashing in or squatting outside. Bradshaw considered this a great waste of time, throwing away precious hours of mellow sunlight. He walked the quiet country lanes with Driver – also afraid of drink – or played chess on a grassy secluded bank with a pocket set of chessmen. Anderton accompanied them several times, but his heart rested in the little estaminets on these occasions, where soldier songs were bawled in all their gross humour. Every evening the lusty lungs declared:

> *Apree le gu'rre finee,*
> *Anglay soldats partee.*
> *Madamersell bokoo piccanninnee,*
> *Apree le gu'rre finee.*

And every night Anderton returned to the barn, cap well back over moist forehead, tunic open at the neck, saying:

'I'll get one of you blighters drunk before we leave Saignville!'

Bradshaw found the greatest difficulty in understanding the Lancashire dialect. Greatcoats became 'top-coits'; nothing but, 'nobbut'. Chorley, from which town many of them came, was pronounced Chorler, and dirty articles – like boots after parade – were 'covered wi' nast'. Everybody was either 'chum' or 'mate'.

One afternoon Bradshaw came across Dickson bent on an excursion in which were concerned a pair of trestles supporting a long, horizontal tree-trunk, and an excavation, in the open field behind the farm.

A few minutes later, with both embarrassingly perched over the excavation, Dickson asked:

'Come across any lice yet?'

'No. Have you?'

'No. Not yet.'

As he left the field, however, Bradshaw looked back to see the other busily searching the innards of his trousers. He was too new – still ashamed – to admit having felt more than once lice creeping on his chest and legs. He wondered if Driver had been troubled in the same way.

The weather remained perfect, and to Bradshaw the days passed like a country holiday. The war was thought of little, and spoken of less. One or two optimists always hankered after news, believing we might have forced a break-through, but the majority had resigned themselves to an indefinite campaign. New articles of equipment were issued daily. New cap badges and numerals, P.H. gas helmets (in duplicate, in case one should get punctured by bullet or shrapnel); breech covers. A three-inch square of plain scarlet material was stitched under each collar between the shoulders to distinguish the battalion, and decorations in the form of a red rose occupied prominent positions high up on each sleeve below the epaulet. In fact, Bradshaw felt that nobody could distinguish them from old campaigners. He would have preferred webbing equipment to the leather he wore, but a time would come when webbing would be lying about spare.

They drilled on a well-turfed field not two minutes from

the billet, dug trenches in the innocent pastureland, marched the leafy lanes happily and vigorously, and after the leisure evenings slept like logs. Bradshaw felt as fit as a fiddle. Training for the war here proved to be far more interesting and pleasurable than at the Base, where the main object seemed to be to get you so fed up with life you'd be glad to go up the line.

On their last night in Saignville, when Anderton had gone for his usual 'allowance', the other two boys sat on an old tree-trunk overlooking a vista of golden-green fields. The village murmured on their right, out of sight but close. Driver sat quieter than ever, absorbed in the view.

'We'll be pretty useless at scrapping compared with a fellow like Anderton, don't you think?' said Bradshaw, knowing Driver to be less a fighter, even, than he.

Driver grinned. 'They can't make soldiers of my kind. I've a feeling already that the first time we get to bayonet-fighting I shall come off second best. I feel too – too young, somehow.'

'Yes!' broke in Bradshaw, 'me too. I don't feel equal to it; not grown up enough. I often wonder if it'd be any better to run a bit more wild. Start drinking and swearing. Might help.'

'These fellows don't seem to worry about things, do they? They're as happy as larks with their beer and cigarettes. Perhaps they don't think about things. . . . That's my trouble. Always trying to imagine what the fighting will be like; my own little share in particular. Wondering whether I'll be a coward.'

'Ah! And I suppose you attested to prove you weren't a coward? I did. Mother was always saying: 'Well, Fred's gone;

thank God it'll be over before you'll be old enough.' She didn't know. I tried twice to get in the artillery with a pal at home. Too small, they said, except for a driver. I'm afraid of horses.'

'I expect they think at home we'll be fighting or chasing each other round like maniacs by now.' Driver grinned again, then added quietly, 'It would break my mother's heart if I got killed.'

His altered tone frightened Bradshaw, who had hitherto felt confident of the issue. Any chum of his ought to feel the same about coming through, too. But your own opinion was no talisman. Thousands and thousands must have felt quite as confident as he; thousands who had been killed months ago. Driver, putting into words a possibility he had beaten away every time it crept into his mind, disturbed him. The possibility became nearer a probability. He strove again to make himself believe that the question of a future for himself was not at all problematical. He laughed.

'Here, don't put the wind up me. Talking like that before we've seen anything.'

'Oh! I'm not getting morbid. Only bullets don't pick and choose.'

Not another word was spoken about the war. Both decided enough had been said. They tried chess, and Bradshaw was twice beaten. He couldn't concentrate. What was left of the evening slowly dissolved itself into a deep, blue-gold brilliance. No bugle-calls jarred. Nothing disturbed the lustrous serenity of the summer night. Because of its beauty, an insidious thought tapped on the window of Bradshaw's mind. The rest was at an end. It would be wasted for many, because they would be killed before they could strike a blow.

Blew a whistle to let 'em know we were coming, did we?

Anderton was already in the billet when they got back, joining in the choruses like any old hand. The sweat-laden air smote Bradshaw as he walked in. Men from other billets had crowded into the barn, attracted by the droning of Chick's mouth-organ. They had 'Riley's Daughter', 'Inky-pinky-parley-voo', and several other old favourites, when, during a lull, a black-moustached face poked itself round the doorway. Immediately there was a cry from the perspiring singers.

''Ow, Fred, cow thi' darn. We bin waiting for thee to give us 'Burlington Bertie'. Wheer's ta' bin —— square pushin'?'

Somebody murmured, 'Georges Carponteer', and after some laughter had subsided Chick said:

'Ay, Fred, show these fellers how tha con do "Burlington Bertie", then tell 'em about "Georges".'   The black moustache cocked up at the ends as its owner grinned. He got no further than 'I rise at ten-thirty' before three or four other red faces squashed in at the door. One of them repeated the last two words of each line, a second late, and nearly buried itself in the straw as its supporting companions vociferously applauded.

'Now "Georges," Fred!'

Nothing loth, the black moustache wagged in the candlelight, and became the centre of a score pairs of round eyes. War was forgotten!

'We was at Bethune, in '15, but the town was out of bounds because there was a Red Lamp there. Me and Joe Lewis was havin' a drink at a little estam. a couple o'kilometres outside

o' t' town, and playin' about wi' one o' them racing machines
– like you see on t' pier at Blackpool. Each puts in a coin,
then you wind the 'andle and the winner gets 'is brass back.

'We was both fed up, an' on'y lakin' at t' racin' oojah to pass
time, but an owd Frenchman watched us aw' time, proper
interested to see who'd win. Well, Joe ses to me, "Ah'm stalled
o' this, Fred. Does ta think this old fogey'll know wheer we
con get a bit o' loose?" I ses, "Ask 'im; you speak gradely
French." Wi' that, 'e gives the 'andle such a vicious jerk that
th' machine jams and won't work. Well, Joe ('e's dead now
– killed at Guillemont) ses, "That's —— it!" and, loosin' the
'andle, 'e turns to the Froggie and ses, "Compree jig-a-jig?"
but the Froggie looks numb, so Joe ses again "Jig-a-jig –
filly – you know!" and makes curves with 'is 'ands. After a bit
the Frenchie suddenly ses, "Oui, oui!" about a dozen times,
and motions us to follow 'im. Then 'e sets off down towards
Bethune, so we pulls 'im up sharp an' tells 'im the Red Caps'll
nab us. Then 'e takes us a roundabout road over some fields,
and we mucked all our boots and putty's up scrambling over
bloody ditches. Anyway, after about an hour's skirmishin' 'e
lands us in the outskirts of Bethune, all eager and pantin'. The
streets was nearly dark, but all of a sudden 'e stops outside a
little pub wi' a sign over it "GEORGES CARPONTIER," and pushes
t' door oppen. . . . Inside, servin' beer, was a right piece,
young and juicy. Joe nudges me and whispers, "That'll be
'oo," and makes to go up for a drink, wearing 'is best smile.'

He paused for breath, beads of glistening sweat trickling
down his face, and chuckled gleefully at certain signs of
impatience from some of the onlookers. He wiped his
moustache slowly, exasperatingly, then opened his tunic neck.

'Phew! It's 'ot! Well, Joe never gets near that wench. The old Froggie takes him by the arm and leads us into the next room, saying, "Voila! Voila!" all the time; and pointin'. In the corner of the room was another of them bloody racing machines.'

Bradshaw went to sleep dreaming that some divining hand went through the company marking out for the B Team – which stayed in reserve – certain members who were destined to be killed in the next attack, and that the company came out scatheless.

Next morning, as they packed up, the most slovenly, melancholy, and overladen soldier Bradshaw had come across shuffled into the billet, and flopped on to his pack in a very dejected, exhausted manner.

'So they've bunged thi' back ageean, Ginger', said Legs Eleven. 'Time, too. Tha's getten too fat for owt. Mak' him a bay'net mon, corp.'

Several others wanted to know why Ginger had lost such a cushy job as officer's servant, and Ginger cursed volubly.

'Cushy be —— ! I'm glad to get back to t' company. That bee isn't safe, makkin' a bleedin' target of hisself. Ah wouldn't do it ageean for a' gold clock!'

'Well, young Crawley jumped at the chance', put in Corporal Hartley.

Ginger grunted indignantly. 'Ay, wait while he's to foller 'im across No Man's Land on a B.F.'s expedition. You know why 'e sacked me? Last time up 'e tuk to walkin' along t' parapet afore we went ower. When I follers 'im – up on top,

o' course – Lieutenant Gillow sez to me, "Come down into
t' trench, man – if 'e wants to commit suicide, let 'im." So I
'ops down from be'ind him, and when 'e turns round a bit
later on an' finds me in t' trench 'e goes ravin' 'airless and
maks me get back up. Daft bee!'

'Ne'er mind, Ginger, we'll mak' thee permanent orderly-
man', said the corporal.

They left Saignville on August the 28th, after serving the
pleasantest period of army training Bradshaw had known.
Instead of poking at your ribs and slapping your puttees
with their canes, the junior officers had acted like foremen,
always ready for a joke, more on the same footing, and as
a consequence getting done what they wanted. Death had
become such a possibility that it mattered less to these old
hands. If you came out, *bon*! If you didn't, well, there were
plenty to keep you company. But Bradshaw hadn't yet got
past marvelling at this stoicism. Midnight found them marching
through the main street of Abbeville in aloof darkness. Their
songs brought women to the open bedroom windows, and
girls who giggled when the officers' flash-lamps whisked on
to their nightgowns. Their adieux touched Bradshaw. Not so
indifferent as they looked during the daytime!

Soon enough came signs to show that their direction was
shaping towards the Somme again. For a short period light,
care-free banter dwindled to reflections of Guillemont. The
peaceful stagnation of Blaireville and Bretoncourt was not
to be theirs again. But by the time Dernancourt was reached
spirits had revived.

'Come on, my lucky lads – up, over, and home!'

They camped in tents at Bouzincourt, near Albert, from where the leaning Madonna was distantly silhouetted against a low, ruddy sky; the reflection of another abounding sunset. The war wouldn't be over till that monument fell, everybody said, and the pioneers had railed off a square of road underneath it. They spent a week of fine, cool nights in a set of exhibition trenches, all beautifully sand-bagged and drained. Two companies attacked the remainder in mimic warfare; they executed raids and patrols. Each morning Bradshaw looked eagerly for the leaning Madonna.

Three miners left the company from Bouzincourt, recalled to the pit. They left envious, well-wishing friends behind them. Birch, the biggest of the ex-Manchesters, got his first stripe. On September the 6th the battalion marched towards the front, the sound of the guns getting stronger and stronger. They learnt that Guillemont had at last fallen. On the roads everything was bewildering bustle and nervous agitation; G.S. waggons, pioneers, water-carts, gun-carriages, and men in never-ending streams dammed and flowing in turn.

CLOUDS gathered with the evening, bringing a steady downpour of searching rain. In the wet dusk 'C' Company was turned into a saturated cornfield near Mametz, and told to do the best it could for shelter. The old hands immediately, almost cheerfully, set about rigging up cornstacks as shelters, showing great adaptability. The new men made no effort to bag their share of the stacks; there were few enough, and the others had prior claim. Bradshaw

had heard a lot about 'roughing it'; he wanted to do the
thing properly. So he slushed about in the sodden, rapidly
muddying grass between corn-stacked couples, and always
with him came Driver, whom he had now commenced to
call Jack. Their greatcoats, trousers, tunics, and feet were
soaked, and it never occurred to either of them to wonder
why more tents – like that little cluster for officers in the
highest corner of the field – were not available.

'The first night we had in the army, down at Codford',
remarked Bradshaw with a genuine chuckle, 'some of the
fellows complained of the blankets feeling damp. Nice
picture, this, of British soldiers moving up for action, eh?'

'Yes, it'll undo all the good Saignville did us', replied
Driver, thinking of the bronchitis he was susceptible to. He
shivered. All night they kept on their feet, trying to pierce
the impenetrable gloom ahead. At times the ridge there
seemed to take on a faintly luminous outline, as though
shells exploded behind it. But they heard no sound till about
three in the morning, when a whining 'sphweee-sphweee'
reached them, followed by several dull crashes and a wild
neighing. A salvo of shells had dropped amongst some
tethered horses on the near side of the ridge. They saw the
red bursts against a sea of blackness; their first shells.

They were on the edge of it!

In the morning rum was issued, and Bradshaw foolishly
gave his tot to a shivering Rimmer. Later the sun came to
dry their clothes on them. On the crest behind perched an
amazingly long naval gun, on stupendous mountings. He
learnt it would fire a shell fourteen miles. Still further behind,
in a deep basin between the ridges, a diminutive battalion

of the Guards paraded, fascinating the overlookers by its precise, machine-like movements. One – one, two! Along the road leading through Happy Valley wormed a toy-like procession of transports. The Lancashires were to follow them, that evening, for two days in front. Their baptism.

Valises, each marked in indelible pencil with the owner's number, were discarded in favour of Battle Order, and the B Team – a skeleton of officers and Other Ranks on which a new battalion could be formed if the existing one suffered extinction – had been picked. September the 7th. Over a month in France. The B Team, all smile and salute, God-speeded them with friendly farewells as they wheeled past towards Montauban. Bradshaw marched obsessed by two thoughts. He might not come back. Jack might not come back. The little fellow in front with 'knock knees' – he might not come back. (Somebody behind might probably be wondering if he would come back.) Then he would feel a certain elation; they credited him with sufficient soldierliness to fight for England! That general wouldn't come now!

A plague of shells had desolated the ground they now reached. Montauban resembled little more than a series of brickwork heaps and twisted ironwork. Guns lurked round corners and under camouflaged netting and futuristic paintwork. Gunners grinned imperturbably as their shots frightened the new men, who ducked scaredly and hurried under their fire. A clump of shabby trees accentuated the dusk, and quickly hundreds of men, horses, and limbers were inextricably jammed at a cross-roads, through Montauban. Officers fretted and fumed; walked up and down with clouded brows and pursed lips. The battalion disentangled itself. Men started forward; crowded on each other's heels. Stopped, started, and stopped again. A battalion of company strength passed them, untidy, straggling. From the line? Neither party sang. Some cross-nodding; a few faint smiles. Bradshaw wished somebody would start singing. He nudged Driver; indicated several gaping shell-holes.

Darkness was touching the stark tree-tops of Bernafay Wood as they dropped down the slope before Longueval. The road got rougher; the guns louder. Several men in front of Bradshaw stumbled over some wreckage on the roadside. A message came down. Two shells burst ahead with spiked slashes of red and yellow, and gruff explosions. A battery on the road bank spat with venom. The men lost their fours formation, squeezing themselves between the flashes. Bradshaw's nostrils twitched from fumes as he hurried across a gap. Vivid flashes silhouetted the men in front. Jack kept near him.

The whine of another German shell was drowned in the fire of more British guns. The night was split by its gleaming red burst. The air-displacement punched Bradshaw sideways. He reeled forward under a spattering of earth, crying 'Jack! Jack!' Something screwed up behind his chest. He felt a strange tightness there; an emptiness lower down. He had the wind up. He no longer seemed to possess a body, but head and feet must have been attached, because he found himself marvellously running into the men ahead. Tree-trunks sprang up at each side in the next flashes. Gruff, gruff, GRUFF! A triple rending crash and a cry of pain. He ran forward again; heard the smacking of missiles cracking into the tree-trunks, splintering. Another flash from the banking,

lighting up three men in front, crouching forward; Driver
nearest. A livid upheaval blotted out everything else in front,
flinging him backwards. He regained his feet, stretched his
arms forward, and ran on blindly; chin tucked in chest. He
tripped, and, crying out despairingly, fell heavily. He heard
curses and a groan; flickering flashes showed several men on
their knees. One wore a dim white armlet. A stretcher-bearer.

The ground rose, and trees on the right disappeared.
Several bright, flickering Very lights lit up billowing smoke-
clouds, casting uncanny shadows among the black trunks.
The path wheeled at the edge of the gutted Delville Wood.
Shells whined incessantly. Three burst with ear-splitting
crashes just ahead in the open ground. Bradshaw recognised
Birch, the new lance-jack. Wounded in the arm. A Blighty
one, the bearer said. Two others wounded; one on the
ground, Fraser standing.

CRUMP! CRRRUMP! SCHWEEEEE – SCHWEEEEE –

The rough track grew suddenly uneven; disappeared in
a background of smoke, dark and menacing. A Very light
peeped brilliantly through the drifting folds, then two greens
and a red. Somebody behind cursed. He looked round;
saw Driver almost abreast, and a straggling file of men. In
front the same, and dirty emptiness on each hand. No other
troops within a hundred miles. One jerking centipede of
scared khaki.

Then came a bounding barrage from the rear, a rushing,
roaring, and whining of shells such as Bradshaw had never
imagined. He didn't know for certain they were British
shells. He bent double, yet felt like a long, wide chimney
with a strong draught blowing up through it. A series of

hideous crashes broke out ahead, red bursts darting and spitting. He caught at the breath whistling through his body, babbling excitedly:

'It's all wrong, Jack! You can't be hit before you've been in action! Firing should stop till we reach the front trench!'

Immediately he felt foolish, growing calmer. More shells dropped near. Men were hit. Bradshaw heard someone say: 'You lucky bleeder!' Then a louder cry, 'Is Drummer there? Gaukroger and Irlam hit. . . .'

The black mass of Delville Wood receded in the left rear, but still they lunged on behind some wonderful brave in front. Flashes and explosions flung the night away all round, creating a perpetual semi-light. A flitting figure passed along, saying quietly, authoritatively:

'Line up behind the trench. Keep down and jump in immediately the others leave.'

They lined up and flung themselves down. A Very light hovered surprisingly near, almost suspended. The shrieking and whining went on unabated, and Bradshaw lay terrified and flat. Two yards away he could see a small depression, but felt incapable of moving into it. He just pressed himself against the dry, smelly earth, believing that all the flying missiles were directed at him. Once he prayed, and several times wondered whether the Germans would attack. Almost sure to; nothing to stop them this side!

He knew himself to be incapable of resistance; pictured his own abject surrender. What he didn't know was that there were no more Germans across No Man's Land than Britons on his side. His mind pictured thousands and thousands of them, ready to press forward. Because he

couldn't see into the unfathomable mysteries behind and
under those graceful, curving lights he fancied all manner of
furtive gatherings. Could they know how few we were? Not
many yards away Chick sat nonchalantly on the parados,
legs dangling in the trench, asking the men there what kind
of a time they'd had. (Not so bad, considering. Went over
yesterday. Bit of a muck-up. Snipers busy in 'Devil's' Wood.)

The whizzings and whinings encompassed him; they
were sure to get him in the end. He no longer felt confident
of bearing a charmed life. What was the placard he had
seen on his last leave in Manchester? 'HELL WITH THE LID OFF'.
John Bull, of course.

The sergeant came along again bent double. Jump in.
The trench swallowed him up in a greedy gulp. It had a dry
bottom and comforting sides. He sank exhausted, glad to
make himself scarce. Corporal Hartley of the big blue eyes
brushed up.

'You . . . you . . . and you. Sentries. You're on first. Get on
t' firestep, tut sweet.'

Bradshaw was the last 'you' referred to. His heart thumped.
He looked round at Driver, the second 'you', then scrambled
on to the firestep, monstrously elevated and afraid. Why
should he be first on duty? Shouldn't an old hand . . . ?

He looked into No Man's Land. Thin masses of black and
grey cotton wool moving regularly to the left made thundery
by the glow of fluttering Very lights. Impenetrable darkness
on each hand – black enough to sting in the few seconds
after each blinding flash. Unfriendly half-lights in front.
Sudden brightnesses that sent stealthy shadows creeping
about the uneven ground at his eye-level. How far were

they off? Was this really the very front line? No wire. No agitated rifle-firing, as expected, across No Man's Land. Just watching. Watching with staring, starting eyes.

THE parapet was newly turned earth, and uneven; on his right hand a higher heap which could easily hide an approaching foe. He viewed it apprehensively, and laid his rifle across a lower pile, bayonet fixed, butt conveniently near his shoulder. Behind, and three feet lower, the others lolled and squatted, but Bradshaw never looked to his rear except once during that first spell of sentry duty.

A burst of red crashes roared and crumped into the edge of the wood where the trench wound. A sickening tearing and splintering; a sea of haze rose. Bradshaw tucked his chin into tense, folded arms; twisted his neck to tilt steel helmet against the showers of earth that rained down when a near one burst. They wailed overhead; shrieked close, quivering the solid parapet. Bits of shell whined musically and thwacked into the parados.

Boom – Boom – BOOM! CRUMP – CRRRUMP – CRASH! WHACK! WHOOSH!

Every few minutes he made sure his companions were still there by a quick corner-eye glance. He was afraid to turn round. Confused, unusual sounds from behind; men stood and squeezed to the trench-sides below. Somebody hit?

'Who is it?' he whispered down. Nobody heard. He snatched back his head, eyes peering through half-closed lids. Wonderfully brilliant, the German flares. Came down slowly, like parachutes, and served our purpose too.

The two hours' nightmare passed quicker than Bradshaw had hoped. The bombardment slackened until only the Germans fired; darkness stole back and enveloped them. Jack's turn up next. Every few minutes the greenish-white glares illuminated the bust of a man leaning against the parados, the shadow's edge thrown by the parapet creeping up over neck, chin, nose, eyes, and helmet as the flare dropped spluttering to earth; submerging them in darkness again. From afar back came the angry growling of howitzers – perhaps that long naval gun at Mametz – from Trônes a nearer, answering bark. Dogs in the night. The last tail-lashings of an infuriated monster settling down again after the disturbing shell-storm.

His next turn on was less solitary, for the greying, waning night brought stand-to. Three others climbed up on the firestep beside him, bayonets all fixed. Attacks often came with the dawn; but nothing happened. The silent shadows assumed human outlines. Stand-down.

The morning brought a cold mist and shivers, calling for something warmer and more stimulating than the bread, raw onions, and currants that constituted their rations. Optimists hoped for a rum ration, or something from the cookers, but nothing came. In England, an officer would have come round asking, 'Any complaints?'

The early hours were quiet. Old hands had scooped funkholes in the parapet, like miniature caves. Bradshaw kept his head down, but caught glimpses of a never-ending sea of dark brown, shell-bitten earth; and dark clumps of skeleton woods. There remained, as during the night, a feeling of isolation; the front line was most inadequately held. The slacker firing and quiet intervals were no less dismaying than the heavier shelling. Something hung over them, imminent. Bradshaw felt this apprehension grow when a sudden single shell dropped a yard or two from the parapet on his left, burying two men who squatted underneath in their funkholes. Other odd pot-shots caused many heart-leaps and a few casualties; Bradshaw stared uncomprehendingly at the burdens carried past on stretchers.

The sun filtered through, finally dissipating the mist. Two enemy planes droned leisurely above, and Lieutenant Fulshaw hurried down.

'Keep your faces turned down. They show white from above!'

The shells came again, creating a dirty, sidling fog over the ruined Waterlot Farm. The supports were catching it. A midday bombardment that coincided with rations flattened them out on their bellies at the bottom of the trench. The earth heaved and spread itself in showers and clods over Bradshaw, who lay distressingly afraid that each next 'whoosh' over the parapet would be the end. Yet his fear had a calmness. He kept his head, and grinned when a near-by voice cursed savagely:

'Where the —— 'ell's our 'tillery?'

Afterwards, he made serious inroads into his handkerchief-ful of currants. He hadn't realised before how much flavour there could be in a raw onion. Several men were cadging water already. Good job they were getting relieved next day; rations wouldn't last any longer.

Walking wounded gathered at the wide bend under knotted tree-roots, waiting for darkness. Envious chums chaffed them good-humouredly. Lucky sods they were. There was no communication trench for a hundred yards or more; stretcher-cases had to be carried across open ground in sight of Jerry. One of the wounded, with a limp arm, sleeve cut away, wanted to run for it, but wouldn't take the risk on his own. They were nervous, dreading a 'Landowner' now Blighty was in sight.

That night Bradshaw wanted the latrine. He hadn't seen one. The word wasn't used amongst these men. He put his wish before Sergeant Todd, surprising himself by using front-line language. Nothing for it but to get out on top, almost at the same spot as he lay quaking twenty-four hours previously. Two big holes there now. He felt calmer on this occasion, but didn't waste any time.

SEPTEMBER the 9th, Bradshaw's sister's birthday. Saturday. From stand-down to breakfast unusually quiet, then in rapid succession three men were hit in as many minutes; alarmingly accurate firing. A Lewis gun team, sitting on its 'pans' one moment, was drowned in earth and smoke the next. Bradshaw, standing stupefied, saw a single twitching hand protruding from the embedded mass. Two men brushed him aside, setting quickly to work with spades. He marvelled at their dexterity. In twenty seconds begrimed men stood shaking themselves like dogs leaving water, spitting out soil and frightened blasphemy. Two others lay contorted, grey white; suffocated. The first close dead he had seen.

Driver came up, brown eyes full of concern.

'Our own guns are firing short. They've just killed Healy and Acton!'

Every minute or more a headlong rushing express train landed with sickening impact from behind, tremendously destructive and terrifying. Men edged away from its line of flight, leaving a gap of trench occupied only by two dead bodies. Lieutenant Armstrong sent down two runners imploring the gun to lift, whilst 'Waggers' worked feverishly in the open rear on broken wires. Fear, resentment, and anger prevailed in the trench. Bates suddenly chattered:

'Let's go over to the bloody swine!'

An old hand swung round on him contemptuously. 'What —— good would that do?'

Bates collapsed like a pricked balloon, pitiable and shaking.

Dying pig, thought Bradshaw.

'Drummer' Fogg, stretcher-bearer and the pride of 'C' Company, quietly performed heroics with the wounded. Bradshaw had never seen anyone so calm and collected. He noticed that Fogg wore a D.C.M. ribbon; that when a call came – 'Stretcher-bearers!' – he scrambled out on the parados; ran, exposed, to the required spot; then dropped down again into the trench. He was busiest where the refractory gun deposited its clamouring shell, applying dressings, congratulating the Blighty ones, sustaining worse cases with cheering words. Bradshaw followed his tireless passings with fascinated, admiring eyes, realising his own shortcomings.

A runner arrived at noon with alarming and quieting news, a message from that detached existence afar back. The tormenting gun had been traced. It was a German, firing from the stronghold Thiepval, now in the Lancashire's left rear. That stopped the resentment and brought an amusing calmness.

Corporal Dawkins said:

'Aa thowt it weren't ours. Th' explosive were too strong!'

The second and alarming news was that they were to go over the top and attack that same afternoon. The Irish Guards on the right were attempting the capture of Ginchy; the Cast Iron Division had to support them on the left.

Bradshaw experienced that strange sensation again. Had they come on Thursday evening with the intention of attacking he could have brought himself to the necessary pitch of preparedness. But now he felt peeved. They ought to have been told beforehand, not had it sprung on them just as they expected relief. The battered trench became a safe anchorage. He fervently hoped there would be no bayonet work; couldn't trust himself not to flinch. Old stagers reckoned that the first time over you made a mess of your trousers. Must remember to have a bullet up the spout; that was easier than sticking a bayonet in, and less horrifying. Impossible to think he could stick that dull steel blade into another lad, except in a mad frenzy. Saw red, did you? They maddened you with a heavy bombardment, perhaps by the loss of comrades; got you so incensed you were temporarily insane with blood-lust. You forgot everything. Forgot that the men opposite hadn't fired the shells; forgot that their artillerymen were too far off to reach by bayonet; forgot that third parties had fashioned and fanned this hatred.

There was fun at Witley Camp, chasing and shrieking across open ground, jumping into a trench; simultaneously driving a bayonet through a straw-stuffed sack; then leaping on. But sacks were not men whose chief aim, rather than killing, was self-preservation. Being the aggressor – going over the top presumably to kill – was too much like liking it; a display of enthusiasm. He would rather stay in the trench and wait for Jerry to attack. One could help to repel invaders – self-defence urged that. Over the top – in broad daylight!

Would he be alive to-night? Some of them would not, that was certain. They would all go mad, he supposed, if the hope that they would be among the lucky ones did not sustain them. Deranging, to know that your life might easily depend on the speed or slowness of climbing over the parapet; or whether you went to left or right round a shell-hole. Straight on, down and up, trusting to luck – that perhaps was best. Jack and he must stick together. Luck was more important than bravery here. The most recklessly courageous of men could stop a bullet in the first few yards; yet a timid creature, dreading the prospect of hand-to-hand fighting, might reach the German trench unharmed.

He heard Rawson say:

'Thowt summat'd happen when t' band played us out o' Bouzincourt. Allus were a bad sign that – same at Guillemont. Wish aa could transfer to t' Flying Corps.'

The rich sunshine mellowed. At four o'clock its serenity was shattered by a palpitating outburst of drumfire, as every big gun turned into a machine-gun, paling the previous bombardment by its accumulated fury. Give 'em hell! That's

the stuff! From a blown-in portion of the trench Bradshaw
saw debris flying in clouds and clods from the German line.
The enemy shelling withered away, but one shell killed
Agnew, who had boasted often enough during the past two
years that no shell had his name on it. An expert polo-
player, they said.

Four Jerry planes came over in diamond formation, one
of our Archies blowing the leader to shreds first shot. A few
minutes later, our barrage fire still quivering air and earth,
Germany squared the account, and the fellows acclaimed
such excellent gunnery as vehemently as before. The lives
that had ended were of no consequence. A diversion.

A quarter of an hour to go. Old hands stuffed sandbags
and shovels up their backs between tunic and haversack.
A few squashed Mills bombs into their breast pockets.
Wonderful how these deadly missiles got knocked about
without damage. In England they were handled as carefully
as incandescent mantles!

With a singing whirr, a nose-cap buried itself in the trench
wall behind Bagnall, a boy from Burnley. He looked round
with dull surprise. Lieutenant Fulshaw ('Oo's nobbut a kid'),
the platoon commander, excited and enthusiastic, constantly
drew their attention to our battering of the German line.
All his patriotism welled uppermost as he watched the
tremendous weight of metal riving the trench in front.

'They'll never stick that, boys! We're on a picnic!'

Bradshaw found the suspense demoralising. He walked a
little way down the trench to where Bates leaned against the
parados, frothing at the mouth and shaking like a paralytic.
Next to him, Carter stood clasping and unclasping his rifle

barrel, face ghastly behind starting eyes. Bradshaw moved
quickly away, wondering if this could be 'shell-shock'. He
saw an old Lancashire sitting on the firestep, staring vacantly
straight ahead through the parados; right away to home.
Driver came up, not nearly so robust as several who had
cracked up; yet he bore himself unflinchingly. His only
comment on 'going over' had been:

'Well, Dick, Brettle's going to have his chance.'

Bradshaw guessed the rest by his own apprehension.
Zero 4.25! Five minutes to go. They'd be playing cricket at
home, if the weather was as good as here. Lucky blighters!
He'd come through all right. Must keep confident. Some
men sensed their own eclipse – he didn't feel like that. Yet
others must have felt the same, and gone west. Driver's
troubled eyes met his, probably pondering the same way.

Lieutenant Fulshaw bent his elbow, eye on wristwatch.

'Look, boys, the way that stuff's going up! Another three
minutes yet . . . they'll all be dead . . . !' The air above
quivered and was shattered, boxing Bradshaw's ears. Earth
rained down.

'Stretcher-bearers!'

He came, half dazed, out of a sidelong reel. Saw Driver's
face, big-eyed, with a tightened-up expression, looking queer.

A piece of shell spun and twanged. German shells rattled
the broken bones of Delville. Dirty grey shell-clouds hid
lumps of the sky, hanging heavy in the yellow sunshine.
Just on zero Carter (in the language of Chick) 'copped a
Landowner's packet'. The roar of our shells drowned the
approach of Jerry's, making them more terrifying. No
warning . . . blinding, crashing upheavals. . . .

Close on now – must be. They'd be getting tea ready at home. Had they had his field card yet? Fulshaw's eyes were brilliant with excitement. The first birthday he'd missed at home. They'd send him some of the cake in his next parcel. Must stick near Jack. One up the spout . . . make sure his safety catch was off. What an uproar. Good job they didn't know at home exactly what was happening.

The burden of shells lifted, the absence of racket stinging his ear-drums. He heard a whistle, a way off. Fulshaw swept his arm upwards, climbing the parapet. 'Come on, lads!'

Bradshaw experienced a moment of indecision. Should he jump over the parapet first, risking getting marked down, or hesitate till the others climbed out? Jerry's machine-guns would rake the parapet; many got pipped in the head in the act of climbing out. Like that film. He found himself on top, enormously magnified and exposed, and joined in the cramped forward walk of the irregularly formed line. Two others had worked themselves in between him and Jack. Better leave it at that. When would that empty feeling in the stomach go? He felt afraid to look in front, and kept his eyes down. They saucered with wonder at seeing a sun-baked face peering up at him from one shell-hole. It smelt. He saw another; a green-white face pressed into the side of the hole, the remainder a limp, ragged bundle of khaki. Some other battalion had been over the same ground.

He raised his eyes slowly over the dry pot-holed surface of No Man's Land; saw in front what might have been an indistinct row of heads and shoulders, some distance away. Impossible to go straight. Some holes had things to avoid in them. They plodded blindly over the innumerable gougings towards the crackling machine-guns and rifle-fire. The impetuous Fulshaw fell first, in Bradshaw's path. The little private bent down on one knee, forgetting the order that nobody had to stop with wounded. His officer waved him on, groaning; other hand to groin. Bradshaw had a desire to stay.

'Shall I get the stretcher-bearers, sir?'

The officer's face grew drawn with pain.

'No, no! Carry on!'

Bradshaw looked round and espied a dud shell. He pulled it up, surprised by its weight, and set it upright on its base near the officer.

'Just to mark the spot, sir. I'll tell the stretcher-bearers where you are as soon as I see them.'

He passed on, a dozen yards behind the thin, extended line. They looked pathetically ineffective. As he caught up, the back of Corporal Dawkins's head fell out; upraised arms sagged to earth. Bradshaw slipped in beside Driver without a word. Dawkins killed. He was post corporal at Bouzincourt – handed Bradshaw his mail.

They *were* men in front there. Germans. Patches of green further behind; unshelled fields. Sergeant Todd called out,

'Don't bunch up, there. . . .'

Bradshaw saw a wide gap on his right, moved right to lessen it. The next man closed towards him, then unaccountably dropped flat. He crouched lower, an attitude that gave a false impression of grimness and determination – men ready to strike. They were merely trying to minimise their bodily targets.

The spasmodic crackling rippled, then sharply cracked in

its sweeping arc. Above it Bradshaw heard a choking sob. Somebody fell. The sergeant staggered but kept on. Another sob. Wounds . . . exhaustion? He didn't know. But he no longer wondered why men walked to attack, even in broad daylight. The ground was abominably loose and uneven. No real surface. A series of craters and holes, with nothing to walk on but the loose rims.

The line thinned mysteriously; became little bunches of twos and threes. They stumbled on exhaustingly, throats dry. He looked up again. No mistaking them this time; less than a hundred yards away. He prayed for something to happen before he got that far. Chick was right, then? The Germans were safe in their dugouts whilst the ground was writhing under our barrage; ready to nip up when it lifted and catch us coming across?

No shells came to aid them now. They were targets. Sweating gunners would be saying:

'Well, if the bloody infantry don't do something after that lot, thank God we've got a Navy!'

The last seventy-five yards might well have been seventy-five miles. They would never get there. Every decent-sized shell-hole clung to Bradshaw's feet, saying: 'Get down to it, you fool. Get down to it! Pretend you're wounded!' Driver was still there, to the left and slightly ahead. He wanted to draw nearer, but felt that, closer, one or the other would be hit. He knew that the slightest swerve or stumble could put him either in the direct track of a bullet or out of its line of flight. To the end of his days the picture of those stumbling men would remain with him; floundering into shell-holes; climbing out. Faltering, dropping, reeling on. Bent figures stumbling forward with distressful gasps; falling, often remaining down.

Fifty yards from the German trench the struggling remnant expended its last ounces of diminishing energy. It gathered, too scattered and demoralised to go farther, into two huge craters, like the sheep that soldiers are.

Their first attack, a washout.

In the hole that held Bradshaw – a huge crater with cracked, blackened sides – there also scrounged a junior officer; Todd, their platoon sergeant, and seven privates, including Driver. Simmonds alone lay on the lip of the crater, potting away for dear life. The remainder crouched more or less unconcernedly lower down. Bradshaw feared a counter-attack. He pulled out his entrenching-tool, adjusted the head, and hacked futilely at the earthy side below Simmonds, murmuring something vague about 'digging in'. He hoped they were not expected to go any farther, and after a few minutes stood up sheepishly. The others were inactive. He saw two steel helmets bobbing in the next hole; Bragg under one of them. One unlucky shell would wipe out all that seemed to remain of 'C' Company. The officer spoke, appealing to the sergeant, who replied:

'Don't seem much good going on, sir. Asking for trouble, us few.'

A bullet had snapped his bayonet, driving a piece of the steel into his cheek. A trickle of blood oozed from a small, dark red blotch. Clearly he had no desire to continue. Thinking of Guillemont, no doubt. Bradshaw saw that another man, named Mason, kept shaking blood from his hand as it ran downwards from a forearm wound. Spots spread over his trousers as he sat flicking his arm impatiently. They were too weak to attack, yet forbidden to retreat: in any case the still bright sunshine would advertise any movement. Bradshaw had a spasm of despair. For the first time he felt his parched throat and dry tongue, but water was precious and he knew that uncorking his bottle meant passing it round.

Machine-gun bullets swished the air above. Jerry knew where they were all right! Influenced by common sense and perhaps by the squad's dog-like expressions, the subaltern decided to 'retire'. Bradshaw, though relieved, was puzzled. He had not yet learnt the subtle difference between retreating and retiring.

In Indian file, on their stomachs, they followed the officer and the sergeant from hole to hole, and soon watchful eyes saw the leading pair glide over the high lip thrown by an extra heavy shell. The third man, hit in the back, slithered back amongst his companions. Another collapsed limply athwart the crater rim, shot in the back. Bradshaw, the next to cross, hesitated, terrified. A sniper had got them taped. He was horrified by the idea of being left so unpleasantly isolated; the officer and N.C.O. had disappeared. He cried excitedly: 'Jack! That sniper'll get us that way. Let's try to the left!'

They took a different direction. Pantingly, frantically, they squirmed over, trying to connect up again with their leaders. Without a word they dragged off their equipment, retaining only rifles, bayonets, and gas-helmets. Flinging their rifles first over into an adjoining hole, they wormed this way and that. Over to the right here, now to the left. In and out, up, over, and down across the pitted barrenness;

all the time imagining the enemy at their heels. None of the others had followed. Here and there they came across dead; grotesquely inert, in horribly contorted flat postures. Some partially covered with newly turned earth, some shockingly mutilated, with green, white, or dark sunbaked faces; and all smelling. Once, impetuously diving down, Bradshaw fell on a corpse, almost embracing it. He felt sick, and straightway flung his rifle into a further hole, hastening after it. The bayonet had pierced another dead body. He cried out; scrambled to the next hole, leaving it. Nothing could have induced him to pull it out. Heart thumping painfully, he awaited his friend. Driver appeared, wild-eyed and grimacing. They lay down exhausted and frightened, sick from the smell and sight of the dead.

They were lost. The blackened bones of Delville, dully glinting in the low rays of the sinking sun, had veered unaccountably. Instead of being slightly to their right, their splintered tops broke the even sky on the left. To stand high enough to get their bearings from Trônes or Bernafay would attract a sniper again. Yet while their heads remained below ground level they were blind. Their loneliness and isolation frightened them. They feared capture, or a false move towards the Germans. They longed for a sight of the company, however small.

A single gun tormentingly dropped its loud-voiced shells around them. Bradshaw wanted to cut and run for it, but Driver preferred lying low where they were till dusk.

Long before the sun's orange disc reached the horizon its lower rim dipped into a princely September evening's haze. The sky, deep blue on one side, green and yellow on the other, slowly deepened. A stillness prevailed, its uncanniness pressing down on them. They peeped over the crater top. Shadows crept embracingly round the skeleton of the wood. They saw no sign of comrades, nor, indeed, of anything living; they were solitary souls on a sea of devastation. Bradshaw found it difficult to believe that a short time ago this same ground writhed and trembled under the lashings of barrage fire; that the air, earlier whipped by the whining shells, could settle into soundlessness. Hard, too, to comprehend that lads so healthily alive then lay thinly spread about in the silence. Near, but an eternity away.

They finished off their rations – tasting of the sharpness of their gas-helmet bags, into which they had hurriedly been pushed – Bradshaw his currants, Driver an onion; half and half.

Their direction was now clear – to the left of the wood towards the lower, and more distant, black bulk of Trônes. Yet they awaited confirmation from the Very lights. The first rose startlingly bright and close, their eyes following its graceful curve and loitering descent. It spluttered amongst the litter, a miniature effervescence, casting graded rays of brilliance in the sudden dimness above. Two others followed quickly from different spots, then a sniperish rifle-crack.

Bradshaw asked: 'Ready, Jack?'

They ran; if headlong diving, feverish scuttling, falling, scrambling, and tripping, can be called running. It was not too dark to discern still, silent figures of wounded or dead. Someone cried out to them, but neither paused. By remarkable coincidence, they chanced across Mr. Fulshaw. He had

had nearly four hours to ponder over the disappointment of his first attack; to conjecture on its success or failure. He was almost under Bradshaw's feet when a flare turned the underfoot unevenness into black pools and shone on Sam Browne buckles. The officer groaned. Bradshaw said, anxious to get back in the trench:

'I'll get hold of stretcher-bearers, sir. . . .'

Jack had disappeared. A few seconds later he tripped headlong into the trench at the spot he left it to attack. Blessed sanctuary! Driver lay blown and panting three yards away.

'Lieutenant Fulshaw's out there, Jack. Must get the stretcher-bearers to bring him in.'

He felt safe again in the trench, but weak as a kitten. Driver and he couldn't have carried the officer in just then. Might aggravate his wound, too. He walked along the trench away from the wood. Except for one man, face upturned to heaven, it was deserted for thirty yards, and often blown in. The shell-shocked and walking wounded must have moved back at dusk. A cry of pain attracted him. He strode farther over portions of blown-in parapet and found the line blocked by a ghastly assembly of dead. The groaning man muttered deliriously, parchedly:

'Haig's a Bloody Butcher. Jeudwine's a bloody butcher. Oh! Christ, water! Water! Oh, matey, water for the love of Christ! A drink, chum. Haig's a Bloody Butcher. . . .'

Bradshaw felt calmer than he had been all day. If he couldn't fight, he could at least ease his conscience by helping the wounded. He searched among them, finding a bottle still half full. The water's only virtue was wetness, but to this pitiful creature it was God-sent. None of these men could adjust his own dressings. Beyond them the trench curved into blackness between two or three gnarled, blasted tree-stumps, strangely like watching figures, barely visible against the blue-black sky. There were no sentries. Germans could pour through. Round the bend an indistinct, unwounded little group lolled and squatted. Ex-Manchesters! Sheep again, too uncaring to be watchful.

'Have you seen those wounded? What about keeping watch? If he attacks now, we're in the cart!'

Not one of them had water. He returned to the ditch of suffering.

'Where you wounded, chum?' he asked in turn, striding over outstretched legs, feeling for field-dressings and iodine tubes. Amateurishly, and, as he well knew, futilely, he applied bandages. No field first-aid outfit was adequate enough to stanch half-severed leg or torn stomach. A heavy piece of shell, to cause that last gaping slash! Blood-soaked trousers and shirt stuck round the wound. In the dimness Bradshaw made out a sergeant's chevrons on a limp left arm; a bandage soiled by his own bloodied fingers, and a wearily shaken head.

'Pass me, lad. . . . I'm . . . done.'

He straightened his back, stupefied by the steadiness of the dying man's voice, and moved on, tears trickling down his cheeks. He went to eleven in turn, two of whom were dead. Several begged weakly for water, but he could find no more. Bottles lay empty and musty. Five of the wounded at least would not – could not – last much longer without expert medical attention. A shadow moved up towards him.

'Dick! Any water left?'

'No. None anywhere. Aren't there any stretcher-bearers on this job?'

What could have happened to 'Drummer' Fogg? Perhaps away carrying wounded, or killed. Nothing less would keep him away from these poor devils. Where was everybody . . . officers . . . N.C.O.s . . .?

Bradshaw refused to believe that somewhere behind keen brains were not still studying their welfare; yet he decided with youthful, level-headed insight that there was something dreadfully wrong about the casualty clearing service.

He expected seeing squads of R.A.M.C. arriving, if not during the attack, shortly afterwards, to tend the wounded lying out. But this task was left to the battalion stretcher-bearers – ordinary infantrymen who carried rifles – of whom there were four to a company. If these four found the number of casualties too numerous to cope with, or themselves received wounds, the system broke down! What yeoman service a few dozen stretcher-armed men could have done that night!

He was afraid of being left alone with those dead. Yet the little attention he might give them seemed preferable to total neglect. Had all the others gone behind? He knew the penalty for leaving the trench. Very lights still went up in front. He rejoined the little knot of survivors, quiet now, speculating on the chances of relief. Dead beat, weak, hungry, thirsty, and lonely, he moved away again. Brooks, Aspinall, Bibby, and three or four others. He knew none of them as friends. He sat down; far enough off to enjoy the comfort of their presence without being disturbed by their conversation.

Back to parapet, legs across the trench bottom, he looked up and down. No sign of Jack. The night was cool and still; a blue-black darkness made blue-green by the occasional fountains of brilliancy behind him; the kind he had always liked for his night cycling. This, then, was war. Had the day been fierce, or merely ordinary? Were such 'attacks' everyday occurrences, happening all along the front, or had he participated in a big battle? Were those wounded part and parcel of every engagement; some unavoidable, inevitable aftermath? Where had Driver got to?

He pictured the Saturday night crowds at home. It would have given a few people he knew something to talk about if he had been amongst the dead out there. Not for long, though. One of many. They should be relieved to-night. Would the relief know where to come? Good word, relief. It would be one when they came. Were Jack and he and that little bunch the only survivors? Another flare went up, brightening the overhead and deepening the trench shadows. The Germans were not far away, behind him; perhaps two hundred yards. Nothing between him and them except casualties. Would they attack? He thought not. They could afford to lose French ground while we lost men. In any case, he could feign death. How quiet it all was now; only a few rifle-shots somewhere.

He heard voices coming near. Two men passed noiselessly along the parados, silhouetted against the darkness. One carried a closed stretcher on his shoulder. Bradshaw scrambled to his feet.

'Eh, chum! Lieutenant Fulshaw is out here badly wounded.'
They stopped and peered down.

'What company are you?'
' "C" Lancashires.'
'We're Liverpool Irish. Our colonel's out somewhere. They say he's dead.'

They passed on. Bradshaw could have laughed. Looking for a dead colonel! Officers first, always. Even when they've gone west. Rations, dugouts, everything. And he was a fool, mentioning only Fulshaw when there were others here. He felt suddenly lonely and weary again; wanting his friend's quiet company. A machine-gun popped far out in the darkness, answered by a second one. The two ripples of fire mingled and trailed away. Half a dozen lads, mere nineteeners, holding the British front in an important sector! Saturday night, and many thousands in England thinking pleasantly of their extra two hours' sleep in the morning. Sleep! Was it two or three nights since he had slept? Carrying on through the night without a definite bedtime break unseated one. Something should be done about those wounded. And sentries. Where could Driver have got to . . . ?

He awakened guiltily, like a man found asleep at his post. Something had touched him. The same vague obscurity clothed the trench; the shadows of two companions at the slight bend leaping in slow motion at each Very light. One leaned dejectedly, tin hat well back, chin-strap under his nose. Bradshaw saw these details by the aid of a foot-wide bar of greenish-greyness that appeared on the parados when a flare reached its maximum height; that gently narrowed and disappeared. Numb and stiff, memory returning, he shivered. Fumbling where his water-bottle should be lay the man who had damned the C.-in-C. and the divisional general; jaws working, but no sound coming. His bandage hung in dirty folds about his knees. Must have crawled twenty yards, dying! He muttered unintelligibly. There was no water. Bradshaw saw that the man's entrenching-tool head had been slung from his pouch straps to cover his abdomen.

He died quietly, quickly, at Bradshaw's feet.

MORNING came with a mist and no stand-to. All authority for ordering it was absent. When would somebody come to take charge? Jerry commenced a random fire that gave little trouble. A shell could pitch plumb in the trench almost anywhere without damage. Delville lay invisible behind the haze. The grimy seven hungered for sleep, food, and relief. Bradshaw looked at the other chins; felt thankful he didn't shave. Three days without a wash! One thing was certain: they were too few to go over the top again yet.

The relief came welcomely at about seven o'clock. Bradshaw never looked at their faces or epaulets. He scrambled up the parados and hurried away back. Somebody passed him running, and he followed suit; a fitting climax to their first stunt. An ignominious flight through the haze to where the communication trench commenced. Men sprang up dimly from nowhere; men who had been in hiding, in the wood.

A few erratically flung shells came over. The second killed one of the old hands, Elliot; out since Festubert. Bradshaw thought he might have been spared after enduring the last three days. A dead, dry figure reclined oddly flat against the side of a shell-hole, as if reading. They reached the trench and jumped between its chalky sides. Telephone wires hung festooned along one side. Two bodies in khaki stood in a bulge of the trench, faces bleached under bloodstains. They were propped up by the trench side. Bradshaw took a frightened glance at their dropped jaws and wide-open mouths, then hurried past. Farther down, two others had been caught whilst carrying water. One lay across the other, limp yet frozen with death. Both faces turned outwards, streaked with dried blood; one half shot away. Four riddled petrol-cans lay jumbled at their feet.

He hurried along in a trance, seeing without feeling emotion, hardly believing his own eyes. He stumbled at the heels of the man in front, urging him on quicker. If he could but rise clear from this beastly neighbourhood; soar away to unbefouled pastures. . . .

The communication trench – Hop Alley or Longueval Alley, he didn't know which – ran down to the point of Bernafay Wood, ending by the roadside. They crossed through a belt of the sickly death smell; encountered another dusty corpse entangled in telephone cables. The mist cleared before a bright new sun. Trunks and stumps became solid. Bobby Peach, their plump and smiling quartermaster, met them with a promise of breakfast where the road was lowest. Cookers came down the slope by Bernafay, and soon they were munching ravenously at thick slices of bacon. It was cold and fat, and had lost nothing in its various handlings. But their degree of hunger overrode any fastidiousness. A

German observation balloon confined them to the trench, and a battery of 'five-nines' barked away in broad daylight from the starkness of Trônes. Gaunt bareness on each hand, razed landscape and chalky excavations. An ambulance crept in view behind the cookers; pulled up at the dressing-station. At times figures appeared carrying stretchers, which they left on the ground fringing the wood. The observation balloon quickly achieved its object, for a terrific salvo of heavies crashed on the defiant Trônes battery. From the rising clouds of dirt and smoke Bradshaw saw more solid chunks flung higher, like balls from a Roman candle. He knew none of the men near by to talk to, but Sergeant Todd was there.

'Have you seen Driver, sergeant?'

'Driver? Who's . . . Oh, I know. . . .'

He turned round, passing the word up, and within a few minutes Bradshaw knew that Driver was all right, somewhere higher up the communication trench. Also Anderton, whom Bradshaw hadn't seen since Thursday evening. Get Fell In, the company sergeant-major, checked their numbers every half-hour, each count showing an increase. 'C' was thirty-five strong at eleven o'clock, most of whom had been lying low in Delville Wood. The old soldiers said more would turn up. One man near Bradshaw frightened him by the tales of dire punishment that would be meted out to him if he was caught without equipment and rifle. Each time the sergeant-major passed above the trench he closed up against the next man. He resolved to sneak out and win both immediately Get Fell In turned his back.

The Irish Guards captured Ginchy. Some of the men saw them going over at the same time.

Darkness came again; Sunday evening. Flares fluttered over the Longueval rise and through the carcase of Delville. Both artilleries commenced yapping and barking, our guns producing strange cracking echoes in the hollow. Bradshaw saw the dull red glows of bursting shells, and felt a horror of going up there again. An S.O.S. went up, followed by a request for help in the front line. He scrambled out of the trench on a pretext of visiting the canvas latrine, and quickly flitted over to the dressing-station; for a moment he feared being pounced upon as a deserter. He found a heap of equipment and a stack of rifles, discarded by those entering the aid post. He selected the best set of webbing he could find in the darkness, and as he turned away two R.A.M.C. men added another blanket-covered figure to the row close by. Gunfire still echoed over the darkened valley as he sneaked back, eyes twitching at the bright blinding flashes of British guns. Single, double, triple, quadruple; all flashing a second before the crack. Fritz replied with fewer, well-directed tearing crumps. The fellows reckoned their H.E. was much more destructive than our own.

Fifty men, including part of another company, also Bradshaw, Driver, and Anderton, together, marched once more up the communication trench. They were moody and afraid. Only the thought of men in distress kept Bradshaw going. It would be an easy matter to slip away in the darkness and somehow rejoin those who hadn't come. He felt they had been robbed of due deserts – a good rest. A halt came in the wood, and they dropped tiredly to the trench floor, quiet; sprawling.

A big fellow named Harrison suddenly spoke.

'What's the delay? Let's get into it, and finished, one way or the other.'

Nearly all were asleep when the message slowly trickled along: About turn. They were not required after all! Weary bones responded willingly, and soon they were back near Bernafay. Much had been granted to them.

Get Fell In passed along the trench ordering them to file out on the roadway. They became a fatigue party, carrying water up to the front line. The shelling died down; became of no account. Hundreds of petrol-tins lay on the roadside by a few small dugouts and dumps. Each man took two, to be haphazardly filled at two waiting water-carts. They went over the top by a rough track – the scene of their headlong flight that morning. Uncertain all the time, it grew worse near the front line. Ungathered wounded cried in the darkness near Waterlot Farm; always for water and stretcher-bearers. This was No Man's Land a week ago. The cans became astonishingly heavy; every step an adventure among holes and stumps and pieces of wire. Bradshaw seemed to be perpetually at the top of an unknown staircase, taking a last step that wasn't there. Every Very light turned the shallowest hole into a bottomless pit, like motor headlights do on a country road. Each man tasted the water he carried. It was petrol tainted; far worse to drink even than the chloride-of-limed stuff they knew. None of them had had time to rinse out his tin, even if such a great waste of water hadn't mattered. Most of the stoppers were missing, and at every slip-up and stumble the tainted and precious liquid spilled.

Shell-burst smells clung faintly to the air, slightly pungent. Farther away, Very lights revealed drifting smoke. Shells fell there. No peace, even, for the dead. Their worldly, bodily cares were over, but again and again the shells fell; burying, uprooting, riving, distorting. Many wounded who should have been safe in clearing-stations were hit time after time; killed. And wounded still lay out. Their cries for water made Bradshaw shiver. Two days; three, four, even a week they claimed deliriously to have lain there dying. The file drew up and concertinaed many times. Once a wounded man raised sufficient energy to grope his way to them, clutching the ankles of the carrier in front of Bradshaw. He heard the splash of liquid as it gurgled into outstretched eager hands. The water was for the men in front, though; they hurried to connect up again.

Bradshaw had a feeling that a bugler ought every night to send the wailing notes of the Last Post echoing over the battlefield, so utterly, outrageously lonely lay the fallen. Too many shells and not enough stretchers on this job.

They marched back through the night past Montauban, dispirited and fagged; moving mechanically without grace, neither swearing nor singing. The guns rumbled and flickered on their right flank. Bradshaw had never known darkness to be so empty and forlorn; there must have been swarms of men about, yet they encountered only one party returning dejectedly even as themselves, their morale in their gait. Driver walked by his side; quiet, contained. They were all quiet. He hadn't heard a song for ages.

'D'you remember the officers at Mytchett Camp coming

round to the huts announcing the Great British Victory early in July, Jack?'

Driver nodded in the darkness, and grinned.

'And we thought they were going straight through and finishing it before we got out.'

Every day or night since men had been going over the top in the same victorious battle. Going to their deaths with smiles on their lips! What rot had been written about this battle. Men were not hoping, now, to come through unscathed. They preferred wounds that would take them away from it all to safety. When they were lucky, and this happened, they became the cheerful wounded so beloved of war correspondents.

Like cattle they were turned into a field. Bobby Peach apologised for having nothing more appetising to offer them than hard biscuits and cheese. The darkness considerately hid their tumbled bunches of undiscipline as they sank thankfully to the ground. Many dropped asleep with rations in their hands. Bradshaw kept awake for some time. He was just learning what the infantryman's war meant. This, over and over again till you got pipped. The old hands became his heroes again. How they stuck it for more than once and remained as they were was incredible.

'Patriotism isn't oozing out of their pores by any means', he said later to Driver, 'but they're positively nonchalant!'

Bowker said it were a bloody shame to put fresh troops into places like Delville; they ducked at bullets long gone past, and shells that dropped nowhere near. Chick argued that new men had the advantage; they didn't know beforehand the extent of the danger. Bradshaw had no

desire to test either theory again. He felt happy at coming
out all right; empty stomached at the thought of going back
again. They had earned a good rest. He realised that seeming
inefficiencies were too big and weighty to grapple with; later
he would joke about them, ponderously sarcastic; knowing
that each man's measure of enthusiasm wilted instead of
flowering; accepting that all a man could do was a duty by
himself and his comrades. Nothing, nobody, else mattered.

On September the 14th, they arrived in Méaulte, a well-
worn, many times second-hand village known to most
infantrymen. Several days' post awaited them, much of it
for the absent. A pathetic but callously humorous sight, this
grouping round a lance-corporal who called their names.
For every letter or parcel not immediately claimed a chorus
of reasons why were advanced:

'On the wire at Guillemont!'

'Nappoo!'

'Landowner at Ginchy!'

'Gone west!'

Unclaimed parcels were opened for the food, though
rations were now plentiful, the same amount having been
issued to the reduced numbers. There were four letters and
a parcel for Bradshaw.

Several of the shell-shocked cases came back. The tanks
passed through, revelations of mightiness, and everyone
spoke enthusiastically of their antics. 'That'll show the
bleeders!' 'Give 'em hell.' They cheered as SAN FAIRY ANN,
FRAY BENTOS, and BLIGHTY passed. The caterpillar 'wheels'
fascinated Bradshaw.

THE Lancashires left Méaulte September the 16th and bivouacked under groundsheets on the road leading up Flers way. On the same road camped dusky sons of India, facetiously known as Bengal Lights, who had rigged up ingenious dwellings with empty ammunition boxes.

Bradshaw forgot his pre-war politeness far enough to stare curiously into these low wooden dwellings. The floors were lined with shallow boxes, and in several of the huts a hole rather larger than a penny in size had been cut in this flooring. Bradshaw was intrigued by the curious constructions some of the fellows built round those holes. Many of the Indians, though quite young men, wore beards, and badges of rank were sewn on their tunic lapels. They seldom spoke except when trading 'mon-gee'.

'Bullee for chupattee?' they would ask, and find a dozen Britons eager to exchange a tin of bully beef for one of the tasty pancakes, cleverly made from 'dog' biscuits, they called chupattees.

'They're waiting for the break-through. Two squadrons went over in July and haven't been heard of since!'

Bradshaw couldn't believe that. No horse could gallop far enough to disappear over the shell-bitten surface of No Man's Land. Its legs would snap. A battalion, that was, of Yorkshire troops passed the bivvies, all looking sick at heart. Tunics open at the neck; tin hats pushed well back over drooping heads; arms listlessly dangling, feet shuffling. They were all silent. To have sung 'Tipperary' then would have been a gross insult to those they left behind. Revived spirits would come later with sleep and food.

Bradshaw wrote to his brother, giving a crude account of his first action. It was childish and bitter, savouring strongly of indignation and criticism. He got it off his chest, then regretfully tore it up. It would be censored. Too risky to use a green envelope; that might be opened. He sent several of those 'All's well, don't worry' notes that so tired the censoring company officers. What could one say beyond asking for parcels, exchanging healths, and exhorting the recipient to keep smiling? What was it Chick said he always wrote?

'DEAR MOTHER, – Please send me ten shillings and the *News of the World*.
'P.S. – Don't forget the *News of the World*.'

Were officers' letters censored, or could they write what they thought?

Rain poured persistently. The papers said it would hold up our offensive, though the weather had been excellent since the attack started, over two months before. They moved up to a slippery reserve line behind Flers, greatcoats sodden and glistening and heavy. Bradshaw slithered and shuffled along unheedingly, his section eventually occupying a shallow depression where the water gathered; a flattened crater with a sliding surface. Given a trench, they could have dug funk-holes and rigged up ground-sheets, but any trench there might have been was obliterated. One or two men, inadequately wrapped in their groundsheets, lay openly on the wet, clayey ground. Others dug oblong excavations like graves, but only sufficiently deep (a foot) to hold the recumbent figure of a man. These were covered with the rubber sheet, and pegged on three sides with bullets through the lace-holes. The occupier crept in underneath. As in the Mametz cornfield, Bradshaw and Driver stood about miserably in the grey drizzle, cheerful enough outwardly. Several incidents made them laugh. A passing man slipped and fell into one of the occupied graves. Another whose hole was a little too deep received down the neck a good quart of rain when his groundsheet, bellying, gave way. An officer passed, wearing the ordinary Tommy's khaki trousers, puttee'd, looking very funny. (So many had been picked off when going over the top that this disguise had been adopted, disclosing the unathletic contours hitherto covered by the officer's uniform.) Every direction was clouded by drizzle, wet and grey. A few shells would honestly have been regarded as a distraction from the soaking inactivity. At seven o'clock an officer appeared, telling them to fall in.

'Fall in!' said Bradshaw disgustedly.

They slid and skidded through the gathering dusk over greasy ground back to a field alongside the road, boot deep in black mud, rapidly becoming a quagmire. Their quarters for the night. Useless to dig; too slushy to lie in. Only half a day's rain! Bradshaw unslung his pack, dropped it, then sat on it. Then he drew his groundsheet round his neck like a barber does, making a miniature bell tent of himself.

'Come on, Jack. Take a pew!'

They watched the rain trickling down ground-sheets; dripping from steel helmets. The gloom deepened, and dozing men toppled sideways into the slop. Couples tried leaning back to back; others trudged about, abjectly miserable.

'We'll be going up to the front line again to-morrow morning, fresh and fit from our rest', grumbled Bradshaw.

He grew stiff and numb; frozen-footed, but he wouldn't admit that he found this roughing it worse than he imagined it. It seemed such a simple matter to erect a few tarpaulin-covered shelters or marquees. They were nearly two miles from the front line. Driver must have been feeling it badly. Could anything be more calculated to distress a carefully nurtured soul like his companion than hanging about in wet, open fields in rain and slime? With what joy they would welcome the oft-cursed trio of bed-boards!

> *Round the old camp fire*
> *A rough and ready choir . . . !*

He felt thankful for Jack's companionship. It seemed to halve the discomforts. The others, nearly all astonishingly good-natured, called them the Twins. They became known as non-smokers, non-swearers, and non-drinkers. Anderton still retained a friendly interest, but had coupled himself with Legs Eleven and Harrison, who couldn't believe that Bradshaw and Driver carried abstention to such a length.

'You don't smoke?' Harrison asked them, brow puckered incredulously. 'Hell fire! I couldn't stick a bombardment without a fag. No booze and no women, either? No pleasures of any kind?'

Low, stormy clouds delayed the dawn, which stole on them, chilled and shivering. Those who had slept stiffly stretched benumbed limbs; raised aching bodies from the trampled filth they had rolled into, swearing at the black mud. It lay thickly on boots, puttees, greatcoats, and equipment. Driver's rifle, one of an unstable pile that had collapsed, was coated with it from bayonet-boss to breech cover. They marched off – to where? The rain stopped. Somebody big-heartedly started 'Rolling Home', but many of them were too wet and wretched to join in.

Two or three went sick. A battalion of Manchesters passed, coming down, apparently at full strength.

'Bin lucky this trip, mate?'

They learned that the Manchesters' bombing officer, all his bombing N.C.O.'s and section leaders round him, was giving a lecture on bombs when the Mills Mark Five, which he held, exploded, killing several and wounding all the others more or less seriously. Beheaded, as it were, the battalion was going back to reorganise.

'Lucky bees!'

'Stripes'll be coming up wi't rations to-neeght.'

During the roadside midday meal, a beautiful blue patch of sky appeared, broadening with the sailing, thinning cloud. Bradshaw heard a voice calling:

'Bradshaw! Two Six Bradshaw!'

His heart jumped. What had he done? The orderly sergeant warned him for a salvage party; Bradshaw looked at him timidly. Was there some perilous duty in the front line attached? (Orderly sergeants adopted divers methods of obtaining fatigue parties, asking anybody who could ride a bike or work a typewriter to fall out on officers' mess fatigue, or guard duty.) (I want two volunteers – you and you!) Salvage? What could that be?

'But I say, sergeant, I don't want to leave my chum here. . . .'

'Can't be helped. I've got you down on my list to go.'

'Well, can Driver come too?'

'No. I'm sorry, but I must stick to this roll. You'll be back with us soon.'

The sergeant was adamant. Bradshaw learnt afterwards that he had obliged two others in a similar way, but one of them, as it might have been Jack, had got killed. The sergeant blamed himself for it. Bradshaw saw the reasonableness of this argument. Foolish to drag away from any direction the army pointed out to you. Let it take you where it would.

Soon the little party was tramping the glistening road through Buire towards Fricourt. From 'C' Company, besides Bradshaw, came Downes, Blakeley, Riley, and Ireland, all privates. The last was to become regimental sergeant-major before the war was ended!

Squat howitzers hurled their whistling loads from the road bankings. Bradshaw looked at them unemotionally. He had been listening to barking detonations all his life, it seemed. A gunner asked if they were the remains of a battalion. What had once been a small church lay spread in little heaps save for one low battered wall. They gaped at a miniature coloured statue of Christ, looking uninterruptedly on the wreck and ruin about. Bradshaw knew about these crucifixes. None were ever destroyed by shells. This one certainly had been protected by its stone alcove, but what about Ginchy church, Longueval, Guillemont?

The lieutenant in charge, an oldish, bespectacled man who beamed every time he spoke, trotted on ahead with bowed legs. His name was Gray, but they called him Uncle. He said their job was cushy. They reached the old front line at Fricourt, a tragic ground of empty trenches and newly growing clumps of grass and weed. The slaughter had commenced here, two and a half months ago. Never had it slackened during that time. Riley and Blakeley found a deep *cul-de-sac* trench, long disused, and decided to convert it into a home. They had no idea how long they were to remain salvaging – till the battalion recalled them, it was assumed – and shells could still pitch this far. So they scouted round for logs and stumps; found a number of planks once used for dugouts, and erected a fairly thick roof over the dead end of the trench; almost waterproof.

As Uncle said, their job was cushy. Simply to scour a prescribed area of the battlefield and collect all serviceable equipment left by the slowly advancing army. Goodly dumps of rifles, packs, bombs, .303 ammo., bandoliers, tin hats, picks, spades, shell-cases, boots, bayonets, periscopes, and other war equipment quickly grew in the days that followed. Most of the time the guns in one sector or another announced fresh attacks, fresh casualties. All they got behind were occasional heavies; sharply thunderous, but few and far between. Bradshaw time and time again wished that Driver was with him, safe at any rate for the moment. Uncle proved to be a thorough sport.

He attached himself to an artillery unit for rations, and won all he could for his men, who were really on nobody's ration strength. They worked hard two hours in the morning on one area, cleaned it up, then moved to another for the afternoon, each man free to roam as he wished. There was

a good deal of private souveniring. At tea-time they made
their way back to Fricourt, eager to see what nature of food
their Uncle had scrounged. It occurred to Bradshaw that any
isolated squad who looked to an infantry unit for spare grub
would fare badly. The weather turned fine and warm again.
It brought forth whiffs of death from crushed-in dugouts and
tangled woods, but real danger was far enough off.

Beyond Fricourt, the ground was unbelievably pulverised.
Bradshaw noted with a veteran's eye what a tremendous toll
must have been paid to the machine-gunners before those
gentle, dark-brown slopes could be crossed. Under the crest
of one ridge lay a huge German dugout; a stupendous piece
of engineering, big enough to house a full battalion. Floor,
sides, and ceiling were boarded, and many thick pillars of
wood supported the extensive roof. No shells could bite this
deep. A wave of attackers might reach and overflow the Jerry
front line, only to get shot down from behind; a simple matter
in spacious cellars like this. The grass grew richly green in
parts of this lashed countryside. Tortured tree-stumps still
stood upright, but of bricks and mortar and stonework not a
sign remained visible. A slow-moving stream of traffic passed
slowly along the straight road to their left, but the stripped
fields they searched were quiet and unoccupied. Dotted here
and there on the rising sides of the slopes, little heaps of
chalk and cut-out emplacements indicated where our guns
had rested before moving with the advance. Blown-in trench
sections showed where the artillerymen had dodged back to
escape the destruction that descended from the sky. Empty
shell-cases sprinkled the ground, and big craters; with here
and there an unbelievable patch of grass that had somehow

escaped the flaying barrages. The next crop that grew over the waste ought to be blood red, not green. Riley found an old dugout, completely buried till a recent shell had once more made an entrance. The hole revealed a ghastly tomb. Half a dozen putrescent bodies fouled the air, proving too strong for their most hardened souvenir-hunter. Germans.

One afternoon Riley came across a sack containing seven loaves, a cube tin of sugar, and one of tea. They had been left by a company of departing Aussies, and afforded Downes a further opportunity to curse and grouse at the better treatment meted out to Colonial troops.

'. . . they know damn well the Aussies'd mutiny if they dished 'em up with four to a loaf, same as we get. . . .'

He would have been satisfied to see those great frames wilting on the ordinary infantryman's ration rather than see his own share increased. There was joy in the little dugout that night, and the three declared they could stick salvaging for the duration.

Next day Bradshaw found himself in Longueval, where he met some cheerful walking wounded of the Cast Iron Division. The Lancashires had got mauled again near Gueudecourt, and were coming out to leave that part of the line for good. Later in the day he met Capper of 'C', and enquired about Driver and Anderton.

'Anderton? He got pipped first day in. Had a shell to himself. Don't know about Driver. A chum of yours, wasn't he?'

Anderton killed! Hardly believable. And Jack . . . he must have been very near, being in the same section. Capper must be mistaken; it was easy to get names mixed up. Without seeing it, he had been staring at a pool by the roadside near a wrecked iron gate. The water was blood-red and stagnant. Out of its edge, buried up to the neck, a devilish face leered, baked nearly black by the sun. The distorted mouth held a fixed, fiendish grin. A square-head! Somebody should bury it. The Blood Pool stank, too. Anderton killed. Bradshaw couldn't grasp it. Going over the top, recklessly, he could imagine it; but standing in a trench stopping a shell. . . . He turned back, sick at heart, and walked slowly back to the little home at Fricourt. As dusk was falling, guns hammered away on his left hand, merciless, brutal . . . it might have been himself but for this salvage job.

When he got back, the other salvagers were standing in a rough group round Uncle, who told them of the impending move to Belgium.

'. . . but though we've managed to push him back still farther, we haven't broken the Old Boche's line. He's sticking to it very tenaciously, and the salient we have forced enables him to concentrate all his guns on any threatened spot. We are fortunate, very fortunate, being here!'

Bradshaw stood silently listening with the others, fingering an array of bullets and cartridges in his pocket. Like all the others, he had a collection of souvenirs. Varied makes of cartridge clips, German shoulder tabs, a 'tater-masher', and a funny little bomb with legs like a tortoise; two red sponges – the rubbers from behind the eye-pieces of gas-goggles.

On the way back to their dugout Riley looked at Bradshaw several times, then said:

'That mate o' thine's getten killed, then?'

Mate of his? That meant Driver, not Anderton . . .

'Mate of mine? D'you mean Anderton?'

'Noa. Well, aye . . . er . . . both on 'em, I hear.'

The war, the world, everything, stopped still for a few lifeless seconds. A pair of serious brown eyes leapt before Bradshaw's vision. He saw them glazing over.

'Who told you that?'

Riley hesitated. He thought Bradshaw knew.

'We met some o' t' lads coming back this after, near Longueval. Old Swish got pipped too, and Legs Eleven an' Haines an' that other mon they caw'd Pip', he went on hurriedly. 'Lucky, being here.'

'How was Driver killed – d'you know?'

'Aye. They say it were wi' t' same shell as get'n Anderton.'

So they'd been killed together, if it were true. But for this job, he'd have been with them, certain.

He walked next day to the trenches he believed the Manchesters had attacked from on July the 1st; the bloodily famous springing-off point of the Great Push. Chalky parapets; fallen-in cubby-holes; wrecked trenches. Disused, old, neglected; long forgotten. A few brave tufts of grass again pushing through. Green, all right. Nothing more to show that in one day a city had been plunged in mourning. Berry, Ingham, Clarke, Gibson . . . heroic figures of the local cricket field; gods, before the war, to Bradshaw. He pictured them marching down Market Street in the early days, the Pride of Manchester. A few pessimistic humorists had looked on and said: 'They'll never go out. The War Office has lost 'em!'

But they had gone out.

And nothing remained but draft-swamped survivors, who

would hold to their dying days the poignant memories of
their first big attack, remembering the inhuman price their
friends paid. It wasn't difficult to picture the trench before
zero that awful day. There would be confidence and courage,
bravado and bravery – not the usedness that had come since.
The trench was shallow here and there, filled in where a
shell had dropped near the parapet. Bradshaw felt a lump
in his throat. Such a shell had killed Driver; and Anderton.
He sat down and pulled out his diary. September the 19th.
(Over two years of war, and really only just starting. It was
only half way to its lumbering, massive conclusion!) The
Somme battle had knocked the bottom out of everything. At
the end of June, when the Germans hoisted a board from
their trench bearing the words 'WE ARE READY', our fellows
had laughed as at a great joke. The higher command had
expected being in Bapaume within two or three days of
the opening attack; and now September was waning, with
the spires of that objective town still faint and far off on
the enemy's side of the line. The higher command hadn't
allowed, in their calculations, for the German machine-guns.

Bradshaw wrote: 'For three months this battle has raged
with a bloodthirstiness curiously cannibalistic.' (He felt proud
of that phrase.) 'Irresistible bodies versus immovable objects,
if conflicting journalism is to be believed. Our side claims
victory because they have bloodily gained, lost, and regained
a strip of putrescent ground; their opponents because an
ensanguined front remains unbroken. It cannot last long at
this pace. One day there will be no reserves to go forward,
late or otherwise; the blood will have run out. However long
the war lasts, the effect of the Somme will remain to the end.'

An artillery officer approached, and, in scrambling to his feet, note-book and pencil slipped to the ground. He grabbed the small book, saluting with it in his hand as the officer motioned him down again, smiling.

'Papers are not read much here, but I have seen one to-day that denies in this carnage any attempt to break through. We are merely relieving the pressure on Verdun. . . . !'

On September the 21st the salvage party was requisitioned to aid in widening and deepening an old trench through Delville Wood. It had to be six feet wide at the top, gradually tapering; with no sharp bends to impede the progress of stretcher-bearers. Sweat poured off them as they laboured in the hot sunshine, and the smell of the dead hung round, sickening. They encountered decaying bundles of leather, ragged khaki and grey; obstacles that with remarkable unconcern were used to strengthen the trench walls. At times the stench was overpowering. A protruding jackboot a yard from where Bradshaw dug was battened by a vigorously applied spade till it conformed with the trenchside.

 He picked up more epaulet tabs with red numbers on blue-grey cloth, and a postcard signed A. Gehring crossed on one side with the pointed script that took him back to schooldays; bits of saw-edged bayonets and a few handle-less German spades. This trench had been taken and retaken seven times, they said. Behind it, in the tangled growth and uprooted trees, lay dead men still undiscovered. Always ahead, the grumbling and growling went on. Always at hand, the sweetish, creeping death smell.

A T the end of September they left Dernancourt to rejoin the division. On their cattle-truck was chalked 'POPERINGHE', an unfamiliar name. Bradshaw enquired of its whereabouts from a bowed French porter, but all the information he gained was a characteristic gesture and a reiterated assertion that it was *beaucoup kilos*. Bradshaw was glad to leave the Somme, a great tragedy whichever way it ended. The weather kept good. Men still went over. But soon the winter rains would come, turning the shell-worried fields into seas of porridge-like mud. Men would have another great enemy to overcome, but that smell might get washed away!

More than once – frequently in fact – had he heard the Commander-in-Chief alluded to as The Bloody Butcher. Without doubt there had been bloody butchery. Old hands said that the divisional general swore to make the Somme either a Lancashire victory or a Lancashire graveyard. Bitter epithets were hurled at his head. A few weeks before, Bradshaw would have been horrified at such talk. Now he classed it with another statement he had sometimes heard: 'There is no God – how can there be?' It was physical and mental pain talking: soul-sickness, fed-upness.

None of them showed that he was either pleased or sorry such a cushy job had ended. They just accepted the move with fatalistic resignation hidden under a 'Don't care a damn what they do with us' attitude. Bradshaw himself had no occasion to rejoice at the prospect of rejoining the 'bat'. He would tell that orderly sergeant that he might have let Jack join him on the salvage party . . . although *he* might have got pipped too by now.

He had lots to write about, but couldn't find the proper words. How explain the difficulties of breaking through to people miles away, who believed we were winning, yet who daily wondered at the size of the casualty lists? How let them know that the German was more of a fighter and less of a beast than they believed?

'One amazing aspect of this tremendous battle, involving hundreds of thousands of men, is the lack of actual fighting, in the true sense of the word. Attackers find that the trench they are ordered to take is either bristling with machine-guns, that polish off the attempt before it can fructify; or they find that their own shells have levelled defenders and objective line. An aeroplane spots an occupied trench, or troops concentrating. A few registering shots come, then a hurricane of shells: unfightable deaths. And the light goes out of eyes; here, then at home. Why cannot infantry oppose infantry, and artillery fire only at opposing guns? Steely, bursting shells versus human flesh! And men endure all this merely because a deep-down instinct has whispered, "Go! Go! Or your head will for ever droop!"'

Down the lines of communication they travelled, slowly leaving the war farther and farther behind. A night here in a siding; a day there, held up while more important freight passed; all the time in a cattle-truck with Uncle. They sneaked hot water from the engine for brewing tea during stoppages (you could creep up and do this without the driver and fireman noticing), and several of the less scrupulous ones sold empty British 18-pounder shell-cases to British nurses as captured German trophies.

It was October the 10th when they reached Calais, and, although the weather had remained ideally mellow, no news of a break-through arrived. When not busy interviewing R.T.O.s, Uncle proved most communicative. With back propped against the truck side, sitting on the floor like the others, he would lay his hands on bony knees and impart what information he had gleaned. The tanks hadn't fulfilled expectations. They made their debut at Flers the Friday following the Ginchy stunt, but did little damage beyond causing a temporary panic. Bradshaw understood they pushed buildings over and climbed trees; that those of the enemy not crushed to death under the caterpillars turned and fled in horror. But, it seemed, vulnerable spots in their armour had quickly been found by Jerry. Within a week, the Germans on the Somme had been completely equipped with armour-piercing bullets, and soon the massive bulks of many of these great land-ships lay helpless and rusting in No Man's Land, their crews casualties.

They turned inland again, passing more and more of those lucky men who enjoyed three meals a day and a sleep most nights. Bradshaw found it easy to understand why rations passing up the line dwindled before they reached the infantry.

For the first time he understood a little the magnitude of the war. Before he came out, lines of communication had conveyed something vague connected with signallers or telephone operators stationed at long intervals between the coast and the front; isolated little parties that kept in touch with England.

Now it seemed that for every man fighting there were half a dozen helping in the rear. Camps abounded everywhere along the journey, with huts and more stable military erections that from their well-built permanence made Bradshaw wonder whether they had been there pre-war. What jobs could all these men be doing behind the lines? Big fellows, mostly, and almost all stronger and healthier-looking than infantrymen. How wrong he had been in thinking that all the men who came to France and Belgium were soldiers – fighting soldiers! These men were as safe here as in England! Downes grumbled unceasingly, and, though Bradshaw disregarded him disgustedly, there was more than a germ of truth in his complaints. The nearer you got to the line, the less pay you got. The danger and the comfort were not shared equally enough. For some it was all danger and discomfort; for the others sleep – and rations – and a roof above your head. All the fit Derby men were pushed into line regiments, so these bees were 1914–1915 volunteers. . . .

  Before the year ended, Bradshaw echoed these grouses. He used to laugh at the fellows who pointed out that Runworth, a violinist who played in the Hallé Orchestra, had been kept off drafts because he gave recitals in the officers' mess. Wouldn't they all have been violinists? But grousing became more and more fashionable.

  The tedious though generous journey ended in the sublime peacefulness of a late summer afternoon, Poperinghe's dinginess faintly relieved by the October sun's gilding. Belgium! Now almost England. Belgians held the shops, but khaki predominated. Here and there the result of a high explosive shell. An engine puffed down the main street by the square on unsleepered lines like an English tramcar. A big wooden hoarding shouted silently 'Wind Dangerous',

and indicated the road to Ypres. The fellows called it
Wipers, Wi-pres, Eeps, Eepris, Eepray. Ypres! One name a
generation would know without having to wonder what and
where it was. A fearful, beautiful name, speaking of gas and
a laughable outcry against 'inhuman' warfare. Ypres, where
the Regular Army perished in saving the Channel ports.

Uncle said:

'Better march in some sort of order through here.'

Buildings turned to tall trees; two straight rows. A couple
of youngsters passed in the strangest of carriages and
pairs – a wooden box pulled by dogs. Two-dog power,
thought Bradshaw. Camps in the field either side; washing
hanging out; observation balloons; sunshine and quietness.
Brandhoek, a name without a village, complete with hop-
poles that reminded Bradshaw of an infinitely more beautiful
place: Kent. The battalion rested in a scraggy wood in a
number of smallish wooden gable huts. 'B' Camp.

Bickerdyke greeted Bradshaw after they had reported at
the orderly room.

'Hello! Wheer's ta bin? Thow't tha'ad getten killed at
Gudicourt. . . .'

Bradshaw smiled weakly, and confessed he'd been
scrounging at salvaging. Nobody else seemed to remember
him. The only face he knew at all well was Bagnall's. Where
had Ditchfield, Mason, Bowker, Bibby, and Sergeant Todd
got to?

The huts held eight men each, giving fair room, and a
craze for cleanliness had bitten somebody. Equipment hung
over each man's place, displayed with greater preciseness
than during training at home. Above each set a small card was

pinned, bearing the owner's name and number. Bradshaw soon learnt by the language that the cleaning orgy was being enforced. All buckles and straps must be polished. Woe betide the man whose boots showed a speck of dirt; or whose rifle's back sight, or piling-swivel, harboured dust. (Nobody bothered, however, to clean ammunition. You merely threw away your old stuff and replaced it with the new that lay about unchecked.) A spot of grease on a man's uniform became a blot on his character and a crime on his conduct sheet if it remained there for two parades. Petrol was issued for the removal of stains. Cleanliness of body, although of secondary consideration, was not entirely neglected. It was of the utmost importance that a half-inch strip of rubber ground-sheet peeped below your valise flap when on parade; that the singlefold of your blanket should show to the front.

Bombers, Lewis gunners, signallers, runners, and other 'specialists' had already been picked, but the company was too depleted for a full complement. Get Fell In pounced on the returned salvage party with the nearest approach to affection Bradshaw had seen him display.

'You look a likely lad; join Bagnall on stretchers.' So Bradshaw became a stretcher-bearer. Get Fell In was evidently blind to the incongruous disparity in their heights. Must always remember to take the feet, he thought. One blessing; S.B.s had been granted a belated concession and need no longer carry rifles. His first parade was devoted to listening to a short sermon on the 'orrors of gas and the prevalence of it in Eeps, and adjusting by numbers the new box respirator. Half a dozen high-up shells passed wailingly over *en route* for Poperinghe, reminding Bradshaw of the war. Later, the tall M.O. lectured all stretcher-bearers, stressing the importance of keeping the hands clean.

The battalion had not yet been up in the line, but went towards Ypres to Vlamertinghe every night on a cable-burying party, travelling by the railway line that ran to Ypres, there decapitated by countless shells. With two or three days' rest in 'B' Camp still ahead, the chaps sang as they neared the mysterious town of fiery activities and still more threatening silences. The sentimental 'Sweet and Low' and 'Swanee River' sounded infinitely pathetic in the darkened coaches as the train gently rocked along. No lights beyond glowing cigarette ends were permitted over the latter half of the distance.

The ground proved to be soft and easy to dig, but at three feet they struck water. Those not 'jildy' soon had the trench-sides collapsing over their feet, so quickly did they sag when unsupported. The cable lay alongside, ready to be laid and covered; any on-the-mark shell could render its whole length useless at a critical moment. An officer moved along, swishing his cane.

'Get a move on, lads. The sooner we finish the quicker we're back in camp.'

Bradshaw didn't realise, till mail arrived next morning, that it was his birthday.

THE Somme offensive fizzled out. Bradshaw wondered how the papers would excuse themselves, but the papers blandly pointed to the rivers of mud at Beaumont Hamel and St. Pierre Divion. The Lancashires assembled in platoons on the duckboard paths outside the huts, in full pack. Considerable haggling and grousing over the carrying of trench equipment – periscopes, flare pistols, Lewis gun pans, and such things. They filed out silently into the road, rows of hop-poles silhouetted against the darkening, frosty night. G.S. waggons pushed them into gutters, upsetting the harmony of their vocalism.

Bradshaw felt creepy. The night grew heavy with silence. Ypres ahead; the name that awed. And perhaps gas. The moon rose higher, spreading a thin green mantle over the disordered wreckage of the station. Then an amazing assembly of jagged ruins sprang up on either side. Tall, angular silhouettes, edges gleaming. Fantastic stage property. Roofless wedges of wall standing brokenly. Glassless wrecks of framework. Gaping holes.

A misshapen dirigible of blackness towered over-balancingly at a corner on the right. A street of ghostly doorways and moon-flooded interiors. A huge fang of stone, the highest about, reared up in the sparkling sky. A dim, arched doorway, piled high with debris: St. Martin's. The jagged, monstrous row of ruins reminded Bradshaw of decaying teeth. They receded suddenly as the troops entered a market square. The Square. Splashes of moonlight poured through rows of window spaces on the left, revealing great boulders of stone. The scraping of hobnailed boots died away as 'C' Company marched past this last formidable upset. Bradshaw felt intimidated; a vague reverence; respect for the men who had died defending the town. Hundreds of Tommies – or Jocks – and civvies lay dead in the cellars underneath this cathedral – sealed tombs since 1914. The company passed silently, eyes and mouths agape with wonder, paying their homage.

A narrow street again, then two banks of darkness; the Ramparts. Across the Menin Gate to open ground. Officers said:

'Quiet now, lads. Cigarettes out!'

They were pulled up alongside a heap of ruin at a fork road, then crossed the field to the right. The files in front vanished into the wine-cellars, invisible from above, bare save for bunk-like rows of wire beds. The old familiar Very lights soared in greeting two kilometres ahead, but gunners held their hands. Too nice a night to do anything but gaze upwards into the mystery of blue-blackness and brittle twinklings. Was this the Ypres front, this alarming quietness and sharp freshness?

They stayed till the following night, then assembled outside again and trickled over the road to a communication trench wriggling and squirming its way to the front line. In places there were no walls to this trench. Two guns fired a long way behind, and soon after a shell rose complainingly, shrieked towards them suddenly, and passed behind quivering. A dud. Quietness again, then a distant muttering on the right.

'That's Armenteers way!'

Bradshaw found that, even when empty and closed, few things can be as awkward to carry down a twisting trench as a stretcher. At every stoppage on the long trail – and there were many – either the man in front or the one in rear received a nasty jab from the handles, sometimes on the chin, others at the back of the neck. Bradshaw resented the curses hurled at him.

Another block concertinaed them near the front line T-joint. The sandbags were very high here, leaving only a strip of star-sprinkled sky between the walls. The men cursed, fretted, and fumed. Those relieved squashed past jubilantly, though they admitted things had been remarkably quiet. A sudden jostling, and Get Fell In appeared, moving agitatedly downwards, bursting his way along by saying repeatedly:

'Make way there – make way!'

Word came down: 'They're coming over!'

A man in front of Bradshaw turned, hurling a scornful indictment after the retreating sergeant-major:

'When that bee spots you with a button undone on rest, he says, "You're a fine bloody soldier!"'

The alarm was false. A nervous sentry had seen life in the wiring stakes and shadows of No Man's Land.

Immediately in the front line began a scramble for dugouts. They were of a very sad and apologetic nature: 'built ups' in reality, because their floors were the ordinary ground level.

Signallers and snipers poked their heads out of the best and said that there were plenty more dugouts farther along; theirs were full up. Bradshaw propped his stretcher against a traverse and said to Bagnall:

'Seems to be nothing else for it but the fire-step.'

A cut in the parados led them to a fragile framework covering a box – four posts and a corrugated iron roof. It looked like an ammunition dump, but smelt strongly of disinfectant. They stayed the night there, only grinning when later they found that their abode was a latrine. Few sounds of firing reached them the whole night; but the infrequent passing of men along the main trench disturbed them. Machine-guns made half-hearted attempts to sound a note of war. Where did all their bullets go to? Several times they made a tour of the trench, the duckboards responding with rusty creaks. Once they met the orderly officer, Mr. Crossley, who kept them talking for three-quarters of an hour; another time Bradshaw toured alone and had a few words with a sentry who could see 'nowt but piles o' muck'. Stand-down revealed a sheen of hoar frost over everything, including greatcoats. Sentries melted the congealed petroleum jelly on their rifle-actions by matchlight. Bolts and fingers were frozen.

Anything less like the Somme could hardly be imagined. The morning came grey, the sparkling freshness of the night lost in what proved to be the most uninviting of trenches. They were duck-boarded, with stagnant water below; a thin layer of ice crusting against the laths. Everybody wanted breakfast.

Between each sentry-post there were wide, unmanned gaps. Bagnall quickly discovered that the duckboards were not to be relied on, one foot crashing through several rotting laths into the wetness below. Officers walked up and down saying that the condition of the trench was deplorable. Two or three inches of ochrey water covered the track on the company's right, where thin ice had already crackled under heavy boot-treading. Those who misjudged the width of the submerged duckboards stamped up and down soaked to the knees: they would have to remain like that for five days.

'Breakfast's late', everybody grumbled.

No sign from Jerry.

A cushy front, this!

Bread was issued – four to a loaf. Bradshaw and Bagnall shared with Brettle and Bates, the company's self-appointed sanitary men. Brettle boasted on every occasion to drafts that came later what a horror the Somme had been, though on September the 9th he had been on quarter guard. Bates, so anxious to go over to the swine on that date, had gone down shell-shocked before the attack. Now they confiscated the loaf and took the major half. Bagnall looked at the S.B.s' share and snorted in disgust.

'When we came up here first t' rations had missed fire, and there were sixteen to a loaf. We tossed up in fours who should stand out altogether – then we found that bee had won a loaf on his own. Bleedin' scrounger!'

The two S.B.s returned to a dugout that everybody else had cold-shouldered. Three inches of water covered its floor. It stood three feet high, four feet wide, and three deep, and had for a roof one thickness of decaying sandbags resting on a corrugated sheet of iron. A cushy little hole when dry.

Breakfast came; bacon and jippo and hot tea, though many expected rum. Sentries lined up in twos and threes, afterwards returning to try the 'old soldier'. Bradshaw took an immediate liking for the Burnley boy's blunt outspokenness, and, smiling inwardly, made no murmur when his companion adopted a protective attitude towards him.

'If any of 'em goes for thee, chum, just let me know.'

Bradshaw submitted silently.

They set about making their new quarters comfortable, lining the floor with boxes of pip-squeaks, to form a mattress of ammunition. This they slept on for five nights. A small wooden cross stuck in the parados, nameless, as if belonging to nowhere in particular. Bagnall eyed it solemnly, and said:

'We could do wi' a piece of wood to 'owd up our curtain. . . .'

But Bradshaw gave him no encouragement and the cross remained for a time where it was. There was also a small black-lettered sign which asked people to 'KEEP DOWN – SNIPER', and Bradshaw wondered whether the cross could have had anything to do with it, and how many other lives had gone before the sign was set up. Uncle came up after breakfast, and, stripping to the waist, washed himself in the dirty cold trench water that had gathered outside their dugout. Bagnall asked him why the shells were so scarce.

Uncle, puffing furiously as he towelled his rather slack body, explained between gasps that it was because the lines were so near each other.

'You see, No Man's Land is only thirty-five yards away, which doesn't allow much margin for shorts. So when the artillery wants to have a stunt we withdraw to the sap until it's all over. Of course, ordinarily, Stokes mortars are used, and the Boche sends over minenwerfers in reply. But he seldom shells unless we start.'

But later in the day, when the continued quietness had aroused some speculation in the company and Bradshaw had retailed Uncle's views, Chick, just returned from a T.M.B. school and feeling fed up, uncharitably avowed that Uncle was a silly old josser.

'Why, mon, it's these Scotch batteries behind as 'as no spunk in 'em. Wait while t' West Lancs. Artillery cooms up fra t' Somme. They'll wakken things up awreet.'

Continuing his notes, Bradshaw surreptitiously wrote:

'This trench is a remarkable affair; quite unlike the deep cuttings one imagines. The ground is too sodden for deep digging – you come to water in no time. Instead of being dug out, the trench is built up, making it more a mark for the Germans. I expect theirs are the same. The duckboards we stand on are only slightly lower than the outside general earth level, and the parapet is a buttressed banking of soil thrown up from the rear, held wall-like by stumps and wire revetments. It slopes gradually downwards from the parapet to the level of No Man's Land, and a row of bursting and rotting sandbags lies along the top, doubtfully bullet-proof. If the breastwork parapet in front were suddenly to vanish into thin air we should be in full view of Jerry.

'The parados behind is, and isn't. In places, no ground has been left over from building the parapet, and we can see uninterruptedly to the broken column of St. Martin's Cathedral and the Cloth Hall, two or three kilometres in rear. The trench is jerry-built and slipshod; no credit to any army that has occupied the same position for so many months. Nice, warm, comfortable trenches. Hot water in every traverse. Chairs, tables, and all modern conveniences. Picture us round the warming braziers, using our bayonets as toasting forks and hoping the jolly old war will last for years. Singing "Tipperary" and cracking jokes as the shells burst around. No, this emphatically isn't the kind of specially prepared trench that visitors to the front are shown.

'One of our aeroplanes was downed to-day; the first seen since we came to the Salient. The British machine was so slow it seemed paralysed. The pilot hadn't an earthly against the fish-tail; he came down like a stone. After the Somme, the Salient is ominously quiet. A bombardier belonging to a Scotch battery on the Menin road told us there was to be a big strafe last night. I don't believe fifty shells were fired; and those spread over nearly half an hour.

'I haven't got used to the front yet. There's always something in the air likely to happen in the next few seconds. A beautiful, sparkling night very considerately hid for us the dark hummocks and plain grey landscape that appear so mentally chilling by daylight. There is a shabby patch of grass between here and the Potijze road – the only vegetation about – but it has a dried, dead appearance, as if the sun shines less joyfully here.

'Winter has come quickly, but no gas up to now. The Very lights almost encircle us at night, and by day Jerry – from the higher ground in front – can see any movement we make. Two great mine craters lie in No Man's Land, touching the front line; they must be thirty yards across, and half full of dirty, stagnant water. What tale have they to tell, I wonder? Duckboard tracks have been run to the far side, from where our sentries are close enough to hear the faint murmur of Fritz's conversation. Bombs could be thrown across easily, either way.

'Twenty yards from the front line, near the end of the communication trench (under a high and unconcealable pile of greenish, sloppy sandbags, which is continually being added to by miners and sappers who burrow under the enemy line), is the sap-head. Down a steep wooden staircase of twelve steps is "C" Company headquarters, in an atmosphere damp, warm, and secure. The sap loses itself in darkness under No Man's Land.

'The trench is in a very bad state, and the prospect of living here five days, and returning after five days in support, is most uninviting. There are rat-holes everywhere, and the pockets of many greatcoats have been eaten away during the night by rats in search of sustenance. We try to suspend our rations in inverted steel helmets from our dugout roofs. The front trench is not uniformly cut or built up; there are no traverses to break the effect of enfilade fire, though these may have been strafed during the last two years into the slow winding curves we now hold. There is much evidence of shelling all round, but at present we are merely on garrison duty, holding a line that no sane adversary would dream of coveting.'

THE A.S.C. brought the Lancashire's rations through Ypres every night, dumped them, and skedaddled back, hoping to miss the evening hate. Ration fatigues from the two companies in support carried them heroically and painfully to the cookhouse and the quartermaster for issue. From the cookhouse the edibles that required cooking were carried to the front line in dixies and vacuum containers, also by the companies in support; a long, weary job via the communication trench, but much shorter at night, when the road could be used. Troops in the front line of a garrison trench win out usually; their comrades behind have the task of supplying all their wants, carrying up supplies, equipment, and trench material.

'B' and 'D' Companies did the carrying for the first five

days, 'A' and 'C' holding the line. Bradshaw only knew that
the rations came up all right. That was all the front-liners
had to do during the day – hang about waiting for meals
and make an attempt to secure some sort of drainage under
the duckboards. They religiously stood-to and stood-down
every dawn and dusk – usually an uneventful ceremony not
too early now the dark mornings approached – and if the
working parties brought up any duckboards (or A frames for
supporting them), those in the front line laid them.

At night there were ground frosts and a gradually waning
moon, and Bradshaw liked it best then. All that the trenches
stood for was obliterated. During the day every twist and
turn of the line, every mound and hole, pained the eyes
with quick familiarity. How many had been killed just here?
Old Contemptibles, a fading memory; Kitchener's Army;
now Derby men. And soon, unless something unexpected
happened, conscripts!

There was some talk of a conference at Stockholm to try
and end the war. Men snatched eagerly at the hope, but
others spurned it.

'Them bees oughter be out here, giving a hand!'
'T' war might be over by Chris!'
'Out, to get it ower!'
'Nowt'll end this bleedin' lot!'
'Peace at any price.'
'Lloyd George wants . . . !'

Casualties were very slight; an immunity not altogether due
to the wide gaps between sentry posts. Shells were scarce,
and the men glad of it. During the day, sentries watched No
Man's Land through a crude form of periscope called the

'vigilance' – a small mirror perched on a stick covering so restricted a field that the watcher must needs keep his eyes glued to it every second of his two hours' duty.

Often enough during the night Jerry's Very lights could be heard fizzing upwards, and his sentries talking from the post in No. 1 Crater. The rumble of wheels as they rattled through the Square and ruined streets of Ypres came clear to the front line; sounds equally plain to the Germans opposite. One of their howitzers came up on rails and loosed a few great thundering shells into Ypres, its clanking and puffing an invitation to our artillery; but no retaliating shots were fired. A cushy war that would never end.

After five days the companies changed over, 'C' moving back behind the ruined château on the Potijze road to a support trench called Congreve Walk. It ran through the château's vinery, one standing wall of which sheltered the cookers. Bradshaw and Bagnall bagged a strong-looking waterproof dugout hidden away off the main trench, and threw off their packs with a grunt of relief.

'I don't see why stretchers shouldn't be taken over like trench stores, Ernie. Do you? Damn silly the way they get carried up and down.'

'Get fell in!'

The S.M.'s voice floated along the trench, and the two S.B.s debated on their chances of discovery if they sat tight.

'Get fell in!'

They gathered outside, grumbling.

'What the 'ell's up now?'

'Pay parade.'

'Holy Jees!'

'What a bleedin' army!'

'Carrying fatigue, already!'

They slouched disconsolately off in the darkness to the Potijze dump, and loaded up with duckboards, A and U frames. 'B' Company sentries cursed them for making a row. Going back, faces towards Ypres, they passed the dark tree-fringed bulk of the château, very ready for sleep.

A subaltern said:

'Only another load, boys!'

A simple task, carrying up along the road. But delays that seemed part of the life encroached so much on the night that two o'clock had passed before they returned tiredly to Congreve Walk.

Few of them had slept during the last week except in snatches, but at five o'clock they were roused and ordered to fall in at the cookhouse.

'What the 'ell. . .!'

'We don't stand-to here!'

'Who wakkened us oop?'

Nobody knew who had done the rousing. Hesitating, a few amongst the dozen or more there slunk off. The remainder lingered; then they too disappeared. Bradshaw's head had just found a comfortable spot on his haversack when the dugout flap was explosively yanked aside.

'Good suffering Jesus! Get fell in, you ——. How many more times. . .?'

Greasy bacon tins had to be cleaned; dixies washed and filled in readiness for the breakfasts of 'B' and 'D' Companies. An unholy task that might have been devised by a Base provost-sergeant for the torture of defaulters.

After much floundering over the broken ground they found an elusive pump in the yard of a Potijze ruin. Domestic duties were completed in rough and ready fashion by the aid of spasmodic matchlight.

Very lights flickered through the tree-trunks round the château, and the nervous ones cried for no more matches to be struck. Much of the water was spilled in the obstacle-race back to the cookhouse.

'Hang about, me lads. No use of going back to kip. You've got to carry this up as soon as it's ready.' The cook grinned and passed a mess-tin of tea round.

'Well,' thought Bradshaw, 'somebody has to do it! The others did it for us. Thousands of men at this moment are sleeping peacefully a few kilometres farther behind, blissfully unconscious of the trials of this handful. We came out only yesterday. Last night, wasn't it? Bedless nights are confusing.'

Three-quarters of an hour later, laboriously weighted with dixies and tins, they trudged up past the château again. After the château the road led to nowhere – a black nothingness made vague and ghostly by the Very lights. Swathes of mist with heads above and feet below. Flatness all round and no distinction between land and sky.

They stepped off the truncated road on to the duckboards a foot below. Dark shadows closed in on them with a rattle of mess-tins.

'Quiet, men, quiet. We don't want him shelling.' 'Now, me lucky lads. One at a time, and no coming the old soldier on Ginger!'

The vinery again. They refilled and cleaned up in the greying dawn for their own breakfast: drifted back to Congreve Walk. Breakfast over, more housewifery; an hour's grace, then dinner was ready for taking up. On this journey the heavy vacuum containers were used, slung on a pole, a man's shoulder under each end. Daylight barred the road; the only alternative was a long trail up Haymarket, during which men had to stop frequently to ease their sore shoulders. Two hours later the carriers had dinner, and, after again patronising the Potijze pump, the cook, grinning sardonically, informed them that tea would be ready in half an hour. They wondered if anybody else was winning the war besides them.

On cold nights there was also an extra issue of tea, sparingly 'rummed', necessitating another trek at ten o'clock.

('Call this a rum issue! Just enough to spoil the tea. . . .'

'Ne'er mind. Some day quarter's 'and'll slip.')

Get Fell In awaited their return. He lined them up and superintended gifts of gum-boots and spades. Some God-forsaken trench to dig somewhere; and getting on for midnight already.

At two o'clock they sleep-walked back to Congreve Walk. Bradshaw wondered how men could have grumbled at those 'night ops' at Witley Camp. A few hours later penal servitude would commence again – ration-carrying.

Three and a half hours' sleep! Before noon Bradshaw and Bagnall, stretcher-bearers, dumped their container for a breather outside a T.M.B. post in Haymarket, viewing with great interest the simplest gun they had seen. A mere tube. You dropped Stokes bombs down the barrel; the detonator hit

a striker, and up and out the missile soared. A clever gunner
could have fourteen in the air before the first one landed.

Two of the gunners commiserated with the infantry-men.
Their little war was to pepper a mound behind our front
line if Jerry should break through. Two to a loaf, and bags
of sleep!

That night's working-party was disturbed by shells, one
man being hit. At the moment he heard the cry 'Stretcher-
bearers!' Bradshaw was wrestling with a badly fastened
bundle of curly wiring stakes. Red rusty, by their feel,
leaving a deposit on his hands.

One o'clock again, with the carriers flinging themselves
down in the Congreve Walk dugouts too tired to sleep.
Bradshaw stared straight up at the little roof as Bagnall cursed.
Sentences passed through his mind; he had a score of things
to put down if he could remember them. No exaggeration,
either. Bitterness was forced down your throat here.

'Life in the trenches has resolved itself into a series of
working-parties. Where all the stuff we carry up goes to, no
one can tell, for all the roads leading out of Ypres are alive at
night with working, carrying, and ration parties. By day they
are lifeless and deserted, converging into a grey, uneven
saucer broken only by the sharp fang of St. Martin's and a
few observation balloons. You couldn't credit the difference
after dark.

'Somebody is unaware that fifteen men are doing the work
of fifty. Unless a draft arrives I can see desertions ahead, or
a little mutiny. There is a thick trunk in Congreve Walk we
call the Blighty tree. Its base is almost cut through by the
machine-gun bullets that sweep round during the night. Two

men wasted a precious hour of their rest standing against it trying to get wounded in the leg, last night.

'We are horribly fed up. Some day it will dawn on those at home that Fritz isn't giving himself up in huge numbers and filling the air with cries of "Kamerad!"

'We go in front again to-morrow, and most of us are profoundly thankful. The last few days have been more than any human being could stand whilst hoping to remain decently fit and alert. I have a strong suspicion – nay, certain proof – that several members of the company are evading their rightful share of duty by hiding under their "specialist" cloak. As new hands, we cannot complain.

'I could sleep for a week.'

Leather jerkins were issued, and north pole gloves; then frost gave way to rain. Bagnall got soundly cursed each night because his long legs strayed out into the trench and tripped up others, but such diversions came like sunshine to Bradshaw. He liked the way Ernie, rising in a hurry at stand-to or when a passer-by cursed his legs, would crack his head – fortunately helmeted – against the cross-beam of the low dugout as he rose.

A Jerry opposite No. 2 Crater aroused further interest by calling out 'Good morning, Tommy.' Bagnall said:

'Some silly blighter'll stick 'is 'ead up afore long, Dick.'

Only two casualties that turn up! The days following came drenched and desolate. The poor devils on the Somme were having a wicked time on that thousand-times churned stretch of abomination.

Casualties were light, numbering only four – one of them

a man who mistook, in the darkness, a tin of creosote for water, and nearly burned out his throat. Another went down with a blood-poisoned finger, the result of an argument with an obstinately reserved bully beef tin. (The key-opener of one brand invariably broke off, leaving no alternative – except throwing it away – but hacking the tin open with a jack-knife.)

Two more, in the support line, were gassed by coke fumes, through keeping a brazier burning in a tiny, unventilated dugout.

They landed at the Magazine after midnight, an uncanny stillness in the streets of Ypres. They slept like logs; some too fagged at eight o'clock to get up for breakfast. The Magazine – a low, immensely thick building with a rounded roof – was one of the few whole buildings standing. The walled-in enclosure at the entrance made 'A' and 'C's' parade ground. Over the road, in the Prison and the Asylum, were billeted 'B' and 'D' Companies. This was the back of the town, least damaged. A ruined water-tank – the dirigible of their entering night – tilted at the street corner, dented and drunk. In a yard at the side of the Asylum lay a twisted piece of machinery bearing a familiar, out-of-place name in embossed letters.

BEYER PEACOCK & CO. LTD.
GORTON, MANCHESTER.

All the streets were lined with wreckage. There was too much of Ypres to blow, like the Somme villages, completely out of existence, but the jagged teeth and stark, crumbling walls

provided far more impressive memories. Every shell that
burst on the ruins heaped a thicker cover on the basements,
strengthening the roofs above the cellar-dwelling soldiers.
Ground-up plaster and brickwork, broken slabs and pillars
of stone, twisted rails, lay everywhere. If some terrific force
had lifted the whole town a mile high, then released it to
crash down plumb and flat on its own ground, the result
could not have been more tremendous. A breathtaking
place. To think that some day this ruin of wonder would be
desecrated by returning refugees . . . a pawnshop here . . .
a tripe-dealer there!

The first working-party from the Magazine carried short
iron girders and bags of cement up Threadneedle Street –
the sector adjoining Haymarket – to a strange part of the line.
Bradshaw eyed interestedly a private-looking mackintoshed
man who superintended operations at the dump and told
their officer that two journeys would be enough. Bradshaw
discovered he belonged to the Royal Engineers – a sapper.
This seemed an insult to those men boring under Jerry's line
up at Mud Lane.

The sapper led them, at long length, to a smashed-up
M.G. emplacement, then vanished.

'He might have carried a load, anyhow!'

'What, at six bob a day?'

Another time they were called out from the Magazine to
assist in excavating on the site for a new baths, a project
so substantially lasting that it dismayed Bradshaw. It would
never be over if they were making preparations like these!
It was a wet day, and the rain depressingly filled in the low
level where they had to stand and dig, but Bradshaw felt

ashamed, when the officer returned, at the little progress that had been made. A quarter of the men should have done as much in half the time. But all working-parties were the same now: grousing parades, where you did as little as possible or dodged the column entirely. There were too many.

A daily dose of lime-water was issued in the Magazine. Nobody knew why, or what for. Riley suggested it would keep their natures down.

They all felt safe under the thickness of the Magazine. Fritz started dropping heavy stuff at intervals; great shells that burrowed and belched, flinging debris and raising brick-dust clouds. Thick concrete walls reinforced by steel plates would stand any amount of that! You could undress in there. Ease your limbs of puttees and boots; have a jolly good scratch and 'chat', and join blankets with your chum, kipping together – though this was against orders. Every morning, a good thick slice of bread and toasted cheese or bacon. Plenty of jippo (if you were pally with the orderly man), and a R.F.A. canteen up Lille Gate when you ate up. For there was a pay parade in the Magazine, where the click of your heels and the smartness of your salute was regulated by the number of francs you received. Often, too, a parcel would arrive from home, crammed with hard-gotten delicacies scraped together with loving care. The great grey waste lay bare and warrened behind you, forgotten till the nightly working-party took you up on the St. Jean or Potijze roads. But always, when you got back, the Magazine. There, relaxed senses brought infinite relief. Tight chests expanded freely again; weak knees became well braced. All round the walls of the broad room men slept, rifles stacked down the centre. A heavy, gloomy building, this strong retreat; given over to kit inspections, sleep, and sing-songs. And they were sing-songs, those. Everybody could join in; Chick, with his girlish tenor, beating time with an entrenching-tool handle, or playing a xylophone of a row of tin hats. All the others in a rough circle; bawling the choruses, laughing, interrupting, shouting; lost in a gaiety that threatened the roof, thick as it was. Or perhaps dividing into two schools, one trying to drown the other:

> *Oh! I wish I was single,*
> *My pockets would jingle.*
> *I wish I was single again!*

or

> *I sat down by Old Riley's fire,*
> *Winking at Old Riley's daughter.*
> *Suddenly a thought came into my head –*
> *I'd like to kiss Old Riley's daughter.*
> *Iddy I-ay, Iddy I-ay, Iddy I-ay*
> *To the One-eyed Riley*
> *Iddy I-ay, Iddy I-ay,*
> *Jig-a-jig-jig,* très bon!

or (to the tune of the 'Red Rose' regimental march):

> *I have no pain, dear mother, now,*
> *But, oh! I am so dry –*
> *Connect me with a brewery*
> *And leave me there to die!*

And more disgusting, humorous songs, but nobody to hear who mattered!

A great place, the Magazine. Now and then you could hoodwink Ginger into giving you Jimmy Perrin's ration, who, you would say, hadn't returned from sick parade. But all the queue knew that Jimmy Perrin got a 'landowner' at Guillemont! And when anybody complained about Ginger dispensing pieces of bacon with dirty fingers, Ginger challenged him to bring an officer. By the time one could arrive, Ginger's hands were pinkly, greasily clean, only his fingernails showing a blue-black frame. The dirt complained of had vanished, washed off by constant dippings in the warm jippo.

Daytime fatigues and leisure Sunday hours found them sightseeing. Bradshaw felt at once gratification and fear at wandering over this famous ruin. It thrilled him much the same way as those mornings at Étaples, when the musical notes of the cavalry réveillé tinkled through the crystal crisp air; (tales of decimated regiments and thoughts of the Bull Ring not yet gathered). What tremendous thicknesses covered the dugouts and built-ups near the Ramparts! He counted fourteen neat rows of sandbags, reinforced on alternate rows with steel girders, over one home! You couldn't take everything in. Debris had poured through the entrance of the Cathedral, and if you looked carefully at the scarred stone heading curving over the doorway you could decipher the lettering: ST. MARTIN. There were papered bedroom walls, naked to the passer-by; and huge boulders on the site of a second big church. A river flowed near Lille Gate which the old sweats said ran red with blood in the early days. The

Menin Gate proved to be no gate at all; a bottle-neck passage between the Ramparts over the moat. Hell Fire Corner wasn't far away on the road that led to the right, but the Lancashires used the Potijze and St. Jean roads mostly.

As he saw all these things, a queer sensation affected Bradshaw. He felt an imposter; a trespasser who had no right to be let in on such sacred ground. He wondered more and more every day how he came to be included with soldiers.

ANOTHER turn up, then 'B' Camp again, with its excesses of polishing. Several men arrived from the base fit again. Also Baker, Slater, Spud Murphy, and a few old hands from another battalion of the regiment. Slater proved to be a tonic, bubbling over with mock courage. He wanted to go up again there and then, and get the job finished. 'We'll ne'er get it over wi' here – let's go up now and get stuck into 'em.' A mystery man also came, attired in breeches, puttees, and spurs; a bandy-legged Cockney over thirty years old, Merrill by name. His greatcoat – British-warm fashion – boasted a full corporal's chevrons, his tunic but one. The company took an instinctive dislike to him, dubbing him 'Cavalry Joe', each man hoping he would be attached to some other platoon. He kowtowed to the officers on parade, and to the men off; occasionally baring his teeth. By discovering two more items that had hitherto remained unpolished – tunic belt-hooks and respirator sling press-studs – he put himself beyond the pale. He boasted that no man went on parade sprucer than he.

Leather equipment had to be glossy, with shining buckles, and, lest those with webbing should consider themselves at an advantage, a special preparation was issued to turn the blancoed equipment a reddish brown. Merrill's leathers shone like piano polish.

Everybody was lousy, too, and all grumbled about baths and new underwear. Bradshaw often felt he wasn't really lousy, but discovered his error every time he got warm. Braziers had an infallible knack of rousing the desires of lice. 'Chatting' parade became part of the day's routine – men on their haunches, tunics open, contorting and twisting to reach farther round; scratching under their armpits, busy searching shirt seams. No wonder the great French soldier Napoleon was always depicted with fingers in his tunic!

The baths at Poperinghe maintained a frigid efficiency. The room resembled a knacker yard, containing a dozen big tubs. A naked 'C' Company wallowed in dirty but warm water; hopped about on a wet, stone, partly duckboard floor under unwilling sprinklers, and tried to dry itself on very soiled, very small towels. A piercing draught speeded up operations.

November the 5th passed unnoticed. Bradshaw had meant to mark the date and see if the artillery displayed any more activity than usual. Every night the guns growled away on the right, comfortably distant. Bradshaw, who had always doubted the existence of No. 1 Field Punishment, saw a Lancashire of the old Festubert days tied to a limber wheel near the cookhouse. Sleety snowflakes settled on the delinquent's shoulders. Men – company colleagues – passed by indifferent and spiritless; the Aussies would have cut him free very quickly!

While Bagnall went boozing one night, Bradshaw visited a hall in Pop where the divisional concert-party nightly entertained an audience of troops. The most attractive turns were a man giving 'Cohen on the Phone' and a youth, with a pleasant treble voice, known as the Lancashire Nightingale. His maiden's get-up evoked appraising, wistful comment among the audience. Curious, that the song 'When I Leave the World Behind' should be so popular with troops!

Bradshaw found that a Bradbury went nowhere in Poperinghe, so grasping were the shopkeepers. The tricks they played with the rate of exchange! He went to one place for a coloured silk card, and was offered obscene ones. (You could see packets in the windows, bearing a note, 'These postcards must not be displayed.' Many Tommies carried a selection about with them – coarse or pathetic-looking naked prostitutes.) Probably the Belgians were resenting the fact that, rather than saving their country, we had merely confiscated it, and were reserving any fuss and friendliness for 'if the Yanks come in'.

Over the Menin Gate again to Mud Lane and West Lane; wet, dark, cold, and misty. Men had shortened their greatcoats to miss the mud. The wine-cellars lay under eight feet of water, only the top row of bunks unsubmerged, and two sentries swayed over an automatic pump in their efforts to lower it. Bradshaw was detailed next for duty at pumping. After nearly two hours, which made no impression, he went to where the exhaust pipe spilled its load, to find that, as they pumped, the water ran back circuitously to the cellars.

Next morning they were evacuated in favour of a ruined monastery, or convent, off the Menin road. They crossed over in fits and starts, heads twisting to watch a Jerry plane spit bullets at a British scout. The scout escaped by spiral dives that brought both planes low, and Simpson dropped on one knee, preparing to fire at the Jerry. A lieutenant saw, and stopped him.

Black, white, and mottled puffs of smoke burdened the grey rising ground over Messines Ridge. The Salient remained quiet, and ominous.

The Monastery made a fine billet: an intact row of cubicles on the Ypres side, cold but dry, with square tiled floors, alternately red and blue. The side of the building nearest the front was blown to wreckage; a crucifix lay in fragments. Men picked up pieces as souvenirs, and copied a crude poem written in pencil on the cream-distempered wall.

Next day Ellis received a letter which told of one of the Lancashires' success in wangling out of the army; or so Bradshaw gathered from snatches of conversation amongst the old hands. As he lay wounded at Guillemont the man exchanged identity discs, pay books and letters with a dead body in a shell-hole, then made his way down wounded. He gave the dead man's name and number on every necessary occasion, and was eventually reported killed in action, August the 8th. After hospital leave he disappeared down a Welsh coal-mine. A tit-bit for the company, this. Bradshaw tried to find a snag in the incident, but found so doing unpopular.

Mud Lane again, and Jerry still calling 'Good morning, Tommy!' A draft of subalterns arrived, and sorely-overworked men wondered why they were not privates. The officers all expressed astonishment at not encountering bursting shells and murderous men. The company quickly weighed them up. (Officers fell into two categories. If they passed dirty rifles, handled a spade, or carried a bag of cement, they were 'aw reet'. If not, they were 'no bloody *bon*'.)

The next morning brought their first real strafe in the Salient, and one fatal casualty – Rowbotham. Duckboards and men lay under a spray of earth, and the cross near the S.B.s' dugout had been blown ten yards. Bradshaw stuck it again in the parados, as near the original position as he could judge from the altered contours.

A LL day the sound of gunfire rumbled Armentières way; in Mud and West Lanes only spasms of machine-gun fire. Fritz got so accustomed to our 'Emma Gees' playing – with shots – the familiar 'pom-tiddley-om-pom', that he himself added the completing 'pom-pom.' That night little fat Sergeant Bell got a bullet in the arm whilst patrolling the narrow strip of No Man's Land in front of No. 1 Crater, and, after assisting with a bandage, Bradshaw said enviously:

'That's a Blighty one, sar'n't!'

Later in the dugout, Bagnall said:

'Daft idea sending patrols out so close.'

The cold bit again, and sentries glued to their posts became stiff and frozen. S.B.s could stamp about.

A 'bullet-proof' body protector arrived in the mail next day for Bradshaw. The flat cardboard container was split; all the company knew what it contained, and Bradshaw felt an ass, wanting to disclaim ownership. Sergeant Stevens came along.

'Doan't forget to wear thi' chest protector, Dicky – tha'll be joinin' t' Tank Corps now, wonter?'

It proved to be an ill-fitting contraption. In the scant privacy of their dugout, Bradshaw wriggled into it whilst Bagnall adjusted the straps.

'Tha waint be able t' scratch i' that, mate!'

In the afternoon the artillery had a strafe, 'C' Company withdrawing to the sap whilst the bombardment lasted.

Bradshaw lay asleep when it started. He wakened fearfully to find the line deserted, great shells whistling and crumping. He scuttled to the sap. When down, a begrimed miner led him crouching between dripping pit props under No Man's Land. The constant, deadened plonking of shells quivered the candle-flames. The sap vibrated. Bradshaw's ears ached.

'If Jerry was to come over now, we're caught like rats in a trap, but no doubt he calmly waits for quietness in the security of his own borings.

'These miners have rotten jobs. They dare feel safe only when Jerry can be heard working, and expect trouble if enemy operations stop for long. An ingenious clockwork contrivance, arranged to perform a steady picking, is often set in motion to delude Jerry into believing we are at work. I expect he has similar devices.'

Bradshaw's body shield proved a bigger washout than at first believed. Some unscrupulous advertiser was making a fortune out of the gullibility of parents and relations. Bradshaw propped it up against the parados at a point where he could get over twenty yards from it. Borrowing a rifle, he put five shots through the centre. He then placed the shield at an angle, and shot four times more, the last aim dislodging the thin sheet of steel. Each shot had cut through both sections like a hot knife through butter. He kept the back, and smaller, piece for a time; planting the heavier chest section in a place from where it could be retrieved. It was too big to go under his tunic; too long for his valise. One was Christmas-tree enough without adding burdens of that nature, and, as Bagnall said, wearing it prevented you from chasing the 'chats' in the spots where they troubled you most.

A smooth-running ration system – what agonies of sweat and fatigue that meant to companies in support! – gave them a loaf each day for four men, which meant, approximately, two slices each per man per day. A loaf or two extra per company would have been a godsend. Bully beef was plentiful enough to be scorned, but Bradshaw never saw Maconochie, and concluded it must be too nice a titbit for Other Ranks.

At dusk, Birtles ran to the dugout, crying:

'Ay! Lieutenant Dalton's just been hit near the sap.'

Bradshaw hurried down the trench. Their Lewis gun officer; a nice, quiet-voiced man, getting on.

The officer lay at the foot of a mound behind the front trench, opposite the sap-head, the gun he had been mounting – a new position – at his feet. A vigilant sniper's victim. Several officers stood by in the trench. Bradshaw stepped over the low trench wall, and an officer said, 'Keep back, there!'

Bradshaw went on, crouching, affecting not to hear. Mr. Dalton groaned painfully, turning his head slightly.

'Get back . . . get back.'

Bradshaw hesitated; then ran back to the trench.

After dusk, Bagnall and he carried the dead body exhaustingly down the narrow communication trench. The arm sockets of both felt pulled out. Bradshaw said:

'Fancy, Ernie, getting pipped like that. A few minutes too soon trying to mount a gun. A keen-eyed blighter, that sniper!'

Later on, Bradshaw fell asleep dreaming the Germans had invented wonderful new sights for their rifles which, even in total darkness, gathered the rays of light like a cat's eyes. None of our working and wiring parties dare go out. He wakened with Bagnall's elbow in his chest. One of them should have been on duty, but things were so quiet that they kept to their dugout, knowing they were not needed. A machine-gun popped distantly, and two men passed the dugout, unspeaking in the darkness. A rat scuffled and hesitated on the ragged sandbags behind his head, then the low hum of a quiet commotion. He shook Bagnall vigorously.

'Ay! Got a match, Ernie? Tea's up!'

The next five days in Congreve Walk afforded little time for anything but hard work and sleep. Bradshaw's notes were jotted down on his memory's pad, the inclination to write having left him. The war troubled him not at all; he was just one of many. They were all in the same boat. What vexed him was the 'dodging the column' by men in the company whom he never saw on fatigue.

Baker, a good soldier possessed of more than average

fearlessness, wanted to take the rations along the road
by the château in broad daylight, because it took only a
quarter the time going by communication trench – one of
those foolish ideas resulting from lack of sleep. Normally
he would only dream of such recklessness as an individual
escapade. Two hours' clear gain over the Haymarket route,
utilised in rest, proved a strong attraction even to Bradshaw,
who had sworn many times never to run any risk. He wasn't
surprised when Baker said to him:

'Will you come, Bradshaw?'

How refuse a Festubert man? Bagnall said, with the wrong
effect:

'Bloody daft, Dick.'

Bradshaw knew it was daft, but promised to go at noon
with the heavy containers.

Noon found them scrambling out of the communication trench on to the road by the château, where a strip of
camouflaged khaki hid their movements. The others passed
on, up Haymarket. Baker insisted on leading, Bradshaw
thankful for the little cover afforded by the container slung
between them. They passed beyond the château's black,
leafless trees to open ground, and Bradshaw felt gigantically
a target. A gradual upward curve exposed them to half a mile
of German trench; Bradshaw saw clearly over the breastwork
into No Man's Land; the irregular line beyond; a belt of wire;
fields. He felt spineless and weak-kneed; empty inside. He
breathed fast. How far bullet-proof would the container prove
if snipers got busy? Baker carried on imperturbably. Fools, to
have come; every sentry in Jerry's line must be watching. The
front line, a hundred and fifty yards away, seemed ten miles

off. An old ruined cottage appeared on the right of the road, a few yards high. A ditch, now, too – somewhere to dive to! A cold sweat broke on Bradshaw's forehead. Only twenty or thirty yards . . . they could run for it. Jerry must be waiting till they got almost to the trench before he fired.

'Thi' waitin' on us, mate!'

Bradshaw looked up as Baker spoke. In front, 'B' Company watched them from the parados-less line; two officers, too. Hell, there'd be a fuss! Two shells fell on the right. Bradshaw urged at the pole, sweating in desperation, dry-tongued. Phew! Home!

'What the devil do you fellows think you're playing at?' One of the officers accosted them – a new one.

'Gettin' t' rations up quicker, sir', replied Baker.

'Quicker be damned, man! Do you realise you've endangered our position . . . drawn the Boche's fire? What company are you, "A" or "C"?'

Bradshaw lay back panting, unable to speak. Baker muttered, ' "C" . . . sir.'

The rest, awaiting the others, more than compensated for any trouble. Where had Jerry been? Enjoying a midday nap or appraising a foolhardy diversion? They got back to find the Potijze pump broken. The tins and dixies were cleaned with shell-hole water, then refilled at the green, scum-covered lake for tea. The cooks had gathered a bunch of broad grasses from the vinery, to give the stew a bit of body; Bradshaw wondered what they would get next to eat and drink.

After ration-carrying they took up U and A frames again; duckboards and corrugated iron sheets. Nothing else under

the low, heavy sky seemed alive, so still was night and
war. They clanked along the road, a row of weird-shaped
silhouettes, and dumped their loads none too quietly where
the front line cut across. A machine-gun suddenly sogged
away at the breastwork parapet; several angry shadows
gathered round them.

'Quiet, you noisy bees!'

'Remember tha' art gooin' back, out o' it!'

One bullet struck a wiring stake; ricocheted, pinging, like
the singing of a string instrument. Slater said:

'Out of it? We're coming every 'orf-hour, all t' neeght. Want
to get this waar ower wi', as you bees aren't shaping so well.'

Another day, then the Magazine. Five more days in front;
after that ten in 'B' Camp!

MUD LANE, unchanged and bitterly cold. Bradshaw
stamped the length of their front, hands tucked
in armpits. Prickly sharpness everywhere; bluey
red noses, snufflings, and dewdrops. Hands and feet
unbelonging; stiff movement; an effort to speak. Spasmodic
attempts to coax the circulation by the cabman's method
soon relapsed. Every man shrunk into his clothes and
equipment; chins into collars; hands into cuffs. Ice lay on
the water below the duckboards. When pulled up about
their chins, men complained of the difficulty of shaving, so
their beards grew in an atmosphere of cold disapproval.
Bradshaw's down-covered chin had not yet seen a razor, but
he could imagine the torture of shaving. The fastidious ones

who did shave used the remains of their tea as hot water.

Rations came up to time. Hot, but too short to keep the cold out for long. Slater, mock serious, would burst into a little group and say exasperatingly: 'Ast 'eeard, lads? T' cooks is makkin' a special effort to-day. Thi' sendin' oop a great plate o' spud pie apiece. Then there's apple dumplin' and rice puddin' – as much as wi' con ate – and sarn't-major's tea wi' bo-koo rum and –'

'Ere – stow it, y' crazy bee!'

'For Chrisake stop!'

At night, many regretted the shortening of their greatcoats; you needed all the warmth you could get. Gum-boots were issued, the duckboards being so untrustworthy on the right of West Lane – long ones for small men, short ones for the taller chaps. The thigh straps were either missing or weak, and Bagnall and Blakeley both slipped one foot over the duckboard side first morning. Cracklings of ice and muddy water poured in, soaking them both to the knees.

During the quietness of the afternoon a frightful, long-drawn groan floated over from Jerry's line.

Men looked at each other wonderingly, turning colder. The guns were silent. An accident? A self-inflicted wound? Bradshaw went into No. 1 Crater, curious to see if anyone had been sniping.

Lieutenant Hautz stood there pondering. No one had fired; they'd never know what it was. Bradshaw learnt there was to be a strafe that night; the West Lancs. Artillery had come up from the Somme. The company would be withdrawn to the sap, and Mr. Gray (Uncle) had volunteered to stay in No. 1 Crater firing flares.

A Jerry sausage balloon spotted carryings-on in Ypres. The Ramparts writhed under a hail of shrapnel and H.E., whistling and rushing high over the trenches. Backs to parapet, men stood watching the rising clouds of black and dun-coloured smoke. Near to Bradshaw, Stansfield looked down to Ypres fascinated. The last few shrapnels burst, black and bushy; thinned; vanished.

'Sithee, chum. Fritz 'as getten a shell as bursts twice', he said, eyes a-goggle, to the S.B. 'Watch t' next 'un. . . .'

Bradshaw looked up, surprised. He heard the flutter and whine of another shell; saw the black puff of the burst expand and elongate, high above the ground.

'That's once!' cried Stansfield.

Two or three seconds later came the sound of the bursting shell.

'There thi' art. It's gone off agean!'

Bradshaw tried to explain that the shell burst only once; that the sound of the explosion, when the shrapnel burst in the air, took some seconds to travel their distance; but Stansfield interrupted, unconvinced. He'd seen it once with his own eyes, as shrapnel; then heard it with his own ears crashing on the ground somewhere, as H.E.

The strafe came, bottling them in the dark, underground bore. Plonk! Plonk! Plonk! went the shells above, shivering the air. One of the miners told them that a Fritz gallery had been located.

A wily bird, Fritz. His reprisal for the strafe caught them next morning after stand-down, when thoughts of revenge had been lulled by a long cold night of quietness. Half a

dozen nerve-racking whizzbangs came over. Z-z-z-z BANG!
Z-z-z-z BANG! Z-z-z-z BANG! In ten minutes little heaps
of crumbly, smelly black earth covered the duckboards.
Walking along the trench with Bagnall, Bradshaw heard a
zip! and ducked as he noticed a gaping bite in the parapet.

'Duck, Ernie!'

Another whizzbang had scattered the roof of their dugout.
Great chunks had been bitten from the parapet; warning
zips from snipers sent them stealthily to their knees. More
working-parties!

Four men hit, Hucknall seriously. Peel went down with a
scratch on his leg, in the face of a volley of hearty contempt
from Bagnall.

'Tha'll get bumped back reet quick!'

But Peel got to Blighty.

'No, sir', said Bagnall to Mr. Hautz (whom many believed
to be a German, decent though he was). 'Them 'as 'asn't
sin t' Somme 'as sin nowt. Wi' lost three parts o' t' battalion
under an hour. Should 'a' bin' there, sir, to see summat
lively. This is nowt. Why . . .'

A tearing, triple explosion interrupted this hyperbole.
Everyone started up in time to see earth spattering and
smoke billowing twenty yards behind the sap-head. Bagnall
shouted, 'Come on, Dick. 'Swan of ours! Bring the stretcher',
then raced away. Bradshaw followed him along the
duckboards to a track that ran in rear of the front trench. A
T.M.B. man lay across the duckboards, a mass of wounds. An
officer, on one knee, feverishly applied patches of bandage
to the worst of the punctures.

Bradshaw, forgetting himself, said brusquely:

'That's no use, sir. There's only one thing to do; get him down to the M.O. quickly. He'll bleed to death while we're patching up all those wounds. It'll only take a few minutes over the top.'

Two of the victim's friends helped the stretcher-bearers. They hoisted him gently up on four shoulders, Bradshaw and Bagnall taking the rear. Stepping over the track, they made a bee-line for the M.O.'s dugout.

They rose higher over the pocked ground, a fifty-yards target for Jerry. Bradshaw refused to look round. He had a spiked feeling between his shoulder-blades; wondered if the stretcher would topple over if he fell. All the way, as they bobbed up and down over the dark, flayed mounds, and dropped to patches of dried, dirty grass, Bradshaw's stomach felt low down and empty. However much he tried to brace up, resisting a possible shot, he couldn't shake off a sense of coldness in the small of his back. But they got there without a shot being fired at them.

The two S.B.s stood by for a few minutes watching the M.O. deftly at work. Bradshaw counted forty-one separate wounds, mostly small. One of the T.M.B. men awaited them outside. His eyes said:

'How is he? . . . D'you think he'll live?'

They discovered that the T.M.B.s had been carrying up Stokes in sacks, in readiness for a proposed strafe. A pin of one of the three bombs in the wounded man's load had entangled itself in the canvas sack, gradually being drawn out.

Bradshaw grimaced.

'Fancy detonating them first, and carrying 'em up after!'

Back in the front line, Lieutenant Hautz told him that a mine was being blown within the half-hour.

A whispering wind sighed along the corridor by the sap-head – the aching quiet before stand-to.

Thousands of men in Ypres Magazine, the Prison, Asylum, Ramparts, and innumerable cellars, were being detailed for their nightly labours. Soon the silent road down to Potijze, past the château he could still dimly see behind its mask of trunks, would echo with the clank of fatigue-parties.

The ground rocked and stirred pleasantly like a gently disturbed hammock. No sound of any explosion came to the little dugout, but the gallery had been blown. Bradshaw felt torn between a savage desire to hear that dozens of Germans had been killed and a hope that they'd discovered our intentions and cleared out of harm's way. You never knew; Jerry might have had a mine right under them at that moment.

White hurried along the gloomy trench; bent down to lift up their dugout flap.

'Ay, quick! There's two men in t' sap, deead!' They rushed to the sap-head. Two miners lay at the foot of the steps, one slightly moving. After a tremendous tussle they dragged the nearer one up the narrow entrance and laid him along the communication trench duckboards.

'Try and get him round, Ernie.'

Bradshaw raced down the steps again; found three more sappers lying in their death sleep, facing the entrance they had been trying to reach before being overcome by gases. He bent to lift the second man; a dead, immovable weight. He felt helpless; groaned at the weakness brought on by months of steady underfeeding. Several small glass tubes containing oxygen tinkled in his iron ration pocket; the M.O. had issued them at one of his lectures. He pulled them out, looked despairingly for somewhere to crack them; then crushed them in his palms, holding cupped hands to the insensible man's nostrils. Up the stairs again, Bagnall, jubilation in his voice, cried:

'Ah've getten him breathin' agean, Dick!'

'There's half a dozen more down there. . . . Where is everybody?'

Only White there, who dare not leave his post. Company headquarters, usually busy with one or two officers, batmen, or signallers, was deserted. Bradshaw adjusted his respirator, and, remembering far back that the heaviest man could be carried by one of slighter build, descended light-headedly again; sinking, as if in water. Behind him followed Bagnall.

'Get back, Ernie . . . make sure of one.'

Bradshaw strove ineffectually to lift the prostrate miner, but the bad air already in him made his efforts, in the confined space, feebler than ever. He flopped back dizzily on the bottom step, a warning instinct whispering caution. He turned and crawled gingerly up the endless steps, senses going.

One . . .

Two . . .

Three . . .

He'd never do it!

Four . . .

Five . . .

He collapsed limply against puttee'd legs.

Midnight in the château aid post. All that Bradshaw remembered of getting out of the sap was of Jem Fletcher, the M.O.'s big assistant, applying pressure with his huge palms to Bradshaw's stomach in an attempt to squeeze out the gases, and Bagnall standing by saying pathetically from a great distance:

'Dick! Dick! . . . He's aw reet, isn't he?'

Now he lay back on a stretcher, when he should have been up in West Lane. An oil lamp and two candles flooded the room with yellow light. Two Jocks came in, gasping and coughing; one a sergeant who cursed the other for whimpering. They'd been badly gassed; Jerry was soaking their front with it. Gunfire vibrated through the walls.

Bradshaw was so little in tune with the war that speculation on the outcome of the sap incident never entered his head. He learnt the next day that the blow, being unattended by any surface upheaval, had trapped all the 'after damp', and the noxious gases, seeking an outlet, had filled the sap before the miners could reach the trench.

By the time the reviving oxygen apparatus arrived, all the men save the one Bagnall had saved were dead. The M.O. told Bradshaw that box respirators were useless against 'after damp'. Also that the badly wounded T.M.B. man had died that morning. If Bradshaw had been himself he would have made some sarcastic allusion to the absence of the oxygen apparatus, which, instead of being on the spot, had to be brought from somewhere behind.

Belcher fell a victim to one of Jerry's snipers the morning Bradshaw went back to duty. A dirty business at first glance, yet psychologically inevitable. One of their sentries called

across again, 'Good morning, Tommy', and Belcher, fears
of treachery easy from repetition of the salutation, bobbed
up. Immediately a bullet came from the flank, and Belcher
stepped down with a purple puncture under his left eye,
saying:

'I'm wounded.'

When the two S.B.s got to the crater, they saw the
wretched lad leaning against the sandbags, the life running
out of him.

Bagnall said bluffly:

'Well! Tha'art for Blighty, chum. Jump on t' stretcher.'

Bradshaw, astonished at the wounded man's resignation,
thought: 'He'll never come back.'

They carried him down the main trench, then passed the
sap-head, and several times the stretcher struck the trench
side jarringly. Half way down, after another jog, Belcher
said:

'All right, I'll walk.'

Bagnall turned his head quickly.

'Tha'll what? Thee stay where thi' art. Trench gets wider
here.'

But Belcher slid his legs over the stretcher side, stood
up, and walked calmly down. Behind, in amazed silence,
foolish and expostulating, followed the stretcher-bearers.
The man had a bullet in his head!

After reaching the M.O.'s dugout, they never saw him
again. Bradshaw wondered many times afterwards how
much venom had been in that sniper's shot, and how much
sporting instinct. Often the two didn't seem far removed.
The very men who swore bitterest at Jerry getting Belcher

laughed loudest when Slater had pipped a fat Fritz who sat dozing in a trench across No Man's Land. This Jerry, unaware that a shell during the night had bitten away a huge chunk of his parapet, sat unconcernedly in the morning light, partially exposed. Slater levelled his rifle, then said to the others about him:

'Ah'll gi' t' poor sod five minutes to move!'

He timed the minutes by wristwatch, raised his rifle, then said amid laughter:

'Noa! Ah'll gi' him another five!'

But the German didn't move till Slater fired. Then he toppled over.

Christmas was coming! Luck had already favoured the Lancashires; they would be out of the line for both Christmas and New Year. Their next turn in front terminated on December the 23rd, when they moved to the Magazine. New Year would find them in 'B' Camp! Hardly fair to their sister battalion the Lancasters, who would be on duty on both occasions. Would there be any fraternising?

All eyes turned skyward. A line of wild ducks flew above in perfect alignment. Several men shot at them till Lieutenant Marriott came along angrily forbidding them. A rattling fire came from across No Man's Land. No restrictions there!

Shells wailed across on their flight to Pop, and men said: ''Ello! T' leave train's coppin' it agean!' Who went on leave? Bradshaw didn't see anybody. Officers disappeared from time to time, but none that he knew of went from the ranks. Yet who had earned the right more?

For most of them, leave was an elusive something that was always 'stopped'.

That day the colonel sent word up to his companies informing all ranks how well pleased Division was with their work since coming to the Salient. He had been awarded the D.S.O.

Under a silvery moon and over the parados, Bradshaw and Bagnall filled sandbags to repair the roof so rudely shattered by Fritz. The soft, smelly earth made their nostrils dilate. Bradshaw was just wondering how many of the millions of sandbags along the front were filled with sand when his spade struck something hard. Bagnall, cursing angrily because his box-respirator insisted on swinging round every time he bent, straightened up, then peered closely. It was a bone. They went on digging and filling, and five minutes later an almost complete skeleton lay jig-sawed at their feet. A grisly relic, with the moon striking it.

'He's a "square-'eead," Dick.'

They carried the bones as far back as prudent, burying them in the deepest shell-hole they could find, where further disturbance would be less likely. Doubtless some mother still hoped faintly to hear from this member of the great army of missing.

'How're your hands, Ernie? Mine are filthy.'

It wanted but two days to Christmas when the Lancasters made a big bombing raid, the Lancashires holding the line an extra day to enable the raiders to thoroughly organise their stunt. Two hundred and fifty of them passed the château, Bradshaw and Bagnall watching them from Congreve Walk. What devils they looked! Hands, faces, and bayonets had been blacked, and on each of their backs glowed a square of white. Rain fell heavily: an advantage, some might say.

Land and sky became one on a dark depressing stage as the preliminary bombardment shook the night; a short and bristling overture reminiscent of Ginchy. In Congreve Walk the two stretcher-bearers stood near the Blighty tree, craning their necks and straining their sight in an endeavour to pierce the wet desolation in front. Rain blinded them.

The raiders came back past the château wretched and soaked; caked in filth. Gaps here and there; the usual stragglers, trailing. . . . No prisoners.

Christmas Eve in the Magazine; very little doing.

No working-parties that night. The front lay quiet.

Taking out a pad, Bradshaw propped himself against the solid thickness of the wall and stuck his knees up as a desk. A little group in the centre of the room sprawled on their blankets playing pontoon.

'I'll stick!'

'Twist one!'

'Busted!'

A series of exclamations, blasphemous and obscene, signified that Chick had turned up another pontoon. Several other men wrote. Bickerdyke, the good soldier, rubbed his already shining rifle with an oily rag ('Treat your rifle like you would your wife, or best girl' the instructors advised. 'Rub it down daily with an oily rag',) and Bagnall left the pontoon party in disgust and squatted beside his colleague.

'Broke agean! 'Ast seen ony post, Dick?'

Bradshaw wrote:

'The first stunt of any note came off last night, when sixty casualties resulted from an abortive bombing raid. The raid has been the topic of conversation in the Poperinghe estaminets for some weeks; the Belgians appeared to know as much about it as we did. When the raiders reached Jerry's front line, he was not there, having got wind of the stunt. Alternate duckboards had been removed, providing waist-deep mud-baths for nearly half the party. All the dugouts had been cleaned up of any informative material. And whilst our fellows wallowed about confusedly in the dark and rain, Fritz shelled his own trenches!

'Jerry is peculiarly inoffensive these days, but doubtless considers it a profitable policy to stonewall while we swipe out recklessly.

'We should have been relieved last night, but stayed in an extra day for the raiders. Tramping back through Potijze to the Magazine was most un-Christmas like. It was damp and cold, and in spite of these colleagues, and in particular Bagnall, very lonely. We grow callous very quickly out here, but it is impossible not to give thought to the raiders who didn't return. We are mostly single men in "C" Company, but up and down the front and away to the bases, thousands of men who should have been playing Santa Claus created visions of home.

'Pantomimes; brightly lit shops; stocking-hanging; carol-singing; dances and parties – all seem some remote dream.'

The Christmas mail brought many parcels and letters; many exhortations to keep smiling. For half an hour Bradshaw and his chum wolfed grub.

CHRISTMAS DAY in the Magazine; the strangest that many would ever spend. Peace on earth! Little to do but lounge about; no officers fussing around. Gifts from the press came: puddings from the *Daily News*; biscuits from the *Manchester Guardian*. Sweets, fruit, fags. Beef and pork. FOOD, FOOD, FOOD. As much as they could eat, then more! No eating the day's ration at breakfast, then falling back on tile-like dog-biscuits. For months their first opportunity to be greedy!

As they sat down to eat, the hefty Lieutenant Rushton, temporarily in command of 'C', roared: 'Men of "C" Company – the King!'

Lieutenant Gore, the company's late commander but now with 'A', and showing signs of whiskey, followed suit dramatically:

'Gentlemen of "A" Company – the King!'

Everybody sprang to attention for a moment, and mugs of beer and ginger beer were raised. Bates said to Bradshaw:

'Hell, that stuff! Get some beer down you!'

A dinner to be remembered in the mixed months that followed.

A new draft arrived; men from Shropshire. Henceforward the housework in Congreve Walk would be lightened. Old Lancashires were definitely in the minority now. Standing, one of the company snipers (who signed his letters 'Sniper Standing') was heard to sneer something about tribunals and starred trades, but on the whole the newcomers looked a more intelligent crowd than the war-beaten men they joined. 'One or two are old enough to be my father', thought Bradshaw.

They had an easy week in 'B' Camp, with some snow and sleet, then the officers arranged a concert in the Y.M.C.A. over the road from the camp. A sudden air of patriotism stirred.

On New Year's Eve the seven in No. 11 hut sat round a choking, eye-smarting fire. (All seven became casualties before 1917's New Year's Eve. Two were killed at Passchendaele and two at Cambrai.)

'Don't put ony more on; you'll ha' th' hut afire!'

'Who gathered all this green wood?'

'Oppen t' door a bit!'

'Good job Cavalry Joe is on leave!'

Bradshaw bought some Quaker Oats. Bagnall sneaked up behind the cookhouse and came back with two tins of Ideal milk, a piece of reconnoitring loudly acclaimed. The two S.B.'s mess-tins were used, being cleanest, and after a deal of mixing and stirring they fed. One or two unfinished parcels came to light, and after eating they sang and joked, the war neglected and forgotten. Near midnight the songs turned sentimental, with crude attempts to harmonise. 'Auld Lang Syne' was encored several times, then everybody felt that here were good hours that might be used for sleep.

They quietened down at last; blew out the last candle. Inevitable cigarette ends glowed. Queer little settlings and splutterings came from the cooling brazier.

'Good neeght, Dick!'

'Good night, Ernie!'

Duties in that winter of 1916–1917 became unendurable in the stiff, frozen trenches, and hundreds went down with

trench-feet and frost-bite. Beards grew again unchecked,
and water-supplies froze. Ice was smashed on the château
lake and in certain of the big shell-holes to get water for
cooking. Snow fell, sticking at once where it let; men
washed themselves raw and sore in it; gathered handfuls
to melt for tea-making. Cold, brilliant dawns; frosty suns;
wan, bleak afternoons, terrifying in their contemplation of
the approaching long night.

To allay frost-bite, whale oil was issued to the stretcher-
bearers, together with an order that every morning after
breakfast each man's feet had to be vigorously rubbed.
Bradshaw and Bagnall had the greatest difficulty in
persuading the sentries of the efficacy of the oil. Some men
flatly refused to bare their feet. In the end, an officer started
at No. 1 Crater with them, and, burdened with a heavy jar
and a few old sandbags, the two S.B.s followed. Men cursed
through chattering teeth at this latest imbecility; swore they
got colder through standing barefooted. Liberally oiling his
palms, Bradshaw massaged toes, ankles, soles, and heels
whilst the unhappy victims shivered, blue.

Then Bagnall rubbed with his sacking till the sentry
howled for him to stop. An icy job, and no towels. If Jerry
had come over at that particular hour any morning he would
have found the defenders in various stages of ineffectiveness.

'If this job were done properly, Ernie, you and I would be
installed in the sap at company H.Q., where it's warm. The
chaps could come down in twos as they could be released.'

One afternoon Lieutenant Hautz said:

'Bradshaw, you're going on a course soon.'

The S.B. was naturally tidy. Orderly officers commented

on his clean equipment and scoured mess-tin. Two days later he was made post corporal, without either stripes or pay. The possibility of promotion troubled him. He knew that the ordinary private soldier had the dirtiest job in all the war; that even the despised lance-jack enjoyed some compensations, whilst a full corporal or a sergeant had comparatively a cushy time, and could often wangle 'buckshee' rations. Despite what men said about being privates, and proud of it, stripes had certain definite advantages. But promotion would mean leaving the S.B.s for a more responsible job. And the S.B.s were cushy, at least at present.

He wouldn't volunteer for anything now. Do his best when detailed, but nothing further! The idea of agreeing to gamble with death didn't appeal. If you were ordered, well and good; but don't sign your own death-warrant. The motives for carrying on with the war had worn threadbare, so individual effort mattered little. When Mr. Hautz told him of the course he didn't say he'd rather stay behind. Better just let things happen. Besides, he guessed the officer had had something to do with wangling the course, out of his generosity.

On the last day of the next spell at 'B' Camp, where everything also lay in the grip of frost, Bradshaw received word to proceed to the 8th Corps School at Proven, where officers learned to handle men and men became N.C.O.s.

The school was strongly constructed of wooden huts and zinc and wood dining-halls. Spotless tables to sit down at; cushy quarters for all ranks and no rousings from sleep to stand-to.

The Commandant, a keen Scotsman who drilled them

marvellously on the big parade ground from horseback, could bring them all to a halt like the crack of a whip.

The second in command – a small, wiry major – seemed to think the war could be won merely by crisply cutting the preliminary word of command from 'Company!' to ''M'ni!' He criticised the officers on parade before the Other Ranks, making them mark time before the whole school.

The fierce frost held; the water-pipes froze. They became schoolboys again, sliding on the lake near the Proven baths. Snow fell again – Christmas-cardy except where heavy boots trampled it hard and brown. At night in the estaminet on the Proven-Poperinghe road congregated Belgian soldiers who boasted they should have been in the line near Poelcapelle.

The month passed quickly. Bradshaw found that the regular meals and sleep, the general comfort of the school, were making him a coward. Badly as he wished to see Bagnall, whose two brief lurid notes made light of the battalion's privations, he hoped for still longer away from the front.

When they got back, the battalion was busy trying to thaw itself a little in 'B' Camp. Definite proof came to hand that Cavalry Joe had been ransacking parcels. Or, at least, presuming and anticipating deaths.

Bradshaw got a letter from Tewson, an older, fellow-worker in the distant cotton warehouse. He had been a Terrier pre-war, and proud of his marksmanship; but before the Derby Scheme he joined the A.S.C. The letter gave A.P.O.S.1. as his address.

'That's Rouen', thought Bradshaw, 'a marksman, at the base, making his fortune flogging rations to the French!'

IN March the 164th Brigade changed sectors. Instead of the Magazine and Congreve Walk as reserve and support they took over the Canal Bank and several Ypres cellars near Lille Gate. The big 'elephant' dugouts set in the Canal Bank looked cushier than Congreve Walk. They paraded on the narrow path during the day, hidden from the front by the high bank. Occasionally three warning whistles announced the approach of a Fritz plane, and they dived out of sight till the anti-aircraft battery on the other side of the canal announced a diversion. At night they carried 'gooseberries' of wire up the raised duckboard track that led to the front line, or gathered at the St. Jean dump for A frames and steel girders. Sometimes a man would rush into the dug-out and shout, 'An S.O.S. has just gone up!', and a hurried scramble would bring them to the battery near the dugouts. If you were lucky you got there in time to see the first blazing reprisals shot out by your own West Lancashire Artillery. (During a night summons they worked like demons, clad only in their shirts, strong to maintain a reputation of being the quickest workers on the Western Front.)

On the last night before moving up to take over in front Sergeant Stevens buttonholed Bradshaw:

'Tha' art for patrol wi' me t'neeght, Dicky!'

No Man's Land lay under a mantle of snow when a subaltern, Stevens, Bradshaw, Walker, and four other privates climbed over the parapet. A rumour that white smocks were being issued to the patrollers didn't materialise.

Jerry, who, everyone agreed, would never have done it with a Lancashire division opposite, had pushed two saps out into No Man's Land, which was nearly two hundred yards wide here. The patrol crawled stealthily between them, and lay quietly to listen at a point not far from the main German trench. Bradshaw had no idea what they were to do if sounds of movement rewarded their efforts. They crouched in the darkness, hearts thumping as a Very light soared and shed pale green daylight all round them. It hissed and died out, leaving an aching blackness, full of apprehension. It was Bradshaw's first patrol, and he felt horribly surrounded. If the Germans manned their two saps the patrol stood a poor chance of getting back unseen. Another Very light shot up, impaling them underneath in suspended anxiety. They had been seen! Bradshaw's heart leapt as the light spluttered, blinding him again. Somebody gripped his knee.

'Look!'

It was Walker, directing the officer's attention to the rear. Faintly silhouetted against the floor of snow and the dark background behind them blacker shadows moved. More issued from the sap on their left. A stupendously calm whisper from the sergeant comforted Bradshaw. He heard a muttering between officer and N.C.O.

'When I give the word, move to the left over the sap. If they see you, run, and make for our trench!'

Panic seized Bradshaw. Their only exit was blocked. They had to cross the German sap!

'Now!'

They crawled swiftly on all fours across a level patch directly at right angles to their original direction. Too slow. Several got on their feet, bending low but moving faster. Bradshaw found himself behind. A black strip loomed underfoot. He made a too-late effort to jump the sap; fell inside; and, like a Stokes bomb, shot up again terrified. Throwing discretion aside, he ran, swerving a way between the black blotches that were holes. The snow pointed a clear path, or Bradshaw would have fallen headlong a dozen times.

The next night they went again, nerves quivering, but didn't venture so far. After two hours' listening and lying in the snow without incident they returned like boards. Bradshaw drank unfeelingly, untastingly, so cold had he become, from a cup of rum. Thawing, he stumbled back to the dugout he shared with Walker. (When Bradshaw went on his course, Downes joined Bagnall on stretchers.) He remembered giggling nonsensically and their poking fun at each other. Next morning he was too drunk to stand-to, and carried a bursting head about all day, as heavy as lead.

The frost broke, but winter had other cards to play. Within a few days came rain, sleet, sunshine, snow, frost, and rain again. Then a thaw pierced everywhere, slowly turning the hard ground to thick, gluey dirt. Rain thinned this: boots turned it to mud and mire. The Lancashires slushed from canal bank to dump; from dump to supports; from supports to front line; then from firestep to dugout, and over the top on patrol. Mud everywhere.

The leave rumour cropped up again; Bradshaw wondered if the ex-Manchesters had any right to expect consideration.

Attempts at bodily cleanliness had long been abandoned. Lice held the upper hand. Periodically they managed a lukewarm tub either in Ypres or Poperinghe, and renovated body and soul with fresh but second-hand underclothing; but khaki could not be changed, and it was here the lice lurked. So quickly did the pests regain their grip that men declared washing and stoving didn't kill them; they hid in the seams. Only squashing them between thumb-nails was effective.

I want to go home,
I want to go home;
I don't want to go in the trenches no more,
Where the Jack Johnsons are bursting galore.

Take me over the sea,
Where the Allemongs can't get at me,
Oh, my! I don't want to die;
I want to go home.

This dirge – popular, poignant – best of all expressed the infantry's fed-upness at this period. Bradshaw entertained no delusions over the quality of the present British soldier. He sometimes wondered why Jerry didn't come over and mop them all up. He knew most of them possessed the courage, born of despair and misery, that might see them fighting for their lives in dogged defiance; stubbornly resisting all efforts to overwhelm them. But in this life of garrison duty they were all, in their cliques of ones and twos, selfish – living for their own ends and existences. A few really courageous ones, whose spirits had survived two weary years, still showed willingness to volunteer for any stunt that came along. Most of the others carried on cheerfully grousing whilst engaged in the semi-safe occupations of trench routine, but immediately this security was imperilled by duty over the top, fear showed behind the eyes of those detailed.

They ate rations that, often enough, had spelt the death of brother carriers. It was common, too, for one member of a quartette sharing at a loaf to become a casualty before evening, leaving behind him an extra portion for the other three. This was eaten without more than a passing, sympathetic thought. It was all in the game, like swapping parts of a dead man's equipment if they happened to be in better condition than your own. Unsafe to think seriously about casualties. In some future reflective moment you would realise that those casualties had really died. Not a little of this callousness resulted from the craving for more food. Men would have choked each other for half a loaf. Behind, they still had enough and a little to spare.

Front-liners had few privileges save that of airing their grievances, and they did that to some length in the lowest language. The foulest obscenities, the ungodliest blasphemies, became everyday words, inseparable from all conversation; merely sounds for expressing their disapproval and fed-upness, their significance lost in constant reiteration. Snow was bloody, khaki was bloody, the sky was bloody, green envelopes were bloody.

To Bradshaw the war was a begger.

To Lieutenant Hautz war was a bagger.

To the others it was the same, pronounced slightly different. Bradshaw learnt that a clean mind could accompany an unclean tongue.

Odd cases of self-inflicted wounds came to light, wretched men who were called cowards and dealt with unceremoniously. To Bradshaw, it needed more courage to

blow off one's fingers or toes than he possessed. He'd stick
it, half coward, first. Some men had reduced it to a fine art.
The first cases had gone down to be unsuspectingly treated
as ordinary casualties; then the burning of the flesh caused
by a shot fired from close quarters aroused suspicion, so
now men fired through a sandbag or a tin of Fray Bentos
placed against the part to be wounded.

This desire to get away from it came to most privates.
For the majority, it stayed at a wish to be nicely wounded;
a cushy, honourable, Blighty one. To others it became an
obsession. It came to Bradshaw, when Tilson, Mr. Hautz's
servant, mentioned whispers he had heard concerning a
spring offensive. Bradshaw's mind flew back to Waterlot Farm
and the wounded crying out in the darkness for succour; to
the stripped, pulverised fields; to battalions reduced in a few
minutes to platoons. He could have felt less pessimistic had
he believed that the next offensive, however murderous,
would be the last.

As he sat near the canal, writing, two officers fired at an
empty bottle on the water. That, and rat-shooting, formed
their pastimes. Their revolvers, like infantrymen's rifles,
were seldom fired otherwise.

It was Sunday afternoon, typically springlike. The men
lolled about basking in the warm sunshine, enjoying Sabbath
leisure. Two bridges crossed the water from bank to bank, and
a small wooden hut on the other side, Bradshaw suspected,
housed the material for demolishing them. Against the blue,
flying low, three British planes circled and glided like fishes
in a globe; in and out, up and down. Probably joy-riding.

Outside the dugouts men wrote, dozed, and 'chatted'. Near to Bradshaw a man stood on the duckboard track 'pulling through' his rifle for an inspection at three o'clock. His calves, heftily puttee'd, were level with Bradshaw's eyes; at the baths they had been proved impostors.

A sharp whistle cheeped over the canal, quickly repeated. Heads turned upward, to see a big Fritz plane sweeping down; a bolt from the blue. Before even the sound of machine-gun fire reached the watchers the first victim burst into flames; dropped blazing to earth. Quickly the second and third were dispatched, to fall limp and stone-like near the canal's dead end. The Fritz made a bee-line for home, pursued by our bursting Archies. Somebody shouted, 'They've got him!' but the bank blocked Bradshaw's view. Slater regarded the whole thing as a great show arranged for their pleasure; a diversion.

One. Two. Three. All over.

Bradshaw wrote:

'I have not yet seen any confirmation of the journalistic assertions that we are masters of the air. Incidents – they are regarded as incidents and not as disasters by the infantry – like the one to-day are exceptional. A single plane seldom is presented with such an easy chance of downing three adversaries, but certainly just now the Germans are losing less men, and machines, than we are. Our airmen are superior, or they would never attempt the risky stunts they do, but Jerry's planes are nippier, adding a hundredfold to the confidence of their pilots. But we can never claim the mastery of the air while German machines cross our lines high up and penetrate unmolested, save for our Archies, to the areas far behind.

'We have a painfully slow machine; a biplane with a framework body. A moderately skilful German can always triumph over a more expert Briton piloting one of these ponderous tanks of the air. He has half won before the duel starts; but several times lately we have made offerings to Jerry of this suicidal plane. It ought to be scrapped before any more good lives are lost in it. When I mentioned its feebleness to one of our officers, he told me that the machine was, probably, only in use until a later type arrived; to prevent front-liners from thinking we hadn't many planes!'

One bright evening a Jerry plane shot like a rocket along the main road at Vlamertinghe, firing at the transports making their way to and from Poperinghe. But he came too far, and Bradshaw noted with glee two British planes following behind and cutting off the raider's rear. Could it be true that a crowd of Aussies, watching the surrender of the two German airmen to our own, flung tins of bully and other missiles at victors and victims because they considered the affair was treated in too light-hearted and trivial a fashion by both lots of officers? Possibly the Aussies were thinking of the men and horses lying on the road.

'We are fairly cushy here on the Canal Bank, but over the water at Tattenham and Salvation Corners heavy stuff crashes for hours at a time. Shells and supplies come up on those routes. We feel as safe inside the arc of this long-range firing as if we were entirely out of its reach.

'Jerry's prolonged inoffensiveness seems remarkable. No attack of any weight since 1915! It bears out reports that his bolt is shot. He is cunning enough to know, however, that defence is the best weapon of attack; he may believe that we shall commence throwing away our substance again, as on the Somme.

'Rats are quite as numerous in the new sector. No Man's Land is wider, but not too wide to prevent the intrusion of "Minnies." Fiendish missiles, these!

'Patrols go out every night. They consist of half a dozen men, a subaltern, and a sergeant. Too many if the object is merely to listen for sounds of activity; too few to combat the larger bodies of raiders Jerry usually sends over. Generally, our object in going out is vague and intangible. If we hear Jerry working, what can we do? We know he is there. The officer, too, is uncommunicative. All we know is to stand and fight if enemy patrols are encountered. One night the Germans almost surrounded us between two saps; we had to run.

'Another night we spotted a patrol of similar strength. Luckily, we were scared enough to withhold our bombs. They were "A" Company's men.

'We never carry rifles on these night excursions, but stuff bombs in our breast pockets. Woollen helmets are worn instead of the heavy tin hats. Numerals, pay-books, letters, and other objects of identification are left behind in the trench. If we are captured, Jerry will then be no wiser, not knowing to which regiment we belong. Some of the fellows have a disc of cloth stitched on their sleeves, with the Red Rose of Lancashire worked in red and green silk; but this is not detached when the wearer goes on patrol.

'There is little discrimination shown in selecting who

should go. S.M. Wiles (Get Fell In has left us – ill, I believe) comes along and says, "You're for patrol to-night!" The sergeant taking the patrol has already said to the S.M.: "What! My turn again? Well, give me some good men – no duds!"

'The subaltern also has intimated that, this being his first patrol in the new sector, he would like men who know the ground. Consequently if you happened to be on patrol the first night, you are landed for regular.'

Winter's dying snaps petered feebly out, and generous warm sunshine flushed away the effect of frost. The British success at Arras in April hardly heartened, so remote did it seem. Each battalion had its own little war; cut off in these days of quietness from those on either side. Like the warehouses in that city of cotton, each run on similar lines: directors, very remote; managers, foremen, and workers.

They went up to strengthen the line one dull grey afternoon, in charge of Corporal Fogg. In the front trench Graham dropped his spade, and a sentry turned on him angrily:

'Y'clumsy bleeder! 'Ave 'em strafin' us!'

At night the job would have been simple; shovelling a loose parados into sandbags; using them to strengthen the lower parapet. From reaching up, Bradshaw's sleeves soon filled with earth. Walker said:

'I'll fill, chum. You hold and tie up.'

Bradshaw bent down to shake his sleeves. He heard a faint but increasing whizzing:

Zzz-rr! Zzz-rr! ZZz-rr! ZZz-Rrr!

A Minnie!

He glanced up, seeing it immediately. A lazy, black tub, toppling menacingly; slowly gyrating.

His chest tightened.

ZZZ-RRR! ZZZ-RRR!

He scrambled a few yards, fell with one leg down over the duckboard. The whirring ceased abruptly. A splitting, tearing roar behind – the most sickeningly dreadful he had ever heard. Earth rose, and something kicked him hard behind, collapsing heavily on his back, squeezing out breath with a gasp. His forehead struck the duckboard. . . .

When Bradshaw came to, a mountain lay on him. The barred edges of the wooden track bored his thigh; loose clods and crumbs of earth littered the duckboards, within an inch of his eyes. Boots moved.

'Give a hand, quick!'

'All right. I'm O.K.'

More boots. The burden was lifted, dragged aside. 'Dick! Arter hurt?' It was Corporal Fogg.

'No, I'm all right!'

Bradshaw turned on his side; raised himself stiffly; pushed a leg on one side. Hands, under his armpits, lifted again.

He stepped over the bashed figure lying at his feet, stared hard; looked up. It was Graham.

A dozen aeroplanes circled round each other very high up, crow-like, thousands of eyes watching. One, two, three, came down in flames; two others broke away *hors de combat*. Someone asked:

'Which is which?'

Slater replied:

'What does it matter so long as they come down?'

There were weeks of hard work at this period. Bradshaw found that keeping a day-to-day diary provided monotonous reading. Life was a succession of fatigue-parties from the Canal Bank, patrols from the line, increasing cannonades, and heavier casualties. A considerable livening up of operations heralded the summer: everything indicated hectic happenings in the near future.

Jerry knew the exact time every evening when carriers gathered at the St. Jean dump. There were many hurried stampedes. Of working-parties Bradshaw wrote:

'Those who haven't experienced them could never understand the tragedy of these nightly working parties in the rain: men trudging wearily back and to between reserve, support, and front trench, month after month; when all they had in mind in England was a great yelling, a scrimmage, then either a Blighty or a "landowner."'

'The course of the war troubles us little. By the time we reach them the fruits of victory will be sour. The prevailing feeling among infantrymen is that some day both sides will leave their trenches, fed up. Yet we know further attempts to break through will soon be made. That is why these nightly patrols, these overhead M.G. shoots, these livelier strafes, have commenced. To harass Fritz. As far as patrols are concerned, they have the opposite effect. Instead of worrying him into a nervous wreck and weakening his morale, they make us jumpy. It is difficult to believe, but sometimes there is no more reason for our patrol than the acquiring of a few inches of enemy wire! I dread these visits across No Man's Land, because it is inevitable that some night we shall be ambushed. Fritz is learning to watch for

us. He is exacting a small but continuous toll from these
nocturnal stunts, knowing we never miss a night. Every time
I approach his wire my heart thumps in fear. Who knows
but that a hostile party has our silhouettes already covered,
and lies low in wait to make surer aim?'

'Yesterday, Tilson, carrying his officers' flare pistol,
somehow fell down the duckboard side, accidentally
discharging the S.O.S. rocket. Quite a lot of our shells went
over in amusing retaliation.'

None of the patrollers believed that the excursions into
No Man's Land had any value, or were calculated to speed
the end of the war. That may have led to a slump in warring
instinct, for Brigade insisted that samples of the German
wire be brought back. And German wire didn't lie all over
No Man's Land; you had to crawl, usually, within a few
yards of their front line to get some. Walker, keenest-eyed
of them all, volunteered to go forward single-handed the
first time such an order came through. Thus Bradshaw
was coerced into another stunt he had no taste for. How
leave his dugout partner to go alone? Midnight found them
before the German trench, the rest of the patrol lying low
at Admiral's Road behind. Their slight sounds magnified
terribly, especially the tinkling of the wire as cutters severed
a length. But they got back uneventfully with several strands
resembling hacksaw blades – proof that a patrol had crossed
No Man's Land.

Several more new officers came. The patrollers had no
compunction in curbing their enthusiasm in a way that
usually made the sergeant grin and turn a blind eye. The

whittled stumps that had once been a hedge lining Admiral's Road were pointed out as the wire in front of the German trench. Parties of the enemy working in front were invented; at pre-arranged signals messages of caution passed from both forward flanks to the officer in the centre. Bradshaw discovered that most subalterns tempered their pugnacity with discretion. The formula which made the ex-S.B. chuckle in the darkness was:

'Oh! Well – er – we'll lie here for a time and listen.' On their return to the front line the officer would sometimes throw out a feeler: 'What does one say on these occasions?' And Bradshaw would reply: 'Well, sir, I should suggest there was a strong wiring-party out mending the wire, and that on ascertaining their strength you withdrew the patrol and asked for a Lewis-gun strafe.'

Then suddenly Fritz would emerge from his shell and send a big party of raiders across, twenty or thirty in number, and sometimes by daylight. He generally contrived to snatch away a British sentry or two. During one relief, the front line packed with Lancashires and Lancasters, a Fritz arrogantly appeared on the parapet, looking down on the jostling figures in the trench. He disappeared after dropping several bombs. Afterwards, a man near swore he had said:

'Share those among you!'

Our men were too handicapped to get their rifles working.

It verged on the uncanny, the way Jerry anticipated their moves. Everything they attempted received an effective counter, yet some nights they could walk along sections of his line. And a facetious rumour gained ground that there were only two Germans holding the opposite trench; a father and son, who walked about firing Very lights from different points. British patrols raided the two sap-heads, strongly fortified by thick belts of wire. Very lights rose from one as they encircled it; a machine-gun swept round occasionally. Yet it was unmanned and empty when they entered.

They took a Bangalore torpedo one night – a long tube of explosive – pushed it gently under the belt of wire at the nearer sap. A Very light went up even as they tinkered about outside the wire. The torpedo blew a good-sized gap, through which the daring subaltern, Mr. Agostini, rushed. There was nobody there. They searched around, but came back empty-handed. Before they reached their own front line, Very lights were again rising from the sap-head.

Other things went wrong, and the fellows groused about the unending monotony. Brass hats were trenchantly criticised as having no bloody tactics.

'Scraped 'em off me putty's', they would say, with a grimace. Our strongest suit seemed to be Bull-dog Tenacity. . . .

Bradshaw had seen but one general in the line. A quiet period, because he was a venerable, white-haired old gentleman appropriately named Snow. Bright, multi-coloured ribbons covered his breast – 'tea-party' ribbons, they were called. If the Staff depended on battalion reports, and these were 'cooked', how could they know better what happened in the trenches?

A general stocktaking took place – a gingering-up that came unpleasantly, following the winter's slacker discipline. Officers paid more attention to the men's bearing. One said to Bradshaw, eyes on downy face:

'You don't shave?'

'No, sir.'

'Well, you'd better start!'

The few ex-Manchesters automatically became veterans, still faintly despised by odd members of the dwindling originals, but volunteers to the late Derby groups. Bradshaw went to great lengths to hide his association with this scheme.

In unguarded moments he heard the 1914 volunteers admitting the war was 'no *bon*'.

'By hell, I'd a bin a conchy, too, if I'd known then what I know now!'

Williams, nettled by one Festubert man's continued efforts to evade fatigues, accused the 1914 and 1915 men of being less deserving of honour and glory than the first Derby men.

'The New Army Saviours! Pooh! All you saw when you joined up was six months holiday at Blackpool, and the war over by Christmas. How many of you expected seeing active service when you enlisted? You think everybody who wasn't out here before last July a wash-out. Why, the fighting didn't start till then!'

Bradshaw liked this kind of talk, yet he would always retain a feeling of superiority over later comers. Those who weren't in at the Somme offensive had missed the fiercest engagement of the war! Never again could Jerry show such tenacity and doggedness in defence! Yet Williams had once said to him:

'That fat old swine could invent a thousand Derby Schemes without hooking me again, coward or no coward!'

Odd times anger would flare up; only once did Bradshaw

see blows struck. Hesketh, smarting under some indignity, had hit out at Brettle. Whilst calling him one or two foul names, Hesketh had yet surprised and amused Bradshaw by addressing the other as 'chum' and 'mate'.

'Sithee, chum, A'll knock thi' bleedin' 'eead off if tha does that ageean! Now, mate, A've towd thee!' But though they might get irritable, disheartening conditions were usually met with good-humoured stoicism. Parades might be a nuisance; having little more use for a rifle than to keep the bore shining might be a bore. But there was always the other fellow in the same boat. Blows were uncommon. If bitterness welled up, harmless bickering followed, seldom overreaching the bounds of ponderous sarcasm.

And always afterwards, Bradshaw would say to himself: 'I'd give something to be where fields are fresh and green. To go bare-headed again, and throw this steel dome away!'

FOLLOWING an affair in which a rum-bottle was concerned, Sergeant-Major Carnforth of 'A' joined 'C' Company as a private; a tall, rough-looking man, whose pet aversion was Derby men – in particular the later groups. He planted his kit next to Bradshaw, and didn't bother going on parade. Every night Bradshaw dreaded the ex-S.M. coming in drunk and sprawling over him sick.

Orders came from behind that identity discs must be worn round the neck on a cord, instead of on the wrist. Missing hands and arms were leading to doubtful identifications.

Time also changed. 'One o'clock' and 'Half-past two'

became 'Thirteen hours' and 'Fourteen hours thirty'. The eleventh hour became the twenty-third, but midnight was ruled out and called either 'Twenty-three hours fifty-nine' or 'No hours one'.

This Continental time had to be used on every occasion, and men giving evidence at orderly-room were often pulled up sharply for lapsing into English time. Sergeants, too, became flustered, often making mistakes in verbal or written evidence.

'Sir, at eleven fifteen – I mean – er – twenty-three hours – er – fifteen – prisoner was found drunk on the line of march.'

(Strange, that the only N.C.O. in the company who went about threatening to 'crime' people couldn't make out a pukka crime-sheet!)

Odd times an N.C.O. was killed or wounded; some private got a stripe. Just like the warehouse – dead men's shoes!

Bradshaw learnt that to less calculating men it was a simple matter to appear as a hero. All you needed was a few grains of gumption. After many earlier adoptions of the prone position, and an equal number of sheepish risings, he found that most of the shells that came over were not dangerous to him. A little judgment placed them immediately left or right, short or behind.

On patrol the single crack of a rifle was once a signal to fall flat. If you stood, realising the bullet had already passed, you became a cool customer to your colleagues! Thus could a craven give an outward appearance of fearlessness.

Bradshaw – and Walker, because they spoke of these things together – stuck where he was when things grew hot and lively. So easy to dodge into the way of a shell! When a new man said, after a bombardment, 'Oh! I don't know how you manage not to duck or run', Bradshaw would feel pleased inside and answer:

'What's the good of moving? Every step you take might be towards the spot where the next shell will fall.'

As bad to Bradshaw as most bombardments was the mental hurt of a quiet, wet day in the line. Dripping, depressing desolation on every hand; everything muddy to the touch. Wet shoulders, wet hands, wet knees, wet puttees, filthy boots. Rain dripping from steel helmets; everybody quiet except Slater.

'Now lads! How about a roastin' fire and your feet on t' mantelshelf. Rain beatin' on t' winders, and t' cat on t' carpet. Tea nearly ready, real sergeant-major's, wi' plenty o' sugar and milk in, an' . . .'

Then for a minute the grumpy and bad-tempered would feel like throwing things, but always grinned and agreed 'it were a luvly war'.

Nobody could damp Slater's humour. All odd rifle cracks that came across No Man's Land he followed with one remark:

'There's a sniper there – we mun have him to-neeght!'

He declared he would join up wounded next time there was a war.

Once, on a particularly exhausting working party, Slater toiled under a heavy steel girder and said whimsically, between gasps: 'I wouldn't do this job, but I need t' money.'

Of a vastly different type was Lewis; out scrounging since the 'tater-masher' and 'jam-tin' days, Lewis represented the perfect shirker, always prominent at pay parade and cookhouse, but invariably missing when fatigues were wanted. An untidy soldier, with gaping puttees, a tunic two sizes too big, and a belt that dropped below his bottom tunic button. After his pretence at button-cleaning a liberal supply of Soldiers' Friend always pinked his button-holes and numerals. Invariably without cleaning tackle, money, water, and letters from home, he remained a favourite in the company because he could spin good yarns of the earlier days. Also, he had an enviable command of swear-words. His best story, too naïve to be untrue, was the delightful incident he called 'Georges Carpontier'.

Not quite so humorous were his tales of Lancashire and Yorkshire troops sent hurriedly from England to fill up a thinned portion of the line early in the war. These reinforcements were marched up the St. Jean road in column of route in broad daylight. One shell destroyed a platoon.

About this same time a Canadian unit captured a dozen Germans in the Salient, and bundled them down to B.H.Q. The adjutant, eye on wristwatch, ordered the escorting Canadians to march them down to Poperinghe.

'—— and see you're back here by twelve o'clock!'

The time was then eleven fifty-five, and Pop five or six kilometres away.

A few minutes later, short spasms of rifle fire marked the sequel to this order.

Bradshaw experienced a slight feeling of shame, almost resentment, because the Portuguese and Chinese and Ghurkas (with their stealthy knifing) and other foreigners were helping us. England might be bungling it; but better go down than live by outside aid. The Americans, though, ought to come in; they were more like us. But they were on a better thing, prodigiously supplying bully beef and shells. It was no quarrel of theirs. And yet why should they come in, after three years, and share the triumph, however long-winded it was? What did they know of Ypres, Festubert, Loos, Neuve Chapelle, Arras, The Somme, Messines?

Bradshaw wrote in his diary:

'Is Prussian discipline more rigid than ours? We salute in the firing-line and pick up match-sticks, We dare not take off our equipment or move a yard without our box-respirators, which we have never used. If the Colonel comes round, which is not often, and asks of a sentry, "Who is on your flanks?" he gets irritable at the reply, "I don't know, sir," but nobody bothers about educating us in this direction. The last time we stayed in the Magazine billet, a general asked all our platoon, separately, which army corps they belonged to. Only three knew.

'We can laugh at these things – what do they matter? But the drastic sentences for "dropping off" at one's post after sleepless nights of work, for slanging an irritating, punctilious N.C.O., or other conduct prejudicial to good order and conduct, no!

'A man who is crucified to a wheel before all his comrades suffers a degrading, demoralising punishment. When his battalion is kept in the line longer than its recognised spell, he puts in days of overtime with death. Let him hang back, or overstay his all-too-short leave in an attempt to prolong his precarious hold on life, then he is subject to torture spared the most despicable civilian prisoner.

'Again, men whose roads are the duckboards and whose

dwellings are funkholes (in their campaign of cleanliness, nobody calls round to say, "That dugout isn't fit for a pig!") have just cause for resentment against the police who wait behind, outside the danger zone, alert for deserters. Discipline must be maintained, but the existence of these six-foot onlookers is a standing insult to front-liners. Their strength could be utilised more profitably in carrying duckboards and stuff to the front line.

'Unless their senses are impaired, few men desert. Many of us wish to run, but there is a restraining force stronger than the fear of Redcaps; a power outside the bonds of patriotism even – the inner knowledge that we should be letting down the others and ourselves. Any man who runs away when his comrades are sticking it is best let to run. He is no use in the line; often a menace to the safety of others.

'We have a private in "C" Company – a wild-eyed, queer chap bubbling with generosity – who is obviously affected by shell-fire. Men grow alarmed when they discover he is detailed for their post. Several times he has been found behind, wandering, fogged, after days of absence from the line. He was wounded at Ginchy, and ought obviously to be behind somewhere.

'Slater says our blood is like "shell-oil watter" to stand what we do, but what remedy is there?'

Bradshaw looked up from his pad, a chuckle escaping him. He saw Slater, as he appeared two nights before, staggering under the weighty section of an elephant dugout, asking the lieutenant if he couldn't take two, just to 'get it ower and done wi' quicker.'

Remarkable rumours circulated; the latest, one disparaging

the 'Pork and Beans'. Jerry sent 'pineapple' gas over to them
their first trip up – they liked the smell so much that half
their force quickly became casualties.

'Sniff! Sniff! Ah! Bon! Bon!' became a favourite catch-
phrase.

A Chinaman at Proven, enquiring too inquisitively into
the functioning of a Mills bomb, blew his hand off. This
casualty caused the greatest delight amongst his yellow
brothers, who regarded it as the funniest of jokes.

The French Army mutinied, and a dreadful reverse was
hushed up.

But rumour lies, thought Bradshaw, or we should have
left the Salient long ago for India, Mesopotamia, Egypt, and
Salonika; and our opponents across No Man's Land would
be lads of fourteen, fifteen, and sixteen.

One afternoon on the Canal Bank, Lieutenant Jenkins sent
a runner for Bradshaw and Bagnall to appear at Company
H.Q. Mr. Jenkins had temporary command of the company.
He wanted details of the mine disaster at Mud Lane.

'I'm recommending you for the D.C.M., Bradshaw.'

Bradshaw knew perfectly well that any recognition
was undeserved. He hid a sneaking pleasure by saying to
Bagnall:

'Medals? Pooh! Men who won them deservedly must feel
like chucking them away, now they're being flung about so
freely. Remember what our papers said about the Iron Cross?'

For some unexplained reason, Ernie, who had saved the
man's life, received no recommendation. But all he said was:

'Tha deserve it . . . tha went down.'

THE little eruption at Arras subsided, exciting no more comment than would a neighbourly quarrel. The fellows preferred it so; quiet continuation rather than volcanic action. If another offensive could end it, well and good. But let it be on another sector.

Bradshaw never really attuned himself to the front. The simple, straightforward duty got befogged and bewildering in its ramifications. Fight for one's country, certainly; but that was all the other chap was doing across No Man's Land.

They'd never make a soldier of him. He was convinced of his own unsuitability. Yet they were all alike. He often went about haunted by his own insignificance. The war was too big, his part too infinitesimal, to matter. Were the other men as confident and used to this sort of thing as they looked? Always came that feeling of looking on; being in the audience instead of on the stage. Or did he imagine things? Imagination, realisation, played the devil if not kept in rein. Lucky if you had no imagination at all!

In April, Bradshaw wrote:

'I often think that a soldier's life is worth while when he can stand before the beautiful husk of St. Martin's, or watch the break of day through a network of barbed wire. I feel glad and thankful, yet sad and unworthy; aching for the power to describe the strange emotions that strive for expression on such occasions.

'Two men from the battalion go on leave to-morrow. They catch the train – so often shelled – from Poperinghe, which travels down the lines of communication picking up other fortunates, reaching the coast packed. There will be infantrymen – pukka front-liners – and infantrymen who work

155

typewriters at headquarters, amongst them. Artillerymen from the Menin road and garrison blokes whose guns fire from safer areas. A.S.C. men who travel regularly through Ypres, and some who unload provisions ten miles and more behind. R.E.s who boss infantry working-parties about, and genuine sappers who advance farther in their saps under the German lines than the infantry can advance on top.

'Across the Channel a few front-liners will boast exaggeratingly about the number of casualties they leave behind every time up; how Jerry blew a mine at the craters and sent a platoon sky-high; how far Bill Jones's left leg was from its right partner when a five-nine got him on the St. Jean road; how close the Germans are at Mud Lane (so close that mythical braves lob bombs across, exhorting the recipients to "share those among you!"). And how Fritz, with a cheery "Gooten Morgen" and a perverted sense of humour, tries to lure simple, unsuspecting Britons to pop up and be sniped.

'And by the time London is reached the whole train-load will become a band of warriors from the front, naïvely recounting to proud relatives second-hand escapades and horrors. Or joking about trench comforts; bayonets used as toasting-forks; rats bigger than sandbags; lice bigger than rats. And mud, mud, MUD; oceans of it.

'Many of these leave men are far safer on the lines of communication than their wives and sweet-hearts living in London.

'I should like to go on leave.'

The cycle of garrison duty remained unbroken. Two or three weeks' penury ended at 'B' Camp with a munificent pay

of five or ten (sometimes twenty if you weren't in debt!) francs.
A couple of nights riotous living in Pop on eggs and chips
and 'vin blong', or cigarettes, biscuits, and chocolate from the
R.F.A. canteen, then possibly another month's poverty.

And all the time the A.S.C. and the R.E.s got cursed because
they drew the fabulous sum of six shillings a day! Bradshaw
gave up arguing with his colleagues. Instead of wanting the
infantryman's pay pushed up to six bob, all they desired to
see was the A.S.C.s' and R.E.s' cut down to their own!

One evening, with Bradshaw leaning against the stale,
heaped parapet as stand-to uneventfully expired, Sergeant
Orrell came along humming, to the tune of 'God send you
back to me':

'Gord send a Waac to me!

— Oh, Riley, I shall want you for patrol to-night.'

Out of the corner of his eye Bradshaw saw, with faint
amusement, Blezard retreat before the sergeant's oncoming
and dive quickly through the parados to the latrine. Less than
six whizzbangs had come over all day, but one of them chose
to burst ten seconds later, and near enough the latrine to
leave a small splinter in Blezard's stomach. He died next day.

One day, Bradshaw heard Lieutenant Jenkins say:

'The Irish got off lucky that stunt . . . only two killed.'

Only two! As if those two hadn't each had a life to live!

Another time, prior to a fighting patrol, Lieutenant Hautz
said: 'They're not expecting to have more than a dozen
casualties.' Everybody had lost their sense of proportion and
value! That was why Bradshaw had refused to volunteer for
this same fighting patrol. Mr. Hautz had seemed surprised,

so surprised that Bradshaw nearly said 'Yes' when his senses protested 'No'. If it had been on a task of rescue, perhaps; but to destroy others . . . !

Corporal Atkinson came down terrified, holding up his trousers in a very embarrassing manner. The fellows laughed at him, chaffing. A shell splinter had caught him, sitting down in the latrine. He also died next day, surprising everybody.

Several interesting patrols took place, giving Bradshaw material for his diary.

'"A" Company patrol had the task on Monday of visiting the old, disused dugouts in No Man's Land. Built by the Canadians in 1914, they were left isolated when Jerry pressed up back on Ypres, high and dry between the lines. The patrol had instructions to find out if Jerry manned them at night.

'Monday's patrol reached them, to discover the wire too thick to penetrate. Brigade weren't satisfied. They sent up a carpet, to be unrolled over the wire, and strict instructions to get inside and investigate. Tuesday night's patrol succeeded, and found an old teapot and a rum jar in one of the dugouts. (Built-ups, really.)

'On the point of retiring with this evidence (which some now claim had lain there since 1914), Fritz spotted them and opened fire. The patrollers hurried back, but frantic efforts failed to dislodge the carpet, so they left it behind, impaled on the barbs. They went again last night – can't you imagine some irate general, feelings lacerated at the prospect of hopping about in a carpetless bedroom? – but Jerry had forestalled them.

'The carpet had gone.'

Two men returned from Blighty the following day, absent

since Ginchy. An A.S.C. corporal joined the company, incredible as it seemed to most, for tuition prior to going home for a commission.

'Gosh, Ernie', said Bradshaw. 'Fancy those two coming back after all this time . . . no nearer the end than before.'

Bradshaw had the opinion that to stay at the front was less painful than going home, tasting comfort and civilisation, and coming back to the unpleasant intimacies of trench life. Next day he resumed his simple chronicle.

'Last night – and this morning – we chased after carpets and woollen helmets in No Man's Land. We had the sandy-moustached, nervous little officer with us, Mr. Stanbridge, Sergeant Stevens, and an A.S.C. corporal (the latter for tuition). We left the front line at the post by the road; the password was 'Beer'. Years of pre-war use made this road plainly visible, dull and shining, in a faintly illumined No Man's Land. We could feel grass under our feet – that dead-looking stuff that somehow survives the surrounding upheaval. We kept the road on our right; heavy boots might have clanked on it. It led to St. Julien in front; down to Ypres behind.

'After five minutes' stalking, the squat bulks of the dugouts loomed up – sixteen of them all told. Our duty lay with the end one, nearest the German line. Indistinctly, a belt of wire ran before them, without any apparent break. Everything quiet and dark, breath-catchy, in front of No. 16 dugout – our objective. Very lights flickered, few and far between.

'A solitary rifle cracked the silence. 'Stivvy' whispered tensely, "That's —— it!" I heard him, being next behind. We had been seen.

'Picture us there, keyed up to top pitch, the cause of our distress doubtless by this time safe and snug between his sheets and blankets. But for Sergeant Stevens's good solid bulk before me, I should have felt like rapid retreat. The officer, too, had more guts than his appearance told.

'Whilst apprehension and indecision held us rooted, came an order in German, unintelligible. A few seconds' aching silence, and a succession of bombs burst about us – over our heads, so close had we crept! A dozen Very lights hissed and soared upwards, to burst blindingly. As we stood fearfully exposed, rapid rifle-fire spat at us, appallingly near. The sudden uproar was deafening. A machine-gun crackled round with a vicious sweep. A sudden scurry from behind. The others were running back! I stood panic-stricken, unable to follow; then dived for the nearest shell-hole. Anything to get below that dangerous fire! As I dropped pantingly, I saw "Stivvy", rock-like, calling softly, "Steady, boys – steady!"

'Fragments of earth dropped round me as I crouched, heart thumping, shaking, against the Jerry side of the hole. From our lines a Very light rose, feebly flickering and fading; in our trench they wondered what the rumpus was all about. A confusion of faint calls penetrated the commotion. I was isolated.

'I soon realised I couldn't stay there. Fritz might pop out any time, to see if he could bag any wounded prisoners. "Give your legs a chance," Slater always advised, but I lay afraid. The brilliant lights fluttered above uninterruptedly, encircling me in a perpetual light, searching out my shallow hole. How tenacious, or windy, Jerry was!

'Dread that they might come searching gripped me again,

and after two hesitating attempts I crawled and scuttled towards safety. Odd bullets still bit into the ground and flung crumbs of soil over me. I can laugh now to think how close they were, but a sickening fear daunted me then. How painful to get one in my rear!

'I looked back, several tufts and stumps taking on the shape of stalking Germans. Sweat broke out on me as I leaped frenziedly to my feet, running madly. They heard my sudden retreat, rifle-fire breaking out again. I twisted and dodged, then came a shaking cropper. Panic possessed me, and I cried out; what, I have no idea. As suddenly, I sobered. Our own sentries might fire at me!

'I found the road again without difficulty, and called "Beer" long before any sentry could possibly hear; reached the wire, wending a way through the gap; repeated "Beer" in a strained whisper. Again fear gripped me. "The sentry perhaps covers me, believing me a Jerry, and waits, to get surer aim."

'I called again, "Beer! Beer!" (Bagnall has often tried to get me to call that in an estaminet). The trench might have been unoccupied for all answer I got!

'"Beer! Beer! It's Bradshaw!"

'I reached the rising earth that formed the parapet, quickly reiterating the magic, futile word, faint from fear. Bending over the sandbagged top, I peered down. In the dimness the sentry sat, huddled in the corner of the firestep, asleep. My mood changed. I dropped a clod on his tin hat, and he jumped, terrified. "You're a fine sentry," I growled scornfully; then left him to regain his scattered wits.

'I felt aggrieved that the trench should settle so quickly to its normal life; hurt that "Stivvy" and the others could go to kip caring so little for my welfare. I trudged down the deserted communication trench almost resentfully; bumped into Bagnall and an excited "Stivvy".'

Bradshaw paused in his writing. What had 'Stivvy' said?

'Hell, Dicky! Where's t' a bin? We've only just missed you. I counted eight when we got back to t' trench, so thowt thee were aw'reet. That bloody A.S.C. wallah. . .! A'd ne'er a' gone to kip, Dick, if A'd a' knowd tha' were out theer. . . .'

Bradshaw learnt what had happened from Bagnall. Sergeant Stevens had included the sentry when counting up, dismissing the party as complete. There had been no casualties in the hurried flight, which had commenced with the A.S.C. corporal.

'Stivvy' insisted on taking Bradshaw to Lieutenant Gore, now back at his post of acting-captain, to explain what had happened.

Bradshaw resumed:

'Mr. Gore is a broken semi-soldier of the Somme days; weedy and pale, but generous and decent. He makes mad, solitary, hair-raising midnight excursions to the Jerry trenches; walks along their front line till he sees a sentry; then hops out and comes back again.

'His dugout was warm, and the spirit of friendly hospitality strong on him. The easy-going sergeant was soon "over the top," that being his second visit to the captain's dugout.

' "I'm not going to have my patrols bumped by those bees! We'll have a special out – Sergeant-Major Wiles . . . Sergeant Whiteside . . . Corporal Fogg . . . you, sergeant . . . Lieutenant Stanbridge . . . and you, Bradshaw? . . . and Walker."

'How can one refuse such requests – refuse the proffered rum that thousands would give their right arms for – point out to superiors the foolhardiness of such petulant attempts at retaliation? I walked to the dugout entrance, the darkness outside intensified by the captain's light, and rather feebly said:

'"Yes, sir! But it's frightfully black outside; wouldn't it be better to postpone it for another night?"

'He came towards me; made no comment on my audacity, but peered out and agreed. We had another sip at the cup of rum, waited for "Stivvy" to have a drink, then disappeared down the still communication trench.

'A working-party had returned just as we got back to the dugout; everybody was awake. The patrollers argued about the number of Jerries they'd been ambushed by, then cursed the A.S.C. Several had torn puttees, following a hectic time in our wire. The faint voices I heard in No Man's Land were their oaths and calls as they got tangled up in the barbs. Two or three found themselves shin deep in the pond that lies before the trench. The stench, as they disturbed the stagnant water, appears to have been atrociously putrescent.

'The S.M. appeared a few minutes later, as we settled down to sleep, to warn us for an immediate special patrol. Mr. Gore had changed his mind. A quarter of an hour later, after another drinking bout, we arrived back in the front trench. It was funny to see the same sentry on duty, scared stiff because he thought the appearance of the captain and the S.M. had some connection with his sleeping on duty.

'I borrowed the revolver that "Stivvy" carried before – he stayed behind to sleep things off in the support line. Walker was the only other private, anxious because the captain had a reputation for eccentricity.

'A more ill-conceived attempt at retaliation would be hard to imagine. We strolled down the road towards the first dugout without any attempt at concealment. The same faint light illumined No Man's Land, and we could see thirty or forty yards before us. Walker suddenly disappeared from my side, strangely, it struck me, because we had come to a whispered agreement to stick together a little apart from the others. Lieutenant Gore chatted to Mr. Stanbridge and the S.M. all the time. My nerves felt crocked, so that I jerked up trembling as a weird clear cough came from in front. The captain hesitated a moment, then motioned us on. Another cough, almost peremptory. A stoppage; a whispered conversation. The idea came to me, as we stood there undecided, that a lonesome Jerry lurked by No. 1 dugout; afraid of engaging us, yet urgently desirous of turning our head.

'And turn we did. A retaliating fighting patrol, purpose defeated by two coughs! Before we had reached our wire again, Walker gained my side. I heard him chuckling, but not until afterwards did it dawn on me what he had done: the biggest spoof ever.

'Walking down the communication trench again, Lieutenant Stanbridge called after us:

'"Oh, Bradshaw. I left my woolly helmet out on the first patrol, stuck on the wire. Would you mind helping me to search for it?"

'It was a present – hand-done – which he valued highly. For the third time I went back again. Dawn glimmered, an established fact. No sudden streaks in the low eastern sky, but a decided lift of the curtain of darkness. Pessimistically, and with doubtful grace, I resigned myself to, at the most, a fifteen-minute search; glad that it would be courting disaster to go beyond our wire.

'Once outside, I put my head to the ground, and immediately saw, like a nest in a leafless tree, a black patch. We unhitched it carefully, undamaged, and Mr. Stanbridge was delighted. I should dearly like to see the letter he will send to-day describing the affair.

'They were standing-to before I got back. The S.M. met me, to say I should be excused all duties to-day.

'Mentioning that A.S.C. corporal savours of a deliberate attempt to besmirch the name of that already much-maligned corps. They got cursed enough; but his defection might have proved a serious matter. He lacked front-line schooling. I wonder if the adventure has upset his desire to transfer?

'I have tried not to write bitterly, but find this a steadily increasing task. If we could only gather some idea how long it will last! This line will never give way – haven't we thousands of guns standing wheel to wheel in the ruins of Ypres? But we get no farther forward; Jerry seems just as firmly rooted across the way.

'Without being either sentimental or patriotic, I feel glad to be one of the British Army whilst Britain is such a powerful nation, for I see in the conduct of this war definite signs that some day her greatness will wane. To be British now is to grant that things are not going as well as expected; that the Germans, with all their strange breaches of "fair fighting," are tough, dogged opponents; that the old myth of one Briton being equal to half a dozen foreigners is going to the wall.

'Why brush truth aside and pretend that the "magnificent courage" and "heroic sacrifices" are anything but the result of disciplined fear? Courage and heroism abound everywhere, especially in the soldier's steadfast acceptance of distasteful conditions, but is most strongly manifested when discipline has carried men into dangerous places not of their choosing. Since we saw the Guards at Mametz, and later in action at Ginchy, we have thought of them with every degree of awe and respect, following their many fortunes. Some men in the company attribute their successes to superior stature and general robustness; others to longer periods between stunts and better "nursing" during those periods. But is it not that individual thought and feeling have been drilled out of them by a much sterner discipline than that enforced in our own battalion?

'This morning "Cavalry Joe" afforded himself a great deal of coarse amusement by assuming the duties of barber. He ploughed deep furrows in the company's hair with unwieldy horseclippers, starting at the centre of the forehead and running over backwards. He mowed off my eyebrows and left another boy bald except for two ugly tufts over the temples. One man swore to put a bullet in his back at the first opportunity, but of course he won't.'

As Bradshaw wrote, Grayson leaned idly against the dirty clay banking, scrutinising the rat-holes and tearing away bits of rotten sandbag. He seemed fascinated by the imprint of canvas on the moulded earth, and sniffed as strange odours tickled his nostrils. Bradshaw noticed the cracks in the sandbagged joints and a number of holes where pieces of shrapnel had whizzed and whacked their way in. How long ago had the trench been made, and where now were the builders of it?

Grayson always looked fed-up, but had proved a willing worker. He waited, mess-tin in hand, for the carriers, weary and dispirited-looking. Probably wondering how his present existence ever came to be termed fighting in the trenches! Marvelling how the numerous duties, the nights of drudgery carrying up costly material that was as quickly blown to fragments, could be war; doing his bit! One of the Shropshire Christmas draft, thought Bradshaw, doubting if he'd yet seen a German!

Two men were killed that day, Howarth and Brook, two casualties occurring so unremarkably and unemotionally that Bradshaw wondered later whether they really were dead. Of course, Bagnall said apropos of Howarth, whose death he saw:

'Another poor bee for the rest camp.'

Both boys had spoken to Bradshaw not long before, yet their going affected him little. His first thought, as always, had been:

'Thank God it wasn't me!'

They must have consoled themselves in similar fashion many times. For all he knew, a shell aimed at the spot he occupied might be on its way! He dwelt on that possibility till he almost convinced himself that the next shriek would end at him. Yet he didn't move. Likely as not the shell would be a few yards wide. Why move into it?

Later, when came the full realisation that two colleagues had gone, he sat head in hands, staring, wondering why he couldn't cry.

Bradshaw experienced transitory moments of elation when he stuck out a pretty stiff bit of shelling, yet he felt deep down that cowardice, fear of moving to a more dangerous spot, held him rooted.

Grayson stopped pulling at the sandbags; put a hand inside his tunic to scratch. The last time they had physical jerks at 'B' Camp, those in the rear rank saw lice crawling over his shirt at the shoulders and neck. He got ostracised daily for allowing them to multiply unchecked. Bradshaw's tunic-collar, shirt neckband, and trousers seams were alive in a week if neglected. He got weary of destroying the pests, yet laughed at the witty remarks of his fellow-sufferers. Bagnall daily laid odds against anybody else's brand racing his own red-backs!

Some used candles to burn them out, others their thumb-nails. One or two merely picked them off and flung them aside unsquashed, getting roundly cursed by those harassed victims who believed they crawled back!

With the warmer weather, the men suffered many minor agonies. The lice plagued at that exasperatingly inaccessible spot under the knee where puttees were bound. Skins were scratched till they bled, and soon great sores appeared, as round as sixpenny and shilling pieces. Many legs were covered with them; they stuck to socks and underpants and trousers, the scabs coming painfully away whenever garments were removed.

Good clean water remained difficult to get. On their next trip up, the whole battalion washed in a trough in an open field near Pop, the water thick and gritty with dirt. Many teeth, including Bradshaw's, were ruining for want of cleaning; of what use a toothbrush, with decent water unobtainable? The opportunity for washing socks or underwear came rarely; towels smelled sourly. Many mess-tins went from meal to meal uncleansed. Finger-nails were neglected.

Bradshaw had charge of a bombing post and six men on the extreme right of their front. The trench twisted and turned emptily beyond him, losing itself in another battalion. He never ventured far towards the next post, but the gap fascinated and alarmed him. Jerry might easily get round behind them. Could the next battalion's sentries be relied on to watch their part?

Rumours of the impending offensive reached home, and Bradshaw received several anxious letters from his mother explaining that as he had never been christened would he see the padre and have this neglect remedied? (What straws you snatched at, dear mother, hoping to safeguard your son's life!) Later, she wrote direct to the padre (Bradshaw never saw him except on church parade), who sent a runner up to the front line with a chit.

A rather shame-faced Bradshaw presented himself nervously at the chaplain's tent, and was baptised whilst a choir of machine-guns and heavies chanted from the Salient's eruptive right.

'C' Company did another turn up, at the end of which Bagnall might have been heard saying:

'Well, lads, t' Magazine t' morn! Ast'a ony brass, Slater?'

Slater's answer was always the same:

'Noa. Sweet F.A.!'

But they didn't go to the Magazine. April the 23rd found them in Houlle-Moulle, out of shell range the first time for months. Bagnall and Slater swore to get Bradshaw drunk on pay day, but Bradshaw and Walker were lugging them upstairs to their bedroom billet before eight o'clock, 'blind to the wide'.

Houlle-Moulle was nondescript, a river – representing the hyphen – running through it. At Houlle he saw big enamel CHOCOLAT MENIER signs, but all he bought invariably tasted like sweetened cinders. Not a patch on that which came from home. No. 9 Platoon had a little cottage-shop standing lonely in a field off the main road, far away from the rest of the company and fatigues. They had been in the billet only half an hour before Baker was at the window shooting rabbits.

A narrow trench filled with water – a cutting from the river, Bradshaw supposed – constituted the baths. They passed through it like sheep in a dip, but revelled in sunlit water. The weather smiled every day, and all day, during their stay.

Four in 'C' Company – including Bradshaw – were given a stripe each. Casey declared he wouldn't wear his, and went on several parades till convinced the stripe was to be paid for.

Bradshaw sometimes wondered what kind of a show the battalion would put up next time it was called on. Any job that human beings stuck at too long became irksome and monotonous. If he had possessed the necessary aplomb and bearing, he might have applied for a commission. He believed that the several months' safety necessary for the making of an officer offered strong inducement to those wearied by trench life. Slater defined the difference between commissioned rank and the private soldier like this:

'Rabbits and other good things come up for the officers' rations. They get knocked about and dropped in the mud by carrying-parties. When they reach the officers' mess they are washed in hot water, and this liquid is dished up to the men as soup.' Remarkable how few of the officers were looked up to and respected. Those who fussed about grease-spots on the men's khaki, and otherwise showed their punctiliousness, were liked least. The Other Ranks made a god of the lieutenant with the Italian name, for his fearlessness on patrols and under shell fire. Beyond him, what other examples were there of forceful and exemplary 'leadership'?

Bradshaw seldom saw Colonel Pringle's soldierlike figure in the line, and never the round, fresh-cheeked adjutant, who looked like an overgrown baby.

Did the same lack of confidence prevail across No Man's Land? Was it imagination, or the dominating influence of their commanding position, that put Jerry's prestige so high? Without showing any activity, he always appeared to hold the upper hand. Professional versus amateur?

Bradshaw wondered how much more seriously the company would take the war were the Salient round Preston, or Bolton, or Manchester. Had British soldiers ever been so impotent in any other war?

Fortunately there was always the indefatigable Slater to enliven the company with his new-angle humour.

Bradshaw was detailed here to make one of a firing-squad, to put an end to someone's poor wretched existence. (It seemed a pity that volunteers who couldn't stick it any longer hadn't the chance of un-volunteering.) With Mr. Hautz's help he wangled out of it.

YPRES again; a new billet behind the Asylum. A battery of howitzers lay close by, and two tremendous guns on a rail track. According to the gunner, Jerry had never managed to silence these two. They nipped out, fired a few shells and took cover again before Jerry could locate their position. Alongside the high camouflaged emplacement was the most tremendously fortified dugout-cellar Bradshaw had ever seen; rows and rows of fat sandbags strengthened by steel girders.

He watched the five-nines fire, and saw for the first time the shell as it soared upwards from the muzzle. He gazed astonished at the high angle; the shell's destination appeared to be no farther than the next field – and all the way to heaven and back before it got there. Astonishing to hear the shells were going well over Bellewaarde Lake.

'Gosh, Ernie! Fancy one of those blighters landing plump on you . . . put a nasty taste in your mouth!'

Captain Phillipson visited the post, swapped from 'A' Company. A heavy, oldish man, reputed by his servant to wear a body shield. (He had his head blown off on July the 31st.)

'Are your bombs all right, corporal?'

Without waiting for any answer, he opened the nearest box, took a Mills in each hand, pulled the pins, and flung the bombs over the parapet. In the quietness they burst startlingly and rudely in the wire. He emptied the box.

'They seem all right.'

He turned and disappeared.

Bradshaw thought, 'Well! Why couldn't he have thrown them behind, instead of giving Jerry the location of the post?' He took up the empty box and said:

'Just going to the bomb store. Shan't be a minute.'

He walked down the trench, had a word with Evans, a sentry on the next post. Lieutenant Hautz came up, white and nervous.

'You're wanted at your post, corporal.'

Bradshaw hurried back. Birtles lay dead at the entrance of the smaller dugout. His head and shoulder were shattered, arm severed; missing.

Harrison said:

'It's them bombs as done it, corp! You'd on'y gone a minute when Fritz sent a couple o' pineapples over.'

And that mild enquiry into a reasonless commotion had brought this. He looked round, but half an hour had passed before he came across Birtles's arm, down the side of the duckboard. The hand still clasped a broken bayonet; his turn on duty had been due.

Bradshaw had learnt that keen eyes across No Man's Land quickly determined the position of a post by looking under our parapet for tins and scraps of paper. He had nailed a sandbag on one of the supporting stakes.

'Put all your refuse in here', he said. 'We want to keep this post secret, so that when Jerry shells he'll have to distribute his fire along the trench instead of concentrating it just here.'

Further, he disguised the top of the periscope with a piece of soft clay, to hide its square top, and asked the sentries always to fire from different bays. These precautions had been followed sensibly, but what could you do when a man in whose charge was the company behaved so thoughtlessly?

Little reading came their way, but in a daily newspaper Bradshaw read of a publication called the *Wipers Times*, written, published, and printed in the trenches, which gave endless pleasure to the Tommies. Bradshaw had never seen a copy of it. Neither had he seen or heard one of the numerous gramophones that turned dark hours into gay ones. Perhaps 'in the trenches' included Poperinghe? That term, and 'up the line', were elastic phrases. To the infantry, Poperinghe was down the line; to non-combatant units, up.

There were other side-issues devised by astute men careful of their own skins; Bradshaw had a cousin who ran a concert party.

Glorious dawns at this period. Chilly, before the trenches were aired, but a pæan of joy to the watcher. Nothing distinguishable before stand-to, but always two black silhouettes rising above the dark horizon of the German trench. Every morning one or other of the sentries would say:

'Look! Two Jerries over there!'

Safety-catches would be lowered; a few shots fired. Half an hour later one would say:

'Silly bee! Ah towd thee it were them two tree-trunks.'

'Well! Aa could a' swore they moved.'

Bradshaw had often laughed at sentries who affirmed that in the darkness wiring stakes, tree-stumps, and other inanimate objects became live creatures, slinking and crouching. But he fired at those two sentinels early one morning. Even when it grew light he found it hard to believe they were nothing but blasted tree-trunks.

Captain Phillipson came again. Did Bradshaw know how to act if Jerry grew offensive?

It appeared that the only course not threatened with

immediate disaster was to leave the trench by way of the parapet and take up commanding positions in our wire. From there, any invaders could be successfully repulsed. Bradshaw couldn't see eye to eye with these tactics. If Jerry meant to attack (which he considered unlikely), their first move would be to destroy our wire. If they left the trench at all, it would be to occupy the shell-holes behind the parados. From there, rifles could be trained on the breastwork parapet, and the invaders picked off as they reached the trench! Definitely against orders, to leave the trench that way, but what senior officer was likely to be there during an attack?

On a clear day, mottled puffs of smoke could be seen drifting along the rise of Messines Ridge. That Ridge was the objective of the next offensive. The Fifty-fifth had side-shows of its own; it would not take part in the attack, but had the task of making Fritz believe otherwise. Carrying-parties worked nightly from dusk to dawn. Unmistakable, wide gaps were cut in our wire, ostensibly for our storming troops to pass through.

Ypres suffered some colossal strafes; the thrashed town writhed under clouds of brick and stone dust. Several times Jerry used incendiary shells, and, from the front line, Bradshaw saw great splashes of flame licking the ruined Cathedral; dying unfed.

FIVE days in a naked support trench further reconciled them to the imminent offensive. They got shelled out once or twice during the day, and at night assembled fifty yards behind the front line to dig a dummy trench.

Bradshaw gathered from Mr. Hautz that all round the Salient similar dummies were in operation, behind the main trench where No Man's Land was narrow, in front where the neutral strip was wide. Sandbags and spades lay about after digging had been finished, by order. Jerry aeroplanes simply must see these activities.

Fears that he might overlook this bluffing were soon put at rest. The second night of stealthy digging in the château wood ended abruptly. Bradshaw had never before experienced shell-fire amongst trees. Sparse as the wood was, there seemed no outlet for crashes, fumes, or men. The trunks groaned and swayed; several crashed and split. Shrapnel and shell bits spattered against them, flicking and cleaving. Bradshaw looked up as a Very light glinted on the stripped timbers: each trunk looked on the point of falling. Pungent fumes quivered and tickled his nostrils, smoke blotted out the tree bases. A shell shrieked behind, then a man. Bradshaw cried, 'Oh, Christ!' unaware he had blasphemed. Bluff. Bluff? What did they mean, bluff?

Two figures flitted by, crouching as they ran. Bagnall embraced the near-side bank. Groans from behind. Where had everybody got to? These new drafts . . .!

'Someone hit, Dick!' cried the S.B. disengaging himself from the banking.

The man was dead. They couldn't tell who it was. The wood became silent, still smelling. Between the upright trunks the Very lights flickered normally. Bradshaw removed pay-book, personal belongings, and identification disc.

In silence they returned to the support trench. This bluffing business was being overdone.

The dead man proved to be Evans.

Bradshaw said to Bagnall:

'Why, Ernie, he gave me a letter only this morning!'

The next day turned out to be a red letter one for the R.A.F. One plane downed two Jerry sausage balloons; another one, a Taube that penetrated, insolent and low, to our supports. At night the digging-parties put in a good half-hour's work before the expected strafe commenced, then retired.

Next night the shell-fire commenced before the men had strung themselves out; and again they went back. Whilst doing so, Bradshaw saw a great gaping crater in the road, so big that it linked up the trench on either side. Long since he and Baker had carried that container over the same spot. Take some filling in, that would; you could bury a cottage in it.

Everybody groused. The dummy trench was deep enough now, surely. Jerry aircraft could see it all right; what did depth matter?

'C' Company moved into the front line.

Rumours floated about of some wonderful new gas stunt, and, if half the reports of sapping and mining were true, the top of Messines Ridge would be blown completely off! The artillery in Ypres daily grew more active; Jerry's reprisals increased. He seemed to be using a far more destructive explosive than before – shells that burrowed deeply before they burst.

Bradshaw got another letter from Tewson, which he answered sarcastically, reminding the sender of his marksmanship at a rifle-range on Southport sands on a pre-war office picnic. Still at Rouen, unloading and flogging rations that belonged to men at the front; (floors of Belgian cottages were reputed to be 'tiled' with flogged bully beef tins!) whilst raw recruits were being killed after three months' service! One way of getting rid of the riff-raff, possibly.

Lieutenant Hautz came up, hand outstretched. He shook hands warmly, leaving a typewritten sheet in Bradshaw's fingers. Congratulations from General Sir A. Hunter-Weston at being mentioned in dispatches.

The next noon dozens of our smoke-bombs trailed their dark, smelling clouds across No Man's Land, and Fritz shelled again; but we didn't attack. Bradshaw eyed speculatively a gap in his parapet, behind which the brown and yellow billows unfurled themselves. He hated stunts like this; you couldn't see ten yards. Jerry might decide to come over under cover of our own screen!

Walker came up with two or three dozen sandbags.

'Know those two Stokes men down Haymarket? They're gone west. You should see the hole. . .!'

Lieutenant Hautz again:

'If the wind's favourable we're trying gas in the morning, directly on your right.'

'What kind of gas, sir? Something new?'

'Don't know. The engineers have been busy in the supports getting it fixed up. . . . Nobody seems to know what'll happen . . . the troops there are being side-tracked past you, in case of accidents.'

Everybody expected something to happen all night but calmness reigned. At dawn the men on Bradshaw's flank filed leftwards, leaving a gaping hole in the front. An hour afterwards word arrived announcing the postponement of the stunt, the wind being adjudged unfavourable.

Another cool grey morning. At stand-to, Lieutenant Hautz stood on the firestep between Bradshaw and Bagnall, looking into the mistiness of No Man's Land. He raised his arm.

'It'll go this morning all right. Don't be surprised at anything unusual happening. The gas is phosgene, I believe, but it's the method of sending it that's new.'

Bradshaw said:

'I suppose that "Wind Dangerous" sign is still up in the Square in Poperinghe, sir?'

The officer laughed.

'Didn't you know it was a permanent fixture, screwed up?'

The two black silhouettes near Jerry's front line looked more realistic than ever – two defiant foes upright on their parapet. Behind, the waning night still shrouded Ypres, but they knew its exact position. On the left, in front, a wide channel cut through our wire.

Two dull broad explosions came from the supports in their right rear. 'Sounds like a dump going up', Bradshaw was thinking, when, startlingly and amazingly, hundreds of ghostly puffs appeared bush-like in No Man's Land. They expanded, grew, and, like an army of spooks, drifted silently, menacingly, towards the German trenches. Bradshaw watched, speechless.

Coloured S.O.S. signals rose. Before the shells came a crackling fire spat across from the opposing line. The three ducked as bullets zipped into the sandbags. Jerry had the wind up. The gas got into the mechanism of his machine-guns, which spluttered and popped spasmodically in frantic efforts to remedy the stoppages.

'There'll be no sortie while he fires like this, sir. . . I'll tell the sentry to keep his head down.'

'Oh! M'm'm. . . . I'll move along. . . .'

Falkner's head was well below the parapet when Bradshaw stalked round the traverse. A new man, he bobbed up again.

'All right, keep down till he shows signs of slackening off. . . . nothing, this.'

Bradshaw and Walker squatted down on the fire-step, a continuous thud-thud, zip-zip at their backs, or pinging and swishing just above. Bagnall went searching for casualties. A few shells burst rather close.

The firing ended. In the next bay lay Lord, a thick-set, bluff and hearty farmhand, dead from a piece of shell. His first time in the line.

'Why! Look here!' cried Bradshaw.

Across the top margin on the first page of the dead man's pay-book a text had been written:

> 'I will arise, and go to my Father.'
> O. Lord.

His Christian name was Oliver.

Next day, on June the 5th, disaster befell Bradshaw's post.

The sergeant-major replaced Lord with Cowan, and during the day another smoke-bomb bluff was tried. The weather remained perfect, the only serene element in the

Salient. Bradshaw looked at Harrison's watch, hanging on a nail over the refuse bag. Two o'clock.

'Care to try and win some more sandbags, Freddy? . . . there's a lot of patching up to be done to-night.'

Fifteen minutes later Fritz retaliated, and again Bradshaw drew the sentries down to a safer level. If he had analysed his feelings, he would have found his strongest desires to be for the safety of his men and a wish to be popular in their eyes. He squatted on the duckboard, back to heaving traverse, listening to the rush of hurtling shells; the sudden flurry and ear-splitting percussion of the near ones; the abrupt thud of an occasional dud.

Harrison's blank face appeared round the bend, scared and white.

'Can we go to t' Retreat, corp? Bloody awful in t' next bay. . . .'

Bradshaw rose. The worst strafe he'd known in the Salient. He dodged to different bays. What a wreck! Duty mattered least; he had never been strong enough to enforce it. That was a disadvantage little men would always encounter!

The shells fell distressingly accurate. To each man he said:

'Hop it back into the Retreat, you'll be safer there.'

The Retreat was a disused dugout twenty yards behind the main trench. From the parados a rough duckboard track led to it; several creosote and petrol tins lay about. The strongest funkhole about, which wasn't saying much.

The five men tucked themselves in, and Bradshaw felt weak at the knees. How explain the inexplicable; that he, in charge of a sentry post, had withdrawn his men to – to mollycoddle them?

Walker wouldn't be back yet; he'd keep watch himself till then. Jerry never came over on these occasions. He squatted again. The bombardment frothed in fury; every few minutes from out the general tumult a rising shriek detached itself and sickeningly jolted him, showering earth.

Bradshaw had several close shaves. He wished Bagnall or Walker were there. No . . . better out of it.

One good thing; no superior officers would be about in this. A subaltern, maybe, who didn't matter. No man on either flank; only his five in that dugout. How alone he felt. . . . Walker might not be long . . . but he'd stay down the communication trench if he'd any sense.

A shell buried itself stunningly in the solid banking of the traverse. It failed to explode, but the traverse quivered. A piece of casing splintered the duckboard by his knee. He reached out, touched the jagged steel: scorching hot. Big enough to have split his head open! Another shriek and a crash. Evil-smelling earth and rotting sandbags dropped heavily on him. Cracks appeared in all the sandbag joints. Old Fritz was going it!

He had a vision of tensely waiting Germans, shaking with excitement, expecting this deserted trench to unleash itself and pour its contents across No Man's Land in a surging wave. If only they had known!

Above the crumps and crashes rose a clear, unnerving cry. Bradshaw shivered slightly. Only one place that could have come from. He rose, and ran. Little Hunter crashed into him at the trench junction; panting, terrified.

'Oh! Chris' . . . corp . . . . They're all dead!'

The Retreat lay wrecked; demolished by a direct hit. All

splintered wood, tumbled earth, and khaki limbs. Bradshaw saw Cowan creeping backwards from under the rubbish, shoulder torn and messed up with earth; straighten himself, shaking. A low moan. Harrison, arm across his face, legs doubled up underneath; smothered in earth and pinned by a chunk of roofing wood.

Bradshaw pushed the one standing sandbagged wall outwards, releasing him. He lifted a riddled sheet of corrugated iron roofing and drew back in horror.

Hunter . . . Cowan . . . Harrison . . . Walker down Haymarket. . . . God! These – this – must be Falkner and Grayson. . . .

He rose about the shelling; shook that danger off to confront this catastrophe of his own making. He stood, numb, and cold inside. A shrapnel bullet struck his foot.

Jerry realised at last that no attack was intended; the bombardment slunk back, exhausted. Bradshaw moved to his ruined post, sat on the firestep, eyes staring and seeing nothing. Who would discover him first?

Walker appeared.

'Gosh, Dick, you've touched out! It was bad enough in the supports, but . . . what's happened?'

Sergeant-Major Wiles pushed past.

'Hullo! Any hit?'

'Falkner and Grayson killed . . . Harrison and Cowan both badly wounded. . . .'

The S.M. sucked in his lips.

'Hell! Where. . .?'

'At the back there.' What did it matter now?

The S.M.'s eyes shot back again to Bradshaw.

'What the devil. . .!'

'They were off duty . . . that was the only decent dugout.'
He hurried on desperately: 'Hunter got scratched and
shaken. . . . I've only got Walker now.'

'Off duty? . . . Bagnall an' Stansfield'll have to join you. I'll
send 'em up.' He was back in a few seconds with Lieutenant
Marriott. Bradshaw heard:

'Two killed, sir. . . . Very few spare men. . . . Shall have
to give him the stretcher bearers.'

That night Bradshaw wakened up sweating and delirious.
When Bagnall returned from two hours' duty he found his
friend tossing restlessly, yet he knew no words of comfort
would assuage Dick's mind. For months he had been looked
on as 'lucky'. Men had chosen to go on his post; and now
. . . several times during the night Bradshaw said wearily,
'I sent them to that dugout. They'd have been safer in the
trench. I was!'

Three o'clock in the morning, cool and grey: June the
7th. The bluffing all over; any moment the mines would be
blown. Men of both sides who had survived other attacks
would be killed during the next few minutes.

They rested from their labours, believing – pessimistically,
as is the soldier's wont – that the next hour would unfold an
oft-repeated failure. Bradshaw felt resigned to it. Meaning
no disparagement of the troops concerned, but aware
that it was only a local action which, even if attended by
unbelievable success, could not achieve far-reaching effect.

His foot ached where the shrapnel had hit him. Not hard
enough for a Blighty!

The mines went up, rocking the early morning silence;

an angry uproar surged over the Ridge and crept along the left flank. In front of the Lancashires Jerry again hurled his ammunition about lavishly; the line was on tenterhooks. On the next post to Bradshaw a shell overtoppled the already cracking parapet on to three men; entrenching-tools and spades extricated only one of them alive. Bradshaw saw the clawing fingers; gained some idea of the frantic effort they made fighting for air.

Another shell, the most disastrous for months, took several men who constituted the cream of the company. The great-hearted, cheerful Stevens, Sergeant-Major Wiles, several other N.C.O.s, and the truculent sanitary men, Brettle and Bates. All were mercifully, instantly killed, but the spectacle of that bit of trench could not be described.

Our aeroplanes went over in swarms, sweeping the skies. Bradshaw had never seen such numbers droning under the leaden sky. Soon Jerry's black Archies burst among the close formations, and Bradshaw saw several British aeroplanes blown to shreds by direct hits.

Two met their fate in peculiar fashion, caught in the trajectory of fire from our own guns. They fell like leaves from a tree, fluttering, spinning, the two guilty shells no doubt continuing their flight to burst as intended in the German lines.

Drummer Fogg came up to say that the shelling in the supports was more severe than ever he had experienced since the Somme.

Early morning brought the long-awaited relief; the sun had asserted itself before 'C' Company reached the supports. One eye of the enemy, in the shape of a sausage balloon,

commanded an uninterrupted view of the land before Ypres.
An early bird.

Lieutenant Hautz looked anxious as the file of men passed
down the unwalled supports, hoping the slight snakish
movement of khaki would pass unnoticed.

A string of coloured lights glittered behind like daylight
fireworks, and, nervously hurrying, they dreaded the first
crash. Shells were always to be feared more when coming
down relieved than when going up. A month up the line,
and any moment they might be robbed of the respite so
dearly earned!

But Fritz stayed his hand. They passed through the streets
of Ypres, strewn with newly-riven holes. Another chunk had
been blown off the landmark of St. Martin's; delayed time-
fuses had laid many cellars bare.

'Cost Jerry another fortune to do this', thought Bradshaw.
Kicking a town that's already down!

J UNE the 15th. Bollezeele. Here the old originals – scanty
in number but still representing the only devil-may-care
spirit in the company – celebrated in no half-hearted
fashion Festubert's anniversary; two years ago, when
men of the Lancashires were all as big as Sergeant Stevens
and Ginger Whiteside!

They marched steadily beyond Bollezeele under a
strengthening sun, the Front far behind. A glorious morning;
open country of a pleasant kind, green and undulating.
None of them cared much where they were bound for;

rest alone was desired. The increasing warmth silenced the singing. White dust from the baking road covered boots and puttees; beads of perspiration trickled down begrimed faces. Up and down jogged shoulders and feet. Rifles were slung left, then right; trailed and sloped; packs were hitched up every few hundred yards, only to wear down again and again, overweighing them.

Bradshaw grinned to himself; he could march. The miles they had carried their equipment and ammunition . . . hardly ever used them!

Helmets were pushed back, taken off, fastened under epaulets; replaced. Chin-straps were chewed and hung over ears. Thumbs eased the cutting shoulder-straps; tunics and shirts were opened to bottom buttons.

Each time they ascended a crest Bradshaw saw hot vapours rising from the quivering ground, distorting his view of the ridge beyond. Always in front the column moved on, stretching well up the next rise. The whole brigade was out!

Towards mid-day heads swayed, not in unison, right and left, but irregularly, from varying steps. The Derby men had learned to grouse inwardly when old stagers were about, but now they cursed aloud. Why should they be driven through the heat of the day, when there were long, cool evening hours ahead? Not as if they were going up the line to relieve someone!

The old hands plodded on just as wearily, saying:

'This is nowt; you should'a' bin wi' us in 1915 when we did our forced march from . . .'

Every hour brought its ten minutes' halt, when they became part of the baked ground: seeking protection from

the broiling sun. No need for the officers to walk down the
column crying:

'Keep to the right of the road there – don't wander about!'

Three o'clock, the sun at its highest and hottest; not a
breath of air to liven flagging steps. The last drops of warm,
putrid water had been drained from bottles; salty sweat
made their eyes smart.

Boots – boots – boots – boots – jogged up and down again
before drooping eyes. Intermittent grousing, and that forced
march again in May 1915. Over two years ago! Another rise,
but still the column moved on, like a slow-moving snake;
dipping into valleys; topping ridges; twisting and turning.

A few dropped out. Sweat dribbled to Bradshaw's lips: he
had long settled into a mechanical stride. He glanced right.
The first time he'd seen Bagnall looking distressed!

Before another hour had passed the roadside was littered
with the fallen out, as thick as bushes. The colonel rode
down the column urging the men to stick it; then the
brigadier-general, thin-lipped and grim. But the troops,
beyond even respecting Brass Hats, scarcely raised drooping
heads. The colonel lent his horse out to other officers; the
Lewis-gunners, Harwood, Casey and Willacey, took turns at
carrying the equipment and rifles of more exhausted men.
Their own packs were on the limbers.

Only twenty men remained in 'C' Company, and the
other three were quite as bad. Bradshaw stuck out his jaw.
His steps faltered; his head sang, bemused by the smell of
sweat rising from his stifled body. Several more men reeled
from the files with sagging knees; the dwindling remainder
sweltered on, mouths souring and dry as blotting-paper.

They entered the village of Vaudringhem in the late afternoon. Bradshaw counted but nine of 'C'; Bagnall had gone. He fell out here at the village pump, done. This was their village; he didn't feel like roaming around whilst 'C' Company's billet was located. Afar back along the road a trail of the exhausted extended into the summer haze, motionless. An R.A.F. colonel, O.C. the near-by hangars, could be seen expostulating with the brigadier, and soon a row of waggons and lorries moved to pick up the worst cases.

Harwood came up, epaulets flapping, accoutrements discarded; 'C' Company's barn was less than a hundred yards away. Bradshaw felt annoyed at not quite completing the course; he would have been the only one who had finished, carrying full pack and rifle all the way. Captain Phillipson gave the eight survivors forty francs.

Next morning the brigadier had the battalion paraded in the field adjoining the billets, where they heard how unworthy they were.

' . . . till yesterday the 55th Division had always been noted for its staunch discipline . . . it has been called the Cast Iron Division . . . but now I am forced to the distasteful conclusion that that discipline is only skin deep. . . .'

Bradshaw heard the words imperfectly. Men muttered:

'The crusty ——'

'That R.A.F. bloke didn't half strafe him!'

'*He* did it on his bleedin' horse!'

Bradshaw heard that yesterday's dose of discipline caused a considerable number of casualties. The rumour that several ended fatally was, for one's peace of mind, best not believed!

The bright, hot days of June were spent mostly in practising operations for a big offensive. They went 'over the top' with great precision, following drummers who beat a tattoo. The drumming represented our creeping barrage. The waves synchronised perfectly; all objectives fell before their steady advance.

'Bladders-and-sticks battles!'

The company tailor spent his time stitching red roses on sleeves, and spirits revived in the pleasant, danger-free atmosphere and cleaner living. The men sang again. They were being fattened up, and knew it, distantly.

The Frenchwoman who ran the farm was a tartar, screeching horribly and volubly when anyone struck a match in the barn. She started work at an unearthly hour each morning; obtruded freely among the sleeping men in search of implements stored in the barn, seeing unmoved many states of undress.

Bradshaw's ankle turned septic, gaining for him three days' excused duty – the first time he had reported sick. When he thought of the smug disciplinarians on horseback, who prated about duty and showed contempt for men whose jobs they were never called upon to perform, he had little compunction in expressing inward sorrow that the shrapnel hadn't gone right in.

They went down to the butts for musketry practice, and divisional sports were held; men who hadn't seen enough scrapping punched holes into each other with boxing-gloves.

Following a twenty-franc pay, the R.A.F. canteen did a roaring business. Strangely enough, there was no counter-attraction in the form of crown and anchor. As Bradshaw remarked to Bagnall, these same men now swallowing *vin blanc* and malaga would be craving for cigarettes next time up, yet they hadn't sense to lay in sufficient stock before funds ran out.

Bradshaw saved his Trumpeters and Red Hussars and Oros ('orrors) till the company were up in the line, when dishing them out in ones gave him as much pleasure as the recipients.

On July the 2nd they arrived once again in the prized and honoured ruin of Ypres. The Square being under shell fire, they detoured by way of the side-streets. The dark, sorrowful husk seemed little changed; had any other town been so dearly a part of the British Army? The Salient without Ypres would have been hideous and loathsome indeed.

Jerry came over the first day 'C' Company took the line again – a surprise raid a few minutes before stand-to, during the stillness that links day and night. Stansfield at his post suddenly cried:

'Corp! Corp! Thi' comin' ower!'

Bradshaw realised slowly. That kind of thing didn't happen every day. He looked round, climbed up and peered over, then panicked.

They were!

He took one quick glance at twenty or thirty figures advancing in rough, uneven line, extended.

'Ernie! Freddy! Bring the others, quick!'

How could five keep them back? He checked a desire to turn and run. Levelled his rifle and tried to fire without first releasing the safety catch. Hell! Mustn't get flustered. . . . Where the devil were the others? Ah! An S.O.S. going up on the left . . . the eighteen-pounders! Go it! Knock hell out of 'em!

The raid fizzled out, but somewhere on the left Fritz bagged two sentries. Bradshaw realised he and his post had cut unheroic figures. What would have happened if Jerry hadn't collared those two when he did?

They heard more alarming rumours – leave was stopped for the duration. The French had mutinied again. Chinamen would relieve them at the end of that term.

Every day the preparations for the push grew more intense.

The end of June and the beginning of July marked a time of unusual activity. All the good old landmarks disappeared. New roads were laid for tanks; broad ones of thick wooden planks, a forest in each. Shell dumps grew prodigiously in size during a night, and a new aid post appeared in the Potijze ruins. One new road ran clean across Congreve Walk behind the château. Much of the preparation was carried out in daylight: of too great a scale to be kept secret.

Jerry's gunners enjoyed themselves immensely.

New planes were used; triplanes that executed amazing spiral descents amongst hovering Taubes. Bradshaw liked the way they manoeuvred and escaped, but hated the manner in which even these new planes seemed to be playing second fiddle. Sausage balloons grew in number, often to be brought down spectacularly in flames by airmen who planed over silently, using favourably drifting clouds as underneath cover.

The efforts of the observers to escape by parachute thrilled Bradshaw, causing excitement in the company. They didn't always land safely!

The Lancashires marched into the fringe of these speeding-up operations and stayed at the Red Barn, a strong-point on the Poperinghe road behind Ypres. Every day they crossed the fields and the railway laden with spades (and a pick for each fourth man) and dug trenches under the shadow of the hedges. The troops massing for the attack were to occupy these invisible trenches. Every night brought a few shells, more in the nature of warnings than efforts of destruction. 'We-know-what-you're-up-to' shells, Bradshaw termed them.

They moved north to a field near Proven, where a good pay left the camp strangely deserted and with no doubt in their minds that another offensive was sucking them nearer. Walker and Bagnall got talkative and spent the night in a guard tent. Bradshaw went to kip longing to be endowed with impossibly magic powers that would spirit him, invisible, behind the German lines. In imagination he carried on a short but fruitful campaign that struck dismay into the enemy's heart and culminated in a remarkable personal triumph. He bearded the Jerry Supreme Command in their dens; twitted the Kaiser's moustaches; issued orders that would end in Sedans; spiked all their guns. Futile dreams that afforded a momentary flush of self-gratification.

They struck camp at nine o'clock: a gorgeous evening of graded blue skies, golden-yellow brightness where the trees struck across, upright in the low west. They fell in outside the tents, tolerantly enduring the hackneyed movements that would bring them to the road. Crossley lay rolling beneath the flaps of one tent, insensibly drunk, and Bradshaw was detailed to stay behind and bring him along later. The battalion moved off. At midnight Bradshaw succeeded in stopping a G.S. waggon by promising the driver a good tip for a lift to Poperinghe, where the new camp lay on the war side of the town. In Bradshaw's absence at the road the taking-over battalion moved into the tents, immediately pushing the recovering Crossley into the guard tent. Bradshaw returned (the G.S. waggon waiting) to find the drunk being held down by force. He had struck an officer and a sergeant-major. Bradshaw explained rather entreatingly that the battalion was moving up ready for the attack and some of the fellows had overstepped the mark. Immediately the captain handed the rapidly sobering private over, making Bradshaw sign a chit as receipt for him.

The spare A.S.C. man on that lorry won five francs from the fumbling hand and muddled brain of Crossley, and when the driver drew up saying that this was as far as he went, he also demanded his fare. Bradshaw felt resentful, but proffered another five francs. Crossley brushed it back again, handing his own last note over. Not until they were sitting in the darkened streets of Poperinghe under the lighted sign of an officers' club did he realise that the note had been a tenner. Fifteen francs for a ten-minute journey in a Government vehicle, that not for a moment went out of its ordinary course!

Next morning Bradshaw swore that Crossley had marched smartly back to camp without throwing disgrace upon the regiment; obtaining for the delinquent a light sentence and for himself enhanced prestige. Mr. Gore – now back with 'C' – allowed him a pass to visit his brother at the 64th C.C.S., a most interesting walk. No less than four Redcaps challenged his right to so much freedom, one examining the chit with the air of a detective searching for alterations. Bradshaw's brother was in a cushy place, though bomb-dropping planes had paid several nocturnal fear-raising visits. The little infantryman's eyes bulged as he saw buttered slices of bread piled on plates at a clean table, but the others were used to it. Everybody round asked him to have more. More! 'C' Company had not had a crumb more than its two poor slices per man per day for months. He restrained a desire to cram his pockets.

That night Jerry's bombers came across bringing hovering terror. No shells ever struck Bradshaw as being nearly so frightful in their straight-down destructiveness. One bomb stupendously burst near the band tent, leaving little blobs of flesh and blood for everyone to see next morning. Bradshaw couldn't have slept anyway. Stabs of venomous pain shot through his ankle; he decided to go sick in the morning. But when he sleepily awakened with a distant bugle tickling his ear, things were different. How go sick on the eve of the first big attack since the Somme?

The Lancashires had an easy day on July the 28th, but the stabbing in Bradshaw's ankle grew no better. A demon whispered several times during the day: 'Wangle it and miss the attack.' The company, distantly aware of the inescapable trouble ahead, played cards less boisterously; wrote home; and wondered why Poperinghe should be barred to them on this, their last day. Considerably less than half the company had been over the top before.

They left the goodness of rest, the cheery heartbeat of camp-life, behind. The poplars that had beheld so many similar marchings looked on silent and frowning in the gloomy evening. July the 29th. The attack was to commence on the last day of the month. Last year it started on the first.

It cast a peculiar feeling of desolation over Bradshaw
when he discovered they themselves had to occupy the
concentration trenches they had shallowly dug only a
few days previously. That left no doubts anywhere. The
march there occupied little over an hour, and a leaden sky
threatened rain all the time. At the end of it, Bradshaw had
ceased to worry whether he went over or not. His foot,
heavy as lead, ached damnably. Pains shooting up his leg
suggested diseased bones and amputations. He didn't want
to lose any limbs; he was too proud of them.

He took off his boot to ease the pain. Bagnall and Walker
called him a B.F. for not going sick.

THE morning came watery and bright, with a sprinkle of
glistening raindrops on the good grass. Bradshaw had
lain awake under the hedge half the night, wondering
again if he dare decently go sick at this stage. What the
company would think troubled him greatly. But, however he
painfully tugged, his foot refused to go inside its boot. The
ankle, three times its normal thickness, looked alarmingly
blue and blown up. It didn't need Bagnall now to urge him
to report sick. Bradshaw, really scared beyond offensives,
was already hobbling, boot in hand, to the camouflaged
bivouac which he hoped Mr. Hautz occupied alone. But Mr.
Gore and Mr. Lonsdale and two other officers were there
besides, all looking up as the little corporal approached,
wide-eyed and lopsided. The M.O. came, showing traces of
annoyance with Bradshaw for not reporting sick earlier, but
Mr. Gore and Mr. Hautz both backed him up.

'Well, you see, he's been with us since Ginchy, doctor, and didn't want to miss the fun. Did you, Bradshaw?'

And Bradshaw blushed.

Fellows in the company called him a lucky sod, ungrudging in their good-natured envy. He felt mean, and not a little of a leadswinger. Next day found him at an aid post on the main road lower down than Brandhoek: Bagnall and the company awaited darkness to move up to the springing-off point beyond Potijze.

That night Bradshaw lay, rather lonely, on a stretcher; listening to the rain pattering on the canvas above him. Out in the sopping darkness 'C' Company – many 'C' Companies – cursed the rain that came like a bad omen. Bradshaw blessed his good star, yet wanted to be with Bagnall and the others. (What was it that drew absent ones so irresistibly to follow the fortunes of their companies?) Would the creeping barrage be a success?

He wondered whether he would get back to the company again on becoming fit, or be sent to another battalion.

On the 31st, when uncut wire had held up the Highland Division and caused the Lancashires to retreat, Bradshaw was sent lower down to a C.C.S. between Pop and Proven. He felt safe, but extraordinarily out of everything that counted. Four tents stood apart in isolation for cases such as his; within twenty-four hours his legs were a mass of sickening scabs and sores. He felt ashamed, unclean; a most distressful condition for anyone careful and sensitive of his bodily cleanliness. Others with long trench service to their credit were the same; one emphatically declared they were right for Blighty, so they all hoped.

Wheezing gas cases came in, apprehensive even as Bradshaw because they couldn't gauge the seriousness of their complaint. The impetigo cases were cleared out down the line, and Blighty became a possibility. Nay, a certainty. Wouldn't Those Above naturally evacuate everybody possible, to make bed-room for the thousands of wounded arriving daily?

August the 4th. The *fourth.*

Le Tréport British General Hospital. Bradshaw had two days in bed, and he wasn't sure whether to be glad or sorry when the impetigo commenced rapidly to vanish. He fought shy of the others in the ward, not wishing to be asked where he was wounded, still being at that stage where he believed that all who wore hospital blues were wounded Tommies. Languishing at the coast with sores on the leg seemed too much like malingering. He wished many times that the shrapnel bullet had gone right in.

Next morning provided some food for the petulant, critical attitude adopted by most thoughtful young men who believed at times that the war was lasting because much energy was being wasted on irrelevant side-issues. He wanted to write home, but had no pad or pencil. He left the wooden ward, and, approaching the canteen, was pounced upon by a R.A.M.C. sergeant, who ordered him back because he wasn't wearing the regulation red tie! That finished Le Tréport's attraction for Bradshaw. The sooner he moved the better.

Each day he sat on the grassy bank overlooking the sea, where other oddments in blue gazed in the direction they thought England lay. A Frenchman took many groups of photographs, in which captured Jerry helmets and skull caps figured prominently. Laughter over the finished prints and a concert in the Y.M.C.A. provided the amusement for a mixed assembly. Blighty lay as far off and inaccessible as ever, and Bradshaw, whose leisurely leaving of the battalion had enabled him to bring down all his belongings, ran through the close-written, spasmodic diary he had been keeping, with surprise and a few minor shocks.

Room for some censoring there!

Hundreds of 'demics' drifted about from hospital to con. camp and back – men passed for service in some momentary panic; passengers. No, worse even than that; grit in the bearings.

The air of stability about everything aggravated Bradshaw. Huge camps, durable buildings, a whole monstrous system of military magnitude that went far to confirming the war's endlessness.

On August the 15th, Bradshaw handed in his burlesque blues and resumed khaki at the con. camp. He slept peacefully between meals and an odd light parade. A big Scotsman in full dress, playing his bagpipes, paraded up and down the marquee lines whilst the others fed – to put them off a little and save rations, it was said. A fine figure of a man, whose impressive wild music brought a breath of heather-covered hills and mountain streams.

Bradshaw found the base a hotbed of leadswinging. Every other man seemed to be doing his level best to stick there as long as possible, practising any threadbare subterfuge. At the Board, a file of long-suffering infantrymen, timid and brazen alike, palpably enlarged on their wounds and ailments. The two doctors were obviously sick of their transparencies.

Men whose shirking had been given the benefit of the doubt openly gloated. One with a forearm wound admitted that if he gave his hand a good whack on the morning of the Board it took on a most disagreeable appearance by the time his turn came for examination. Another with a running wound in the thigh bemoaned the fact that, despite judicious mishandling, he couldn't get it to discharge again. Others hinted at soap pills, even herbalistic preparations, for making their hearts play tricks.

There were arguments over the meaning of P.U.O. – Pains of Unknown Origin wasn't it at all. Some of the men with limps, or coughs, or flabby wrists and gloved hands, went about carefully simulating their troubles on all occasions, hinting darkly that the symbols meant Permanently Under Observation.

Here two great boils appeared on Bradshaw's neck and chin, and here he got his answer to the question, 'Shall I swing it here as long as I can?' Those who stuck it in the line month in, month out, yearned often for a glimpse of the base. Wouldn't they just play the old soldier, while some other bee did a bit for a change! But the best of them would have ached to be back in a fortnight, so overdone had leadswinging become. There was nothing at Étaples in 1917 like the companionship of the front line. At the next Board, Bradshaw told the M.O. that he felt quite all right, knowing it was ten to one on him gaining further respite, but he had decided definitely on no leadswinging. Another week's rest, then away from this back to Bagnall and the others.

But next morning he met in the maze of men – in his own lines, too – one of his best chums from home, one G.P. of the Manchesters, who hoped they could go up the line together. Some hope! They played chess whilst enduring the confinement resultant upon the 'riots', and were two of the few men who managed to break camp on several occasions, using each other's spare cap-badges. They never truly learnt the ins and outs of the rioting cause, but were both quite ready to support it if it meant an end of the war. It came as a diversion, and gained in popularity because it aimed at the much resented Redcaps. Feeling ran high at first. Men really enjoyed this war against the military police, being angry, amused, expectant, and resentful by turns. The rumours that circulated! The Redcap that shot the Jock had been kicked to death by incensed Highlanders: three more had been rooted out and mauled, the others making for Boulogne as fast as they could. Now the Jocks had waylaid an indignant provost-marshal; stripped, tarred, and feathered him! Never had more enthusiasm been put into an offensive. Let the spark spread throughout the army and accelerate peace terms! No more 'Get fell in!' 'Correct them slopes!' 'One pace step forward!' 'Cap off!' and being pulled up for walking between piles of rifles. An end to vexing childishnesses!

Everybody swelled into the little town, borne along in the resentful rush; a peaceful riot indeed. Soon the cookhouse bugle lured them back to camp and confinement – little insignificances, ready to be cowed again by the first military policeman they saw.

Up the line again, with an odd squad of reclaimed base-wallahs and new recruits. An M.O. inspected them casually while they stood naked and almost unlovely, remarking as he faced Bradshaw, 'Ah! One can tell you've been in action before.' He was looking at the brownish blemishes on Bradshaw's legs, the remains of impetigo which their owner had learned to detest. Most humiliatingly, all except the new hands were handed over to two orderlies, who shaved all the hair off their bodies.

O N September the 14th, Bradshaw rejoined the battalion, just moving up again after a long rest outside Pop in bivvies and pleasant weather. Old faces amongst the changes smiled agreeably in welcome; but Bradshaw looked in vain for the one he sought. Bagnall had been badly wounded on the 31st. Walker left a leg near the Frezenberg line and died on the way to the dressing-station. Aspinall and Blakeley had also gone west; but Bradshaw didn't miss them all at once. His second stripe had been waiting for him since the last affair, and a third – lance-sergeant – was to come his way after the next. The genial Mr. Hautz – himself sporting a second pip – imparted this information, and offered, first, to take Bradshaw down to the special model of the ground to be covered in the coming attack ('All tripe, Bradshaw, that will be forgotten on the actual day'), and, second, to do what he could to get Bradshaw leave. The ex-Manchesters had all gone, in alphabetical order, save Bragg, Collier, and Birch. Bragg, one day sooner owing to Bradshaw's absence, went that evening with more alacrity than dignity, for the Jerry bombers came over and men with over a year's trench service couldn't afford to take any chances. That was September the 15th, with the attack on the 20th, and Bradshaw's turn already a day overdue. Would his lapse at the base go against him?

Tilson, Mr. Hautz's servant, told Bradshaw of events on July the 31st, and the new corporal quickly realised he had been lucky, away from it. The 51st Division, on the Lancashires' flank, had been held up by uncut wire, but few obstacles had troubled the Cast Iron lads. Busy in the act of consolidating a captured German position, 'C' Company had been almost happy till Lieutenant Lonsdale spotted Jerries closing in on them in the right rear. His immediate order to 'drop everything but rifle and gas-mask, and run', brought a ready response, and 'C' Company chased back over the ground they had so recently covered, peppered at by the watchful pill-boxed eyes behind.

The advance up the slowly rising ridge to Passchendaele, once started, had to go on; but troops were not going over every day, as on the Somme. Periodical thrusts of greater compass had come to pass, and the creeping barrage. No longer could Jerry lie low in his dugouts, or in this case his pill-boxes, and know that the lifting barrage was an almost infallible signal of our attack. You followed the creeping shells now, and pounced on him still dazed and bewildered. The Somme had not been without its lessons.

Rawson came back from leave with two grouses. He had seen Private Simmonds on leave walking down Fishergate, Preston, flaunting three stripes; and heard his local parson, the previous Sunday, praying for the wounded – *especially those from this parish*.

Collier, also like a cat on hot bricks when Jerry's huge
bombing-planes came over next morning, went on leave
on the eve of the move up; Bradshaw had to wait. The
C.O. explained to Mr. Hautz – who was acting-captain of 'C'
since Mr. Gore's wound – that all N.C.O.s would be needed;
Bradshaw could go immediately the objective had been
achieved. Several men in the company saw fit to remind
him that others had been killed when they should have
been on leave.

The trek up to the concentration trench by Wieltje was
rather silent. Bradshaw saw no familiar surroundings; only
new contours and landmarks, hostilely different. The Salient
was on the rack again. No cigarettes. No singing.

Bradshaw heard, behind, the bubbling of occasional
laughter. Somebody's sally and an exchange of badinage.
Probably Slater. Bradshaw had a small platoon of his own
now. What were they thinking of him – a little child shall
lead them? He had two or three good section leaders,
including the intrepid Baker, and, fortunately, a number
of entirely new lads. They wouldn't need telling. He hated
giving orders. It was at moments like this – the going into
action, the passing of a returning, weary-eyed unit (never
too far gone to scrape up grins of friendliness and good luck
– and pity); the vision of the Cathedral and Cloth Hall – that
Bradshaw wished his pen were better able to describe the
strange emotions he felt. But its power was inadequate. Were
there any great writers now in the army to tell what agonies
of body and mind front-liners suffered? Not journalists or
war correspondents, but pukka authors, near enough to the
heart of things to write with feeling and authority? And if

there were, would they put down their immediate, scalding impressions, or go back to twist and turn their phrases, emblazoning them with the doses of honour and glory that most infantrymen were too plebeian to feel?

Why couldn't it all end? The crisis that put courage into men earlier on was making them cowards now, so long was it lasting. What purpose would it serve, even if they were successful in moving the lines a few hundred yards forward, except to afford encouragement for repeating the process? What such gain was worth a millionth part of the innocent lives wasted; the lives of the boys in his charge, some of whom even now seemed to divine their fate?

Bradshaw had known the Salient for a year, but the view from the concentration trench was entirely foreign. Potijze and Wieltje (shades of working-parties!) couldn't be recognised anywhere. The clutch of the barrage had gripped everything in front. A small battered cottage, roof and bedroom walls blown away, reared shakily behind the trench near the road – civilisation's surviving shred. Part of the crumbling lower wall served as a canvasless latrine, and by climbing on the heap of mortary rubble that was once the bedroom wall you could see the ominous rise that led to Passchendaele, broken here and there by sudden puffs of smoky white. Verlorenhoek seemed to have disappeared altogether.

The trench crossed the road at rough right angles, and no liberties were taken on the sky-line, even though Jerry was two kilometres away.

The day turned bright and sunny, its wealth lost on the

flat, uncontrasting ground ahead. Micky Donovan brought
his cards round, and Sergeant Murphy ('Spud', of course –
and he didn't mind it from privates), Jimmy Baker, and Slater
played pontoon in a way that suggested to Bradshaw the
carefreeness of Witley Camp. Their time come? Not likely.
Jerry was going to have another packet at them – three
of them already carried his shell-marks – but they weren't
downhearted. Yes, Bradshaw had some good companions on
that stunt; always on top of pessimism and the daily grind.

Sshwee-wee-CRASH! Sshwee-wee-wee-CRASH! Go it, Fritz!
You don't know what's coming to you to-morrow.

Bradshaw left the players for the latrine peep-hole. Shell-
bursts effervesced in front, hiding the ridge; above them, pale
and distant, a lone Jerry sausage. As flat as a fluke it looked
in front. A plane came over, breaking up the card-party; then
two or three more shells. A shadow flitted across the sunlit
ground between trench and latrine, like the sun winking;
something struck the flimsy roof of the cottage, raining dust
inside and falling debris out. Bradshaw hurried back.

To the company's astonishment, and Spud Murphy's
great concern, little Donovan had completely disappeared,
and an afternoon's restricted search brought no clue. He
had won the Military Medal on July the 31st (and his right
to membership on the B Team next attack; but Casey had
failed to return from leave at the proper time, so Donovan
had to take his place with the company). After tea, with the
sun obscured and rain in the air, Bradshaw's eyes lit on the
cottage roof twenty-five yards away, and saw a bundle of
khaki that he knew must be the missing boy. He cried:

'Spud! Here . . . look!'

They jumped over the low parados together, followed by Mr. Hautz, and climbed on to the crumbling roof. Donovan had been blown bodily out of the trench, to crash against the last piece of bedroom wall above the latrine. The crushed, limp body still bore its medal ribbon, but the bloodless face they saw wasn't Donovan's. They lowered it gently down to Mr. Hautz and Baker. (Casey! Casey!) Nobody had known such a thing to happen before. Men had been undressed by a shell, but to lift anybody like that instead of blowing them to bits . . . !

In the fading light half a dozen of 'C' attended a short service given by Mr. Hautz. Donovan was quietly buried, and within the hour Casey rejoined the company, delayed by a late train.

A bombardment broke out on the right, and the front, like a huge animal awakened by prods and pokes, snarled and bit and settled wearily down again. But what had happened during that fiery fury? How many more Donovans had gone west?

Bradshaw, who had striven hard all day to keep pitch with Murphy and Baker, became depressed. Unlucky stars seemed to be in the ascendancy, and he was for leave the next day. (Have you ever paused on the eve of an attack and looked at the men around you, wondering which of them, and how many, would be left the next day?)

On the move again, with depression writ large over everything. Only a Spud Murphy or a Slater could have infused a little cheerfulness into the murky, wet misery ahead. For it rained immediately they moved off – an insistent rain that quickly put a slippery surface on everything. The earlier sunshine became impossible: it had rained for years. Rimmer, pale-faced and weary, dropped on the planked road. They dragged him across a path of thin branches to the ditch, one of the three old originals. He looked past it as far back as the dripping Mametz cornfield last year, when between chattering teeth he had offered Bradshaw two francs for his rum ration. Out before Festubert – May 1915? You did your bit long ago!

Bradshaw cracked an old chestnut for the benefit of the new men, and Slater commenced to tell them it was a 'luvly' war in his own elegantly phrased, humorous way. The company grinned, uplifted. Bradshaw looked to the morrow. Forget everything in the meantime; you'll be on the way to Blighty to-morrow! He had sent a short note earlier that day, 'Will be home in a few days.' Many men said 'gone home' for 'gone west', but he refused to let that worry him. He could have done with a new tunic and a decent pair of numerals really, for leave.

Would they let him put three stripes up?

The roughly mended road, still laid crosswise with planks and tree-branches, entered a sea of thick mud, broken erratically by the lighter patches of full shell-holes reflecting the darkening sky. The guards of honour dwindled to whittled stumps, their trunks prostrate in the ditches. The road disappeared into an ocean of mud, men cursing as they slipped and slid. The well-filled holes broke into each other; weighted bodies balanced and tight-roped precariously over the crater lips. More than one man slipped, sank, and drowned in those holes, too hampered by wounds or equipment to fight free from the tentacles of mud that gripped them. Many shells had bitten below the three-foot mark, water automatically draining in the holes. The rain rapidly deepened it, and finding a path between was perilous and heart-breaking.

Three stunted stumps on the left, in line and a few yards apart, proved that a road once existed, but these were Nature's last tattered signs. For sheer, overwhelming unwholesomeness, Bradshaw hadn't seen the equal of this dreary waste. There wouldn't be the same savage intensity, the brutal snarling, the tremendous doggedness of the Somme battle. Those would never be surpassed in any attack – how could they be a second time? But conditions were better twelve months ago. Hope had lived then; anything might happen. A year had passed.

The guns were quiet. Did Jerry know they meant to attack next morning? No Very lights soared. The Lancashires halted and waited. Officers whispered. The men filed to the right, where a string of shell-holes marked by a dirty, invisible tape indicated the front line. No trench. No dugouts. No shelter. But now the rain, having connected every hole to its neighbour with a slimy top covering, ceased. Bradshaw never knew how far the front extended, or what battalions manned the flanks. He was thinking of the morrow. Pile it on now, thick and heavy! Lie in the mud, drenched, all night; to–morrow will bring its beautiful contrast! Up, over, and home!

Mr. Hautz appeared from nowhere, peering in the darkness.

'Ah! Corporal Bradshaw! This is our front. Get your men

down to it. Sergeant Murphy and Sergeant Jackson will
remain on your flanks. I'll see you later. . . .'

He passed on, whispering.

'C' Company 'made itself comfortable till morning',
uncertain of everything save its immediate discomfort.
Bradshaw never quite understood how he, unassertive,
undersized, and distinctly unofficious, should be in charge
of a small body of British soldiers. His platoon contained
several older men – two at least old enough to be his father,
and a number of boys, younger even than he. He valued
their lives far more than the ground they were expected to
cover, but realised that he could make no provision at all for
their well-being or safety. He knew their objective couldn't
be attained without first confronting the ravenous machine-
guns, but he was realising calculatingly rather than being
pessimistic. Any fool can see that men attacking uphill are
under a big handicap. When they are attacking a cunning
foe partially sheltered by pill-boxes – a foe who has already
dealt with a similar attack – the disadvantages become
mountainous. Indomitable spirits might surmount even
these odds, but the ground over which they had to move
was almost impassable in its present state. Were the enemy
rendered mysteriously *hors de combat*, attackers could but
crawl muddily, snail-like, till decent roads had been made.

It served no purpose to blink facts. There was a chance
that the battalion would be annihilated before noon – and
not only their own battalion, or division. None talked of
victory; or to be truthful, of defeat; and therein lay the
beauty of that campaign, the beauty and tragedy of it all –
the wonderful way men went forward in that fashion, time

after time, in order not to let down their comrades, their
self-respect, or those who had already died!

They had half a dozen hours to wait, making themselves
comfortable. That meant selecting a high – and therefore
more dangerous, but that didn't matter – spot between the
shell-holes, and squelching down on to it; trusting to luck
not to fall asleep and roll into the water. Mr. Hautz came
back, stepping carefully amongst the vague, lying shadows.
(Where does even that dim light come from in the middle of
dark, rainy, cloudy nights?)

'This is a —— business, Bradshaw!'

Bradshaw agreed. What difference would it have made
to the attack, his being on leave? An understanding sort,
Mr. Hautz. He stayed whispering for a while, for they had
secrets in common. They had been mentioned in dispatches
together; and Bradshaw was the only man in the company
living who had heard the major of the Eighth Corps School
snort: 'You have no conception of giving a command, Mr.
Hautz!' The officers felt things worse there. They had no
more comfort than the Other Ranks.

The only near sound of war came from the banging wet
burst of a shell that dropped behind every minute. The outline
of the ridge appeared faintly against the sky. All being well,
a few more hours would find Bradshaw homeward bound
on ten days of the very best! That gun was getting nearer the
mark. Wouldn't it be wonderful if the shells could pick and
choose, and only hit the poorer specimens, leaving the best!
But which lot would he belong to?

Bradshaw marvelled at the idea of them lying there in
the imperceptibly lightening greyness, barely distinguishable

from the ground; toneless as this chronicle . . . like cattle
dumped in a dark, lonely, messy field. Between the bursts
of the one gun there was less disturbance than you'd find in
our own Cheshire countryside. (If you are awake, and your
mind has been dwelling on a continuously sustained battle –
accompanied by all the turmoil and distress and fearfulness
– it would give you a little peace to see us quietly, if not
comfortably, resting.) Not very far away – in the next untidy
field, he supposed – the Germans were suffering similar
discomforts, apprehensive as themselves of the dawn, in a
constant state of suspense and preparedness. Behind, lost
in the darkness, were our supports – the second and third
'waves' – and, still farther back, thousands of guns that would
soon be hysterically barking and booming and baying.

The thought of the horribleness that awaited what should
be carefree youth hurt anybody thoughtful. Engulfment for
ever, not for a few years! And now people at home were
making the revolting job worse by doubting its rightness
and properness and the 'common sense' of it.

All this time an agony hung over the heads of parents at
home – a sustained gnawing that unhappily continued when
their sons were really quite safe; and happily, thanks to the
censor, no more acute at times like this, when an attack was
due. The anxiety that would prevail in thousands of homes
if the hour of the forthcoming attack were known!

Hell opened up behind them, fiercely breaking loose
in a mighty, rushing outburst. Bradshaw found himself
standing, and looking the wrong way down to a white-
hot, palpitating Ypres. In its wildest temper, the Somme
never approached this roaring turmoil. Then he turned, and

stepped forward in the gloom with the others towards the snarling and spluttering ahead. No words of Bradshaw's could describe the barrage fire; every gun and gunner on the front had gone mad. The sky in rear blazed with countless eruptions, flickering and scintillating in the clouds over the town; orange, mauve, and steely. It cast a dull glow on the Lancashires' loaded backs and on the cheeks of those who looked, awed, over their shoulders.

There was a little confusion and sorting out. Their direction was clear – the guns saw to that – and after a few yards the mud disappeared. They walked forward mostly upright, sections elongating and bunching. Flares in front; haze; smoke; spitting, rippling bursts. Two or three darted instinctively forward as a rending burst appeared magically just behind them. Bradshaw walked doggedly on. The sooner they reached their objective the quicker he'd be away. What a frightful racket! Patches of grass appeared, faintly visible, and a man clawing the earth. What was in front: a bloody victory or a bloody defeat? Nobody looked round now. The guns drove their steel through the air unceasingly, a fury unparalleled.

Nobody did anything but plod on. Jerry's answer came in disconcerting upheavals that spurted viciously on either hand. Their approach was unheard in the great whining angriness of our own shells. Behind, above, and in front it smothered Jerry's retaliation.

They reached the new-turned earth, smelling and smoking: the barrage crept on comfortingly. It was always a solace to feel something, however unsubstantial, between you and the enemy. (You know the confidence you gained from a mere oil-sheet rigged up to keep out the rain!) But what an extravagance of shells! Bradshaw had yet to see, that morning, the first German dead. A few Lancashires fell, but the agitated convulsions that marked Jerry's shells seemed generally to drop into spaces where nobody walked.

Thompson threaded his way back, actually jubilant, tunic sleeve slit from the shoulder, dangling and flapping as he walked. Already, by his face, he is out of it, in blessed dock. Then came the first Jerry; dirty, unshaven, demented. His arms raised upwards, he walked mechanically out of the hell that had somehow, miraculously, left him unwounded. Then Bradshaw heard a silky swishing at his head that went before he could wonder whether to duck. He knew he had missed death by inches; but there couldn't be much safe space anywhere there!

It grew much lighter. Two or three men falling in a heap for no apparent reason brought a temporary check. The pace slowed, but not the shells. Bradshaw passed two men in a hole, then two in silent, gesticulating argument. Somebody called out, astonishingly clearly:

'The —— Lancasters is holding us up!'

Surely enough, Bradshaw saw men, apparently unwounded, fidgeting in holes like trapped rats. Lancasters! How had they got there? Just ahead appeared the light blotch of a pill-box. The straggling formation faltered: soon 'C' Company had bunched in an uneven line. Mr. Hautz came up with Cavalry Joe; a corporal rushed to them shouting: 'Lancasters – in shell holes, sir ——' The officer stepped amongst the crouching men, revolver poking. The line resumed its forward motion.

For hours, it seemed, a procession of stumbling figures passed Bradshaw unheedingly as he gazed into the sky. The ground revolved round him. Everything seemed detached; distant. The company had left him lying there! The back of his head felt blown away, aching dully. He knew he wasn't dying, because there were no half-measures about head wounds. He'd his leave to go on, too.

He'd been wounded! He remembered now. Something had hit him on the head, yet lifted him off his feet into the air and laid him, jarringly, on his back – a flattened bundle. He remembered Mr. Hautz and Cavalry Joe looking round as he fell, but carrying on. Then it felt as if his head were being rolled about the battlefield, and he went to sleep. . . .

He cautiously touched the back of his head. His hair was matted, fingers came away sticky. He raised himself; a trickle of blood changed its course down his neck. Why, the guns were still at it! He stood up gingerly, then fell again, wondering. His tin hat jerked forward and rolled off, revealing an ugly gash about three inches wide. The broken edges, jagged and uneven, showed the thickness of the metal.

Field dressing, of course! Then leave. . . .

He crawled to the nearest hole, clutching the tin hat by its chin-strap, and rolled in almost on top of Whelan, with his Lewis gun.

'Have you stopped one, too?' asked Bradshaw.

Whelan felt round his hip, said he thought so. Bradshaw pulled out his field dressing and broke the iodine phial. Amateurishly he coiled a bandage round his head and adjusted the gashed helmet, now a few sizes too small. It had saved his life. That, and his shortness. If he'd been three inches taller the shell piece would have passed below his steel helmet's rim into an unprotected neck.

For months he had hoped to be wounded; not too badly. Primarily to gain the respite, however brief, of civilised living; and secondly because there was something tangible about a scar gained in battle. A branding of the skin is much easier to bear than scarless mental branding. But now his wound would rob him of leave! And he'd been so looking forward to being at home to-morrow.

Bradshaw left Whelan to his own devices. The Lewis gunner wasn't the only man that morning, hit by a clod of earth, who dropped out to investigate. There seemed little to choose between volunteers and Derby men. Each, after doing his painful bit to the last gasp, was off like a shot the moment he was hit. The days had gone when men disregarded their wounds and carried on.

He felt steadier. The wounded lay in shell-holes held up by Jerry's box barrage, fearful lest after all they wouldn't get back to the safety now within reach. For Jerry plastered the old lines and supports with an appalling shower of missiles: a belt of liveliness too dangerous to cross. Bradshaw had one interest only: to get to the nearest aid post. Dozens like him cowered at the fringe of the hostile barrage, Blighty passports on the hands and feet, legs, arms, and bodies; awaiting the slightest cessation to scurry through. Some of them had been hit several times whilst waiting there; several killed. Must he, sheep-like, join them or make an effort to get through? Stay here, and risk being hit, or make a bold dash for absolute safety?

Another Fritz came through, arms fixed upwards, mechanical, dead-eyed. A man cried 'Bastard', and levelled his rifle at the Jerry. Bradshaw snatched the barrel aside and rose to his feet.

He set off towards the splashing earth, heart in mouth, gasping and choking, making a drunken bee-line for a disabled tank. Another lad followed, hanging on Bradshaw's heels, but soon the corporal was compelled to drop back and assist him. Crocked in the left leg, another piece of shell had entered his forearm whilst waiting for the firing to lift. They carried on more slowly, arms round each other's shoulders . . . entered the barrage, heads down to ward off showers of damp earth.

CRRRUMP! CRRRUMP!

Elliott, Bradshaw's companion, cried 'Oh!' as a third splinter hit his hand, then they carried on luckily between the shell-bursts. A fourth wound came, on the shoulder, and simultaneously Bradshaw felt a tug at his waterbottle. The bottom half hung limp, cut away as if guillotined. Elliott gasped, trembling and frightened, complaining in a plaintive, childish voice that two were enough. He licked away the blood from his hand. They reached the tank, breathless and choking; sheltered a moment under one of its huge, tilted diamond sides. The worst was over; shells dropped behind. A far-pitched one burst on the other side; the tank heaved over them, and settled. They pushed on, reaching the muddy road. Through!

The hubbub before and behind went on unabated. Bradshaw took one look back at the misty rise and bursting smoke-clouds, then set his face steadfastly towards Ypres.

The ground was unrecognisable; filthily churned. A few dead men lay around, pale but not inhuman; a horse here; a splintered limber there. One man, half buried in the road-banking, looked so natural that both moved forward instinctively to help him. The part they thought buried was blown away. An officer came up the road – the first human being they had seen on the safe side of the barrage, and the only one in sight: an artillery officer who might have been greeting friends at home on a Sunday morning stroll.

'Hello, boys! How have they gone on at the Schuler galleries?'

Neither of them knew. Both were tempted to say, 'The lads are going on fine, sir!' Bradshaw looked apologetic, and said he was afraid he didn't know. Some strong point, it appeared.

The officer passed on.

Bradshaw vaguely imagined that behind the attackers would be a force actively backing them up. Not only guns, but parties of men feverishly energetic. There wasn't a sign of anybody. The guns were nearer, and not so angry now, but before them only a stretch of unoccupied, uninviting land; a gap that got Bradshaw in the stomach. It appeared as if every effort to back up the attackers was not being made. By then the different waves were lapping each other, perhaps overlapping, on the beach of pill-boxes. How were they going on? Everything about was unbelievably clayed up and dirty, as if spurned; left dead. A closer examination revealed that an army had recently passed that way. Several times Bradshaw's helmet fell off its swollen perch, disturbing the unworkmanlike bandage. His colleague rearranged it, and during one stoppage spotted in the mud a neat silver wristlet watch. A peculiar yet perhaps natural place to find such a souvenir. 'I was slow then', thought Bradshaw.

The guns still hammered away as the wounded pair reached the first aid post, though less fantastically than that uproarious, spectacular outburst at zero. Thousands of shells were falling expensively, extravagantly, and uselessly on the unoccupied ground between the pill-boxes. Down a few steps, to be greeted by a kindly-faced padre, who, smiling, said: 'Well done, boys! Why, doc, this one's a corporal!'

'Yes', thought Bradshaw; 'a sergeant, really.' Very few wounded had arrived; others, apparently, had been more decorous in leaving the attack. Looking round the dim dugout, he saw two Germans, one particularly ill looking. The pulverising barrage had missed them.

Inoculation. Dressings. The padre again. A bespectacled, quiet-voiced orderly directed them to a grey marquee. Delighted amazement! A trestle counter of several tables groaned, and certainly wilted, under a most appetising array of sweets and other eatables. Chocolate bars and sandwiches were piled in perilously high erections. There were mounds of cakes and buns; a profusion of square, round, and oblong packets of biscuits; and, most acceptable of all at first, big urns of steaming hot tea.

Bradshaw and his companion started an offensive immediately, hastily wolfing. It must have appeared a greedy orgy to the Salvation Army attendants. They paused for breath, then noticed the two Jerries sitting aside on a form. They lolled dejectedly with the demeanour of criminals brought to justice, dreading a sudden revenge; expecting to be bullied and kicked about. Bradshaw got tea for them; and, after an enquiring look at the S.A. helpers, invited them to tuck in at the sandwiches. A whole bulwark of hatred fell from their already opening eyes. Tears trickled down the cheeks of the younger, more badly wounded one, yet he showed exceptional control in mastering his emotion before drinking the much-desired tea.

They returned to where a South African worked trucks on a single uncamouflaged rail track, having gained a better appreciation of these voluntary S.A. workers – obviously not A1, yet working within shell range. They clambered inside a good, low-sided, roofless truck, followed by a fair, upstanding German boy wearing an Iron Cross. Other men came in ones and twos, one a lance-corporal from 'A' Company, loud-voiced and aggressive. He climbed up, noticing immediately the Iron Cross, and peremptorily demanded it. The German clicked his heels to attention, but looked defiant. To Bradshaw's disgust, the lance-corporal quickly proved himself a blustering bully, threatening to throw the Jerry out of the truck if he didn't part with the decoration. But Fritz stood up to Tommy. For a few apprehensive moments Bradshaw feared trouble, then a private said contemptuously:

'Leave him be, fathead. Happen tha'll find thi'sen like him afore this lots o'er wi'!'

And Bradshaw wondered why he hadn't said it. How had the German won his medal? Up with the rations? Probably by killing one, or more, of our chaps. Or, better thought, perhaps by saving one of his own companions. A man, anyway!

OWN towards the Canal Bank, with its row of elephant dugouts (so recently their peaceful abode!) spreadeagled along the strip of duckboard walk. Over the canal on a newly constructed bridge, alongside which, almost submerged in the dirty yellow water, lay an R.O.D. engine, blown completely off its line. Twelve months before, ignorant of the meaning of those great white letters, they had facetiously applied to them the slogan Roll On Demobilisation. Round the outskirts of the great ruin, forgetful of the men attacking until a near-by battery of heavies thundered. Full realisation of their great good luck had not yet come. Bradshaw still felt as if he had been twisted out of his leave, but who knew how long a head wound would keep him away from it? A good bed to-night – sleep! A wonderful lifting out from weariness and precariousness to cheerfulness and security. Lovely thoughts to dwell on, if you were selfish enough not to think of those unfortunate, uncomfortable others still in their mire and misery.

The train took them to a C.C.S. alongside the Poperinghe road. Thousands of walking wounded had trampled the grass to a black mire, except inside the marquee pegs. More queues and particulars and inoculations, then a long hanging about for the train that would take them out of the war. Little groups smoked and talked. Their manner wasn't greatly different from, say, 'B' Camp, or even the front line at a quiet period; but they had an air of expectancy. Bamber, a joiner by trade, was sure his arm would have to be amputated, but the result was too far off to worry him. Two others with him also had arm wounds; a fourth, one in the head. The latter told the others excitedly how the bullet entered the crown of his tin hat, then whizzed round and round his head, burning off his hair and badly scarring him. A voice behind Bradshaw called him by name; he turned, to see Mr. Hautz sitting on a form with two Other Ranks, right tunic sleeve torn away and a bandaged biceps. They had a trifling conversation, cut short by Bradshaw's anxiety not to be left behind. The train had clanked in.

In the train at last; a definite stage towards the goal – Blighty. Unimportant personages decked out in splashes of white bandage, on whom the God of Battles had smiled. Head wounds and feet wounds, arm wounds and leg wounds, back wounds and front wounds. None of them too serious.

All bawled and sang hilariously, out of tune, pushing and jostling.

'Mind my arm!'

'What about my head?'

'Move up a bit!'

'Who's any gaspers?'

Blighty was the place for them! They all told their experiences of the morning, talking and exaggerating at once. The boy opposite Bradshaw drew his attention to a hole in the loose khaki below his left knee. There was a corresponding hole at the back which, ripped to join the other, disclosed the nasty red sear of a bullet. The train plodded on through more camps, past the stationary troops who always considered themselves 'up the line'. They would be there while the war lasted, unlucky men in many respects with little hope of an escape through wounds!

On and on down the lines of communication, deeper

and deeper into pleasantness and peacefulness, the train not travelling nearly so fast as they would have liked. They sang 'Blighty', 'There's a long, long, Trail', 'Pack up your Troubles', 'Sergeant Brown', 'Tipperary', 'Somebody's Thinking of Me', and many more till they were hoarse. There followed a show of souvenirs, and Bradshaw disappointedly realised that all his were reposing in a valise, heavily initialled with indelible lead but irrecoverable – Blue-grey tabs from German tunics, cartridge clips, bullets (assorted), and other odds and ends ferreted out at Delville and Longueval, Mametz and Montauban – carried about for over a year. Oh! and, worst of all, his diary and the tin hat that had saved his life that morning, removed at the aid post by an orderly, and left!

No. 4 General Hospital, Camier. Two questions seemed very important at the moment. Would he get to Blighty? Would the hair grow again on his head where they had removed it to dress his wound? At times he only half believed in the beautiful cool comfort of the hospital. The sight of English nurses, after the sluts in those Poperinghe shops, was wonderfully refreshing. In the next bed lay a Scotty named Eadie, from the Highland Division, two years older than Bradshaw and extremely bitter. He wouldn't go to the front again, not he!

'This —— war is no *bon* for you and me. I've been wounded seven times, and sworn each time never to go again.'

'Seven times! You've been unlucky. . . !'

'Unlucky? Don't you believe it. I've had seven doses of

dock and two trips to Blighty and it won't be my fault if
I don't get there this time. All the time I was there some
poor bees were still sticking it in the line. And of all the
lousy jobs in this bloodstained war is anybody so mucked
about as the P.B.I.? You exist like a pig for weeks on end,
grovelling and nosing and snivelling for rations. Your
constitution is steadily undermined month after month by
insufficient grub. Your body is lousy and dirty, and covered
with disgusting sores. The hair on you is a nesting and
breeding-place for chats and crabs, and has to be shaved
off. You're unclean; degraded. Any Tom, Dick, or Harry
from the R.E.s can muck you about. You have the most
dangerous, tedious, monotonous, and thankless job of all,
and you get less pay than anybody else.

'Compare yourself,' he carried on heatedly, though
Bradshaw had uttered no word of contradiction, 'with the
bees farther back. Some silly devils say they wouldn't be
an airman for anything. We all know they have a rotten
job, and no second chances, but don't you see that for
the biggest part of their time they enjoy a decent, civilised
billet, and always good grub? You're on duty all day long,
and your mind is never sure that a shell isn't on its way to
blow you to blazes. They get proper rest – mental, moral,
physical, and financial; your nerves are on edge day and
night. Even when you're on rest you might stop a shell.

'Look at that bee who took our uniforms away last night.
He wouldn't go near or touch them, but poked them away
with a brush-handle. That's as near as he'll ever get to being
lousy – till he gets home again.

'All the time I'm up the line I'm wishing I was home,

and all the time I'm home I wish I was back again. The last time I got pipped on the Somme and found myself in a shell-hole with four dead Froggies. Their faces were like pale beetroots and their bellies blown up like balloons; gas, I suppose. Then I came across two of our own chaps. One of 'em had a big hole in his neck, with a swarm of buzzing flies round it. There were some newer dead, too, of my own company, so awful that I swore I'd shoot myself before I'd come out again. One of the first fellows I met at home was a blighter who was swanking about the number of cases they'd had through the hospital since early last July. He'd been given a stripe, and said he needed it. "You don't know how unruly the men get," he said. "They behave like hooligans at mealtimes, dodge in at the windows of a night when they stay out square-pushing too late, and they even raid the cupboard where the blues are kept." I thought of four to a loaf for months, and the eight o'clock hospital bedtime, and the Fred Karno's blues they dish out; so I asked him: "And what do you do about it all?" "Put 'em on the peg, of course," he says. "We must have discipline; and only yesterday one called me a bastard. And us doing all we can for them." "And so you are a bastard," I said. "A lousy bastard." I felt like clocking him. But they don't really understand, you know.'

Bradshaw left Camier on September the 25th, after completing the diary that lay, for the most part, at the aid post in the Salient. The last entries ran:

'So now, after nearly two years in the army and fourteen months overseas, I am returning as a wounded Tommy who has done his bit. The irony of it! I came here with a duty before me – to kill Germans. For months I received instructions on how to drive home into my adversaries' bodies the long pointed blade of steel recently discarded. There has never been blood upon its surface; only a little mud and dust. Hardly more potent has been my rifle – and both have been carried many wearisome miles. My service has been a washout; undistinguished. Yet I have seen many dead men and boys – so many that the sight ceased to shock. Not normal dead, but cruel mutilations that were never on God's earth meant to be.

'The older men who use, and misuse, us cannot realise we haven't lived; that our lives are precious to us, and when once lost are irretrievable. They have had theirs in fullness and plenty, and will live on after this is over.

'Soon I shall be viewing Kent's beauty, enriched by absence, tinted autumn gold. There will be a luxurious continuance of white sheets and good food; plates to eat from; cups to drink from. Night after night of refreshing sleep to replenish those rudely snatched by working-party and stand-to. Water in abundance, clear, sparkling and splashing. Baths. Cleanness. No more soldiering for me, maybe.

'Constantly I think of the good men like Sergeant Stevens – men who were the backbone of England, and who now lie dead, many of them slain in those first eager rushes of 1915; others, like Stivvy himself, moving up and down the front, seeing many changes, and, though disillusioned, still quietly doing their long duty, learning bitterly that those who have caused the trouble are far behind beyond reach of bullet or shell; being offered innumerable times to death, and eventually, inevitably, accepted.

'And that other stalwart, Drummer Fogg, whom I can never think about without wondering why knighthoods are not granted to infantrymen for bravery in the field. For all his danger-bound service he has not yet been wounded. Slowly and sadly he has watched the disappearance of the chums he trained with, cheerfully carrying on, perhaps haunted by the fear that his own turn must surely come.

'It is a desolate thought, the picture of those several millions of men carrying on with their hateful task – the dreary prospect of another winter looming ahead – waiting for Germany to crack up. For she will crack up; she has bitten off more than she can chew. And that will be our victory; not the spectacular decisive triumph everybody hoped for, but a slow starving out.

'In picturing my last few moments of the battlefield, one impression remains vivid, typical, characteristic: that of odd Jerry prisoners who had survived our barrage and who walked through, arms raised. The misgivings that must have possessed them! Expecting each moment to be their last; dreading a bullet or a brutal attack; inwardly elated at the damage they saw; perhaps ashamed at the sight of so many silent dead figures in khaki. Counting the chances of revenge, yet passing down farther and farther, unmolested.

'That is being British: honouring our foes. A quality that will render help *in extremis* rather than do harm.

'It is the quality that will pull us through this rotten business.'

On September the 25th two German prisoners carried Bradshaw out of the war. From his stretcher he gazed at the grey sky above, suddenly becoming aware of the broad back and thick tanned neck of the carrier before him. His eyes tilted up under the white bandage, to see an equally powerful frame supporting the head of the stretcher. It didn't seem quite right; perhaps it was a symbol? As he searched for its appropriateness he smiled thinly at the tired eyes that met his.

He was on the boat! Going home. . . .

THE END

W. V. Tilsley in uniform, 1918

WILLIAM VINCENT TILSLEY
by David Tilsley (great-nephew)

William Vincent Tilsley was my great-uncle, and he died a long time before I was born. Despite never having met him, I was aware from quite an early age that there had been writers in the family, with William, his two brothers, John Frederick and Frank, and one of his two sisters, Iris, all having published books. It has always struck me as quite remarkable that what on the surface appears to have been an average working-class family from Levenshulme, near Manchester, produced offspring with such literary urges.

William – known as Vin to his family, Bill to his fellow soldiers, and W. V. Tilsley as the author of *Other Ranks* – was born on 13 October 1896 to William and Emily Louise Tilsley. William senior was a tailor and had a shop on Stockport Road in Levenshulme. His eldest son, John Frederick, followed his father into tailoring, being a 'presser' in 1911, according to the census. In the same year we find William junior, aged fourteen, as an assistant in a dry goods warehouse. It seems that he had attended the Manchester Central High School for Boys, but family circumstances may have meant that he couldn't stay on. Yet both brothers produced books based on their experiences in the Great War, John Frederick's *Cheerio! Some soldier yarns* being published in 1917, during the war. The third brother, Frank, too young to serve with William and John Frederick, would write about his experience of the next world war years later, part way through a very successful career as novelist and broadcaster.

We don't know when *Other Ranks* first began to take shape in William's mind. Writing in 1931, just after its publication, to a fellow veteran with an interest in Great War literature, Thomas Hope Floyd, William talked of 'the two years that "O.R." lay in a drawer, untouched'. Much later, in the 1980s, William's nephew, Harry Shore, said that William had written *Other Ranks* to get the war 'out of his system'. Harry described the Tilsley siblings as 'a very bright bunch. Keen supporters of City and United. Fond of politics, full of confidence and very liberal in their beliefs. Liberal with a smattering of socialism. They were all very capable artists, fond of music and excellent company.'

I have been given lots more information about William as a result of the present reissue of his single published work, particularly about the military career that prompted it. William's service records were destroyed in World War Two, but his medal card shows his original service number with the 1/7th Manchester Regiment as 5114, and it is possible to trace William's likely movements for August and September 1916. Recruits of the 1/7th Manchesters trained in England before embarking at Folkestone on 4 August for Boulogne; from there they went on to the 24th Infantry Base depot at Étaples. On 16 August the Manchesters were sent into the field to reinforce the 1/4th Loyal North Lancashire Regiment, to which William was officially transferred on 9 September with a new number, 6318. His medal index card, held at the National Archives, shows him to have been a corporal in the Manchesters, but on his transfer to the Loyal North Lancashire Regiment he reverted to being a private. By the end of his service the WW1 Service Medal and Award Rolls record him as a sergeant. William was also recorded in the *London Gazette* on 25 May 1917 as having been Mentioned in Dispatches.

The Regimental War Diary records that during William's service C Company took part in the Battle of Ginchy on 9 September 1916, Passchendaele on 31 July 1917, and Menin Road Ridge on 20 September 1917. Anecdotally, after William was wounded at the last of these his brother John Frederick – a stretcher-bearer in the Royal Army Medical Corps – attended to him at the casualty clearing station. It would be wonderful to confirm this family legend. (Fred served from 3 March 1917 to 2 February 1919 with the 64th Casualty Clearing Station, positioned at Mendinghem.) A record revealed that WVT had suffered a gunshot wound to the head, endorsing his narrative.

It's unclear what the years immediately after demobilisation held for him. William married Alice Bessena (Bessie) Hopwood in 1928, and their son John Alvin was born two years later. At this time William's career was in advertising (initially as a commercial artist?), where materially he did very well. Cruelly, John died aged only ten of a cerebral aneurysm in September 1940. William died not long after, on 1 April 1943, from post-operative shock and haemorrhage following a kidney operation. Bessie never remarried, and lived to be seventy-seven. Among her effects was a copy of *Other Ranks* that William had signed for his son John, containing a photograph of him in his uniform dated 1918.

When *Other Ranks* was first published, William seemed doubtful of its value and relevance to the following generation. He wrote to Thomas Hope Floyd: 'It is terrible to think of what happened to our division, but you know what us old ghosts think cannot be of much vital interest to younger people.'

How surprised would he be to know how highly regarded his work has become – still relevant, if not more so; not ghostly, but rich, compelling and true.

29, Crossefield Road
Cheadle Hulme
25.3.1931

Dear Mr Floyd,

I am glad you found something of interest in "Other Ranks", and shall certainly read your own statement. It is terrible to think of what happened to our Division, but you know what we old ghosts think cannot be of much vital interest to younger people. That is why so few historic records will take – we cannot all adopt the crudities of "All Quiet" "Zero Hour" and "Schlump" without blushing for il [sic] amongst the people we know. Consequently we suffer in sales.

I know of no other record of the Division we called the "Cast Iron" (not confirmed to us, I fear!)

If you had not already bought O.R. we could have exchanged autographed copies: I much prefer unassuming works of art to the more sensational books mentioned. You will have read "Undertones of War", I expect? If not do so!

I wish my own book were fit to put in the same library.

Yours sincerely

W. V. Tilsley

By the way – June 15 was spent in celebration before the famous march. I do not clearly give that date for it, merely mentioning the anniversary "binge" and following on with the march. As the "binge" would of course be night, and the 'march off' morning, it must be read that a day intervenes.

Yours

W.V.T.

29, Crossefield Road.
Cheadle Hulme
May 4. 31.

Dear Mr Floyd,

Your incursion into war literature has been more thorough than mine, evidently. I have no time for Churchill even if I could afford his price; though I don't doubt his "World Crisis" is excellent. I haven't read "The Real War" either, but can say 'yes' to "War is War", have only just read it. It is too much like "Other Ranks" for my opinion, though I liked it immensely. It would have been better if more time had been taken over it – the places are spelt wrongly in several instances; probably through rushing at it to get in during the boom. It makes me regret sometimes the two years that "O.R." lay in a drawer, untouched

C. E. Montagues "Disenchantment" is one of my favourites, also his "Rough Justice" and "Fiery Particles". Amongst others I like are "The Secret Battle" "Spanish Farm" "Grey Dawn – Red Night" The Tiejens [sic] Trilogy and "The Enormous Room". Another one that was little heard of is also very good – "The Price of Victory".

I can recommend, too, Philip Gibbs "Realities of War" and the naval works: "Raiders of the Deep" "Campbells Mystery Ships" "By Guess & By God" & "The Danger Zone"; and the Richtofen [sic] Book "The Red Knight of Germany".

I'm not in Manchester every day, and when I am it is usually to be steeped in jobs that leave little time for friendly appointments. However, if the opportunity comes I shall let you know.

Yours faithfully
W. V. Tilsley

29, Crossfield Road.
Cheadle Hulme
May 14. 3.

Dear Mr Lloyd,

Your incursion into war literature has been more thorough than mine, evidently. I have no time for Churchill even if I could afford his price; though I don't doubt his 'World Crisis' is excellent. I haven't read 'The Real War' either, but can say 'yes' to 'War is War'; have only just read it. This too much like 'Other Ranks' for my opinion, though I liked it immensely. It would have been better if more time had been taken over it — the places are spelt wrongly in several instances; probably through rushing at it to get in during the boom. It makes me regret sometimes the two years that 'O.R.' lay in a drawer, untouched.

C. E. Montague's 'Disenchantment' is one of my favourites; also his 'Rough Justice' and 'Fiery Particles'. Amongst others I like are 'The Secret Battle' 'Spanish Farm' 'Grey Dawn — & Night' The Peasons Trilogy and 'The Enormous Room'. Another one that was little heard of is also very good — 'the Price of Victory.'

I can recommend, too, Philip Gibbs' 'Realities of War' and the naval works: 'Raiders of the Deep' 'Campbell Mystery Ships' 'By Guess & By God' & 'The Danger Zone'; and the Richthofen Book 'The Red Knight of Germany.'

I'm not in Manchester every day, and when I am do is usually to be steeped in store that leave little time for friendly appointments. However, if the opportunity comes I shall let you know.

Yours faithfully
W. V. Tilsley

Ernest Magnall in uniform, 1916

ERNEST MAGNALL

by John Magnall (nephew)

My father Alan was Ernest's half brother. His mother, Martha, a war widow, married Ernest's father after the war. Although there was a twenty-six-year age difference between Ernest and Alan, the brothers were close.

Ernest Magnall was born on 19 December 1895 to Annie and James William Magnall, at 21 Cobden Street, Burnley, Lancashire. Ernest and his younger brother Bill were brought up by their father, although their mother was still alive.

Before enlisting, Ernest worked as a cloth looker at Preston's Rylands Street cotton mill in Burnley.

Most of the information about Ernest's military service comes from papers kept by his father after the war. On 26 February 1916 Ernest attested (the process for men recruited under Lord Derby's scheme) with the 3/5th Battalion of the East Lancashire Regiment Territorial Force, with service no. 4681. It was recorded that he was 5 ft 7½ in. tall, had brown eyes and brown hair, and was a Methodist.

On 7 August, after training at Witley Camp, Surrey, Ernest embarked from Folkestone for Boulogne. He was sent to the 25th Infantry Base Depot, a hutted camp at Étaples, where he remained for ten days. He then joined the battalion in the field, and on 9 September he fought in the Battle of Ginchy.

By then he had been transferred to the Loyal North Lancashire Regiment (service no. 6246). In October he left the Somme sector for Flanders, with the new service no. 202862.

In early June 1917 Ernest was recorded in the Loyal North Lancashire Regimental book as having been wounded, and his family received a letter to that effect from the Army Council. On 31 July 1917 he took part in the 3rd Battle of Ypres (Passchendaele). This time his family received a wounded prisoner of war notice from Germany, dated 6 August 1917, and on 28 September his family was notified by the Army Records Office at Preston that Ernest was a prisoner of war. He was held captive for nine months. He was first taken to a field hospital in Wahn near Cologne and then to Soltau – the largest prisoner of war camp in Germany, with a reputation for being harsh.

In April 1918 Ernest was part of a wounded prisoner of war exchange. He travelled to Rotterdam via Austausch-Station, Aachen, and then boarded the private hospital ship *Sindoro*. While in Rotterdam awaiting his transfer to England, Ernest sent a letter home to his father and brother, written on YMCA headed paper; there he speaks of how well the prisoners were greeted in Holland, and says that more kindness and sympathy were shown to them in the first five minutes of arrival than they had received in the past nine months.

On 14 April he arrived in London, and was sent to recuperate at Gifford House Auxiliary Hospital, Roehampton. It is said that during a visit to the cinema Ernest's father had seen film footage of him being carried off the hospital ship.

By 27 April 1918 Ernest was at the King George Hospital in London, when he was sent a letter from a Government

Committee on the Treatment by the Enemy of British Prisoners of War asking him to report on the treatment he and other POWs had received, 'however unfit they were', from the British Sergeant Lee, in charge of 34 Barrack at Soltau. There is a copy of his reply, where he states: 'he did not get me to work as I baulked him by going sick'.

In June, while still a patient at the King George Hospital, he received a visit from his mother.

Ernest was awarded Silver War Badge no. B121067, and wore an iron on his leg for the rest of his life.

Back in civilian life in Burnley, Ernest met Florence Miles and they married in 1922. Ernest went to night school, and progressed to become Manager of Stuttard's Primrose Mill. Ernest and Florrie settled nearby at 301 Briercliffe Road, and lived there for the rest of their lives.

Together with Ernest's well-thumbed copy of *Other Ranks* there is a letter from W. V. Tilsley written to him shortly after publication of the book in 1931 (see below).

In 1942 Ernest joined the Society of St George Burnley, and was elected President in 1947.

Ernest and Florrie did not have any children. After the death of Florrie's sister in 1949 they adopted their eight-year old nephew Harry, and doted on him. Harry was academically strong, and progressed through Burnley Grammar School and Manchester University to become a science teacher and ultimately a Head.

Ernest was given the moniker 'Nuncs' (for 'uncle') by Harry, and the name stuck.

After retiring from the Mill, Ernest and Florrie enjoyed quiet domesticity. For Ernest, retirement involved spending time across the back street in his garden and greenhouse, tending his rhubarb and his 'tommies'. Beside the garden was a brick garage that housed their car at the time, a gleaming black 1953 Morris Minor. St Andrew's Bowling Green was close by, and Ernest would often walk down there of an afternoon for a game of cards and billiards with a couple of 'gills'.

Florrie died in 1962, when I was twelve. I fondly recall time spent with Nuncs, chatting while playing cards and watching TV in the front room; on one occasion an offending lamp flex that had tripped him up once too often was given short shrift with a pair of scissors. Ernest was unmoved, but the live cable ensured the scissors would not be used again.

Once a week there were trips to the Central Library in what by then was Ernest's ludicrously out of character 1965 Hillman Imp, with its pipsqueak horn. I would nip in to swap a batch of five cowboy books while Nuncs sat outside; if there were two out of five he hadn't read, Nuncs would give the thumbs up and off we would go. The drive home would be punctuated with 'Square-'eaded whotsit' and 'Pardon my French', as Nuncs assumed his path on whichever side of the road he saw fit.

For me and for all who knew him, 'Nuncs' became the natural term of affection for a man who was great fun, a good companion, and since his passing my unsung hero.

Ernest died on 22 July 1970 of heart failure in Lancaster Royal Infirmary.

29 Crossefield Road
Cheadle Hulme, Cheshire
17.12.1931

Dear Ernest,

It is good to hear again from you, and to know that the appeal in "Other Ranks" dedication has met with response. How did you come across it? I am also glad to know that unemployment troubles have been kind to you, as they have been with me. Things could be better, of course, but one must be satisfied to live at all decently and comfortably.

I notice you have been married ten years, but no mention is made of possible 'Other Ranks'. You are an old hand compared with me – four years, one small boy two next month.

I hope I have not misrepresented you at all in my book. I tried my best to make it truthful without being spiteful. Quite a lot of people have said nice things about it, but of course it was a year too late to make any real shout.

You will recognise yourself, no doubt, as Bagnall. I couldn't use proper names without running the risk of hurting certain people. How would you like to be carrying up the dixies from Congreve Walk again, like we were just fifteen years ago? Or sitting in the mine shaft at Mud Lane while Jerry slammed at the roof with his minnies?

The book also raked up for me several other old ghosts of drab history, notably Arthur Wilson, one time runner and officers servant. You may recall him.

I shall be glad to hear again from you. Do you ever get to Manchester?

Your old dugout wallah
Bill Tilsley

29. Crossfield Road,
Cheadle Hulme
Cheshire.
17.12.1931

Dear Ernest,

It is good to hear again from you, and to know that the appeal in "Other Ranks" dedication has met with response. How did you come across it? I am also glad to know that unemployment troubles have been kind to you, as they have with me. Things could be better, of course, but one must be satisfied to live at all decently and comfortably.

I notice you have been married ten years, but no mention is made of possible "other ranks". You are an old hand compared with me — four years, our small boy two next month.

I hope I have not misrepresented you at all in my book. I tried my best to make it truthful without being spiteful. Quite a lot of people have said nice things about it, but of course it was a year too late to make any real shout.

You will recognise yourself, no doubt, as Bagnall. I could not use proper names without running the risk of hurting certain people. How would you like to be carrying up the dixies from Caypore Walk again, like we were just fifteen years ago? Or sitting in the mine shaft at Mud Lane while Jerry slammed at the roof with his minnies?

The book also raked up for me several other old ghosts of drab history, notably Arthur Wilson, our tin miner and officer's servant. You may recall him.

I shall be glad to hear again from you. Do you ever get to Manchester?

Your old dugout wallah,
Bill Tilsley

Letter from Tilsley to Magnall, 17 December 1931

YOUNG MEN'S CHRISTIAN ASSOCIATION
WITH THE
BRITISH PRISONERS OF WAR INTERNED IN HOLLAND.

Tuesday April 9th 1918

Dear Dad & Bro

Just a line to let you know that I am no longer a prisoner of war in Germany. Three cheers for that.

I arrived in Holland about 2 o'clock yesterday afternoon, and we had a very fine reception.

They could not have treated us better if we had been royalty. We had more kindness & sympathy the first 5 minutes we were in Holland that we have had in nine months in that country known as Germany.

I wrote a postcard as soon as we crossed the border, but you may get that card at the same time as you get this letter.

My leg is doing fine, about a month in good old blighty will see it alright again.

We are expecting to leave here for England on Friday or Saturday and it will take us two days sail to get to England.

As soon as I arrive I will let you know by a card or a letter. I am sending you a postcard photo of the boat we are coming home on.

Please tell all my friends I will soon be with them again.

So cheer up Dad & don't worry I am alright, the Holland Red Cross Ladies are looking after us fine.

I am writing this from Rotterdam I have just been for a walk down by the dock side! We are in a building only about 20 yards from the water side.

Please Tell Uncle Tom that I will soon be playing him at
Billiards again

I think this is all

I remain

Your Loving Son

Ernie

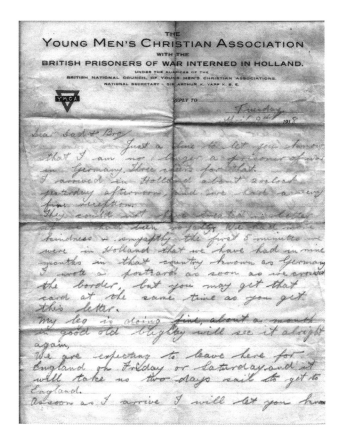

Letter sent home by Magnall to his father and brother from
Rotterdam after his release as a wounded prisoner, 9 April 1918

Charles O'Neill (on the right) with his friend Edgar Dabbs

CHARLES FRANCIS O'NEILL
by Francis O'Neill (nephew)

Charles Francis, the oldest child of Francis Charles and Eleanor O'Neill, was born on 19 January 1894 in Sale, at 32 Victoria Drive. As the first-born son he was named after his paternal grandfather (and father) in the traditional Irish fashion. There were eventually seven children in the family, five boys and two girls, my father being the sixth child. Charles Francis is recorded in the 1901 census as living at 106 Lansdowne Road, Didsbury, Manchester, aged seven. He was first educated at The Hollies, Fallowfield, and then on 19 January 1904 admitted along with his brother Henry Hugh to St Bede's College, Manchester, of which their grandfather Charles O'Neill was one of the Founders. The brothers completed their education in December 1910. In the 1911 census Charles is described as a 'clerk with a provision merchant' aged seventeen, living at 58 Talbot Street, Moss Side. He was probably employed at the Co-operative Wholesale Society, where his father already worked as a clerk.

Only one photograph of Charles is known, showing him as a young boy playing with another boy, Edgar Dabbs, and some rabbits. Edgar Dabbs also fought in the war, but sadly died at Chester War Hospital the day after Armistice Day of shell wounds sustained in battle. Charles's death in World War I was often talked about in the family, but no details were ever mentioned, except that my father, Charles's younger brother by ten years, told me that his three older brothers had all been in the Territorials prior to the war. I initially assumed that Charles was in one of the Manchester Territorial Battalions that fought in the Battle of the Somme in July 1916. It was only gradually that I realised that this was incorrect.

After my Auntie Moira's death in 1966 I was looking through her papers and found documents specifying that her brother Charles was buried in Longueval Road Cemetery near Albert, and indicating that she had visited and photographed his grave. This prompted me to visit the battlefields of the Somme and Ancre on one of our family camping holidays in France. With the help of Auntie Moira's map we located the cemetery, and because I knew it would be a very emotional experience we decided to stop at a café first. I parked the car and trailer on the road outside and ordered drinks for the family, but was immediately accosted by a rather aggressive man who said in good English that I was blocking his vehicle from getting out. I moved my car. Shortly afterwards we heard a loud wheezing sound and a noxious cloud of smoke was emitted by a vehicle which reversed out into the road and drove off with a conspicuous 'D' for Deutschland on the rear.

We then drove the short distance to a small cemetery. There was a short flight of steps up with a pillar on either side, and in one pillar there was a recess containing a book of remembrance. Despite the small number of graves there was an almost daily entry in the book seventy-five years after the events that had caused these deaths; we added our own comments. It was striking how many nationalities were represented in this small graveyard, including soldiers from most of the larger Commonwealth countries and even one German. We were easily able to find the grave of my uncle Charles O'Neill, to which we paid our respects in the warm summer sunshine. The headstone states that he had died on 29 September 1916, aged twenty-two, and that he was a private in the Loyal North Lancashire Regiment, not the Manchester Regiment.

From Auntie Moira's papers it was clear that my grandfather had tried to find out more details of the circumstances of his son's death, but was unable to obtain satisfactory information from British Army sources. According to the family, he therefore used an old Catholic school contact (from Douai or Stonyhurst) who had become a general in the French Army to help him in his quest. This seems to have worked: I have in my possession a handwritten letter from General Jeudwine, the General Officer Commanding the 55th West Lancashire 'Cast Iron' Division of which the 1/4th Battalion was a part, addressed to my grandfather. It is rather formal in tone, but is remarkably detailed and informative about the death of Charles. General Jeudwine was not French, despite the look and sound of his name: he was an old Etonian, considered to be one of the more effective British commanders in WWI albeit somewhat of a martinet.

In my opinion, it would have been unusual for a WWI British general to go to these lengths for the relative of a mere private unless there had been some intervention at a very senior level, so the family story of a French general asking for more detail on behalf of an old school friend may be true. Jeudwine's letter states that he had made detailed

Flanders
11/4/17

Dear Sir

I have made enquiries as to the burial place of your son with the following result:

The Revd W.B. Westerdale nonconformist Chaplain to the forces states that No 5130 Pte. C. F. O'Neill ¼ Loyal North Lancs Regt died of wounds in his presence in the 'Shrine' Dressing Station near LONGUEVAL (NE of ALBERT) on 28th September 1916.

The Revd. HE Maddox Church of England Chaplain to the forces states that he buried No 5130 Pte C. F. O'Neill at the 'Shrine' Dressing Station mentioned above, on 28th Sept. 1916. And that a temporary cross was put up to mark the spot. At the same time he notified this burial to the Graves Registration Commission on the usual forms –

I will make further enquiries of the Graves Registration authorities.

You will note that the regimental number is 5130 not 6319, but I think there can be no doubt that this is your son – Regimental numbers have in some cases been changed during a (mains??) service – especially on transfer.

Longueval is about 6 miles East North East of Albert.

I hope this information may be what you require

Yours very Truly
H. S. Jeudwine

F. C. O'Neill Esq

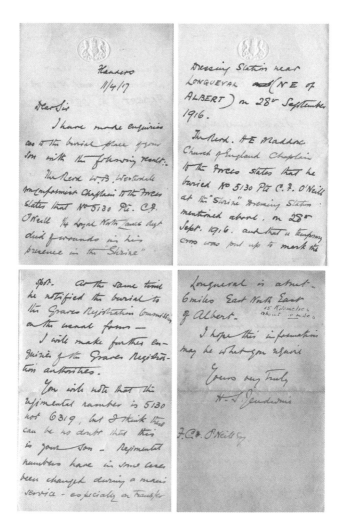

*Letter from Jeudwine to Charles O'Neill's father, F. C. O'Neill,
about Charles's burial place, 11 April 1917*

enquiries and that Charles died of his wounds at a field dressing station known as 'The Shrine' in the presence of a Nonconformist chaplain and was buried the same day, 28 September, by a Church of England chaplain. This would have partly satisfied my grandfather's worry as to whether his son had had the 'last rites' performed and a proper Christian (preferably Catholic!) burial. The chaplains' testimony makes it as certain as can be that Charles was injured and died on 28 September 1916, not the 29th as inscribed on his headstone.

There the matter rested, until by chance in late 2015 I found a website dedicated to the Loyal North Lancashire Regiment which gave a completely different twist to the story. Much to my amazement, there was a very detailed entry for Charles, which stated that he enlisted on 26 February 1916 at Manchester in the Territorial Force, in the 7th Battalion of the Manchester Regiment (as service no. 5130), and had no previous military service. Most of these military records were destroyed in the Blitz, and Charles is the only one of the three O'Neill brothers who served in WWI whose detailed records have survived. This information showed that he was not a pre-war Territorial soldier, and that he only joined the Army after his brother Henry had fought and been wounded at Gallipoli in 1915. Charles had enlisted as a 'Derby' soldier: under this scheme established by the Earl of Derby in late 1915 as a halfway house between volunteering and conscription, adult males of military age had to 'attest' prior to being called up. Charles's home address was given as 35 Gream Street, Moss Side, Manchester. He signed the Imperial and General Service Declaration (there is a copy of his signature on the website) which allowed him to serve overseas. From his medical examination he was 5ft 8¾ in. tall, had a chest circumference of 34 in., and weighed 132 lb: for that era he was relatively tall but slim.

After training in the UK with the Manchester Territorials he sailed to France on 4 August 1916 (over a month after the initial fighting of the Battle of the Somme, which started on 1 July) by the Folkestone to Boulogne route. He was sent to the 24th Infantry Base Depot at Étaples.

There the story ended, or so I thought. The original post by Paul McCormick, the regimental website creator and administrator, had been made on 24 November 2015. I decided to post an appreciative comment on 21 December 2015. Then completely out of the blue on 4 April 2016 I received an email from Paul advising me that Gaye Magnall wanted me to get in touch with her, as she had some information about my uncle of which I might be unaware. Intrigued, I contacted her, and she asked me if I had ever heard of a book with the title *Other Ranks* that had been written in 1931 by W.V. Tilsley. It was based on Tilsley's service in WWI. Unfortunately only a few hundred copies had been printed, so the book was very rarely seen, and very expensive when found. It is generally considered to be a forgotten masterpiece.

Fortunately I was staying in London when I received this information, so I went immediately to the British Library, found the book, and read it every day with increasing fascination. It is dedicated to 'Ernest Magnall who lived and Charles O'Neill who died'. Tilsley is a superb writer. He makes it clear that his account is not fiction, and that it is based on a diary that he kept throughout his Army service. He has changed some of the names, including those of the main characters: he is 'Bradshaw', Charles O'Neill is 'Jack Driver', and Ernest Magnall is 'Bagnall'.

Charles only appears in the first section of the book, where he and Tilsley become close companions: they are both from Manchester, and the other soldiers, who are mainly from Chorley, speak with such a very broad Lancashire accent and dialect that they are difficult to understand. Charles is described as having a 'natural fastidiousness, a nice mind and nice manners'. He speaks the 'King's English' and is 'superior in education, speech and upbringing' to most of his fellow soldiers, but is clever enough to realise that none of this counts for anything in the army. Tilsley says that neither he nor Charles smoked, drank or swore – unlike most of their fellow soldiers – and that Charles was an equable companion, but that there was a six inch difference in their heights (Charles being the taller).

They are first based at Méricourt and then move to Saignville, where they walk the quiet country lanes together while their comrades get drunk at the local estaminet. Charles comments that 'they cannot make soldiers' of people like us and speculates as to what will happen when they have to fight on the front line. Charles beats Tilsley twice at chess and also comments poignantly that 'it would break my mother's heart if I were to be killed' – this being the only mention of his family; he also says that he would 'rather be taken prisoner than lose a limb'. There is no discussion of religion or politics. They leave Saignville on 28 August and then camp at Bouzincourt near Albert, where they have a week of fine cool nights. After hearing that Guillemont had fallen to the allies on 3 September they march towards the front. They stop in a cornfield near Mametz, where Tilsley first calls Charles by his Christian name, 'Jack' (previously only surnames had been used). Charles is worried about camping in the open because he is 'susceptible to bronchitis'. It is 7 September, and they have been in France a month.

They move to Montauban and at darkness are at Bernafay Woods before Longueval, at the edge of the gutted Delville Wood ('Devil's Wood') where there are snipers. On 9 September they are in the front line near the ruined Waterlot Farm (actually a sugar mill). Charles thinks that 'our guns are firing short' and have 'just killed Healy and Acton', but subsequently he is proved wrong: it was the German gun at Thiepval that was doing the damage. The prospect of going into action is imminent, and Tilsley comments that Charles 'bore himself unflinchingly'. He then gives a powerful no-holds-barred description of their unit going over the top and advancing on the German lines, taking very heavy casualties in the process. Seven soldiers, including Tilsley and Charles, survive, taking shelter in two shell holes very close to the German trenches. They confer and decide there is no point in trying to advance further and that retreat is the only sensible option. The first two men out of the shell hole are hit by sniper fire, so Tilsley suggests that the rest should go out of the other side. Both he and Charles make a successful return to the British trenches, which are now virtually unmanned. They cannot understand why the Germans do not counter-attack.

According to Tilsley's book both he and Charles are out of

the line at Meaulte from 14 to 16 September. They expect to be given an extended period of rest in view of their recent action, but they are sent forward again towards Flers on 17 September. Tilsley is put in a 'salvage party', and the next day he hears that the Lancashires were 'mauled again' at Gueudecourt and that Charles had been killed by a shell while in a trench. He then continues his own narrative and refers to the next day being 19 September, which would imply that Charles was killed on the 18th, not the 28th or the 29th as indicated in the information provided by General Jeudwine, by the Army on the regimental website, and on the headstone. It seems that Tilsley may have deliberately changed dates and places in the same way as he altered names. He describes the action throughout as being chaotic, with no clear organisation, particularly for the evacuation of the wounded and the dead, so it is not surprising that there should be inconsistencies between his account and the official reports, but I believe this is more to do with Tilsley being deliberately imprecise.

The time described in *Other Ranks* can be traced in the official War Diary of the 1/4th Loyal North Lancashire Regiment, a handwritten daily account of the regiment's activities during the whole of WWI. A batch of a hundred Other Ranks from the 7th and 10th Manchester and East Lancashire Regiments were posted to join the 1/4th Loyal North Lancashire on 16 August; Charles was given a new regimental number, 6319. His new unit had been in the front line opposite Guillemont since 30 July, as part of the 55th Division. After a rather confusing period of train travel, marching, bivouacking and training, which is described in vivid detail in Tilsley's book, Charles's unit moved into the front line on 7 September, on the edge of Delville Wood, in the direction of Ginchy.

On 9 September Charles as part of C Company went over the top and was involved in the disastrous assault on Hop Alley in which according to the Regimental Book 22 ORs were killed, 125 wounded and 79 reported missing. The figures were in fact much greater: Commonwealth War Graves Commission records show that more than 55 ORs fighting with 1/4th Battalion were killed on that day. Charles miraculously survived and managed to return to his original position, but the numbers of British troops were now seriously depleted. According to the Diary the battalion was withdrawn from the front line on the following day, 10 September, and the brigade was relieved on the 12th. The battalion then remained out of the front line with two periods of training before marching to Brown Trench in front of Delville Wood, close to Flers, on 24 September. This is a week later than Tilsley says in his book. On the 27th the unit moved to Gueudecourt and occupied trenches that had been recently captured from the Germans. On the following day, 28 September, when the early morning mist had cleared a large group of enemy soldiers was visible about half a mile away. They were subjected to heavy rifle and machine gun fire and disappeared. Probably in retaliation, the trenches on the sunken road were subjected to very heavy German bombardment between 12 noon and 3 p.m. According to the Regimental Book 6 ORs were killed and 30 wounded; the Commonwealth War Graves Commission records show 3 men from 1/4th Battalion and 5 from other

attached battalions were killed during this day. I believe that
it was in this action that Charles was fatally wounded, and
that he almost surely died of his wounds the same day.
Ironically, his unit was relieved and left the front line on
29 September, and it was subsequently transferred to a
relatively quiet part of the Western Front.

A book published in 1919 entitled *The Story of the 55th
(West Lancashire) Division*, written by the Rev. J. O. Coop,
Senior Chaplain of the Division, with a foreword by General
Jeudwine (who had commissioned it), is a somewhat sanitised
version of the war diaries but has some interesting information
and trench maps that contribute to this tale. On 9 September, to
quote Coop, 'the task of the 164th Infantry Brigade was first to
take a line of trenches running from the outskirts of Ginchy to
the east corner of Delville Wood and secondly to capture Hop
Alley and Ale Alley. . . . At the appointed hour [5.25 p.m.] two
companies of the 1/4th Loyal North Lancs left their trenches
and following close behind the barrage attacked Hop Alley.
. . . Hop Alley proved to be very much stronger than had
been anticipated and was held by a large garrison with many
machine guns. . . . At one time it was reported that the 1/4th
Loyal North Lancs had captured Hop Alley but, if the report
was true, they must have been unable to hold it and, in spite
of most determined efforts, were compelled to occupy shell
holes in front, after losing heavily in Officers and men.' Coop's
book has a map of the trenches in front of Guedecourt which
shows clearly where Charles was probably killed on 28
September. This account confirms Tilsley's graphic description
of the battle of 9 September in every detail, and also the action
in which Charles lost his life.

The grave of Charles O'Neill, in Longueval Road Cemetery.
It shows his date of death as 29 September 1916; the Grave
Registration Report Form, however, records his date of death as
28 September 1916, confirming the account given in the letter
sent by General Jeudwine to his father.

When the O'Neill family received the official government scroll and plaque thanking them and Charles for their sacrifice there was a naming error – not the usual misspelling of O'Neill, but a transposing of the forenames to 'Francis Charles', adding insult to grievous injury, as both the scroll and plaque had to be sent back for correction. I have managed to get access to Charles's original army file, in which I found a receipt for his 'Victory medal' signed by his mother (my grandmother) Eleanor O'Neill, the only example of her writing that I have ever seen. This is particularly poignant in the light of the comment that Charles made to Tilsley about his mother before his death.

A bag containing his personal effects was sent to his father in Manchester in February 1917. It contained '1 Identity Disc, 1 Letter, 1 Compass, 1 Rosary, 1 Knife, 1 Pipe, 1 Wallet containing 1 photograph and 1 National Registration Card'.

So over almost a thirty-year period I have finally established the truth behind the war service of my uncle Charles and now know much more about him as a person, in his physical appearance, his personality and his character. A pleasant, brave, intelligent man, a credit to his family and his country, and a true hero, who unfortunately I never had the chance to meet in person.

THE MEN BEHIND THE CHARACTERS

CH   Cheshire Regiment
EL   East Lancashire Regiment
LNL   Loyal North Lancashire Regiment
M   Manchester Regiment
The ranks are those of the men at the end of their service
See also the Imperial War Museum website: 'Lives of the First World War'

adjutant (p. 171)	R.N.L. Buckmaster, Capt., *KIA 30/11/17*
Agnew	Albert Askew, Cpl (LNL 2244) *KIA 9/9/16*
Agostini	Horace Simon Frederick Agostini, Lt *W*
Anderton	Arthur Oxley Harvey (M 4730 + LNL 6301) *KIA 25/9/16*
Armour	Emmanuel Armer, L/Cpl (LNL 4504 + 201750) *DOW 31/7/17*
Bagnall, Ernie	Ernest Magnall (EL 4681 + LNL 6246 + 202862) *W, POW 31/7/17*
Bates	Fred Yates (M 4774 + LNL 6304 + 202913) *KIA 21/7/17*
Bell, Sgt	Thomas Bell, L/Sgt (LNL 5601 + 202572) *W*
Birch	Eustace Lander Wood, A/CQMS (M 5095 + LNL 6317 + 202925) *W*
Bradshaw, Dick	William Vincent Tilsley, Sgt (M 5114 + LNL 6318 + 202926) *W 20/9/17*
Bragg	William Henry Wragg (M 4912 + LNL 6306 + 202915)
Brettle	Peter James Webster (M 4300 + LNL 6297 +202907) *KIA 21/7/17*
brigadier-general (p. 188)	Clifton Inglis Stockwell, Brig.-Gen., CB, CMG, DSO
Carnforth, Sgt-Maj./ private	Henry Farnworth, private (deprived of the rank of SGT), DCM (LNL 4741 + 4388 + 201697)
Collier	Frederick William Collier, L/Cpl (M 3907+ LNL 6295 + 202905) *W*
Dalton, Lt	Leon Maitland Walton, 2nd Lt *KIA 16/11/16*
deserter, shot (p. 171)	Richard Stevenson (LNL 2554) *Shot at dawn 25/10/16*
Donovan, Micky	David Rathbone, MM (LNL 12910) *KIA 19/9/17*
Downes	Thomas Lowndes (LNL 4100 + 201532) *KIA 31/7/17*
Driver, Jack	Charles Francis O'Neill (M 5130 + LNL 6319) *KIA 28/9/16, CWGC 29/9/16*
Fletcher, Jem	James Fletcher, CQMS, DCM (LNL 1755 + 200388) *KIA 31/7/17*

Fogg, 'Drummer'	John Hogg, Sgt, DCM, MM (LNL 1762 + 200392) *W*
Fred (Bradshaw's brother)	John Frederick Tilsley (RAMC 45 + 356042)
Fulshaw, Lt	Cyril Henry Forshaw, Lt *W*
'Get Fell In', Sgt-Maj.	James Elijah Farnworth, A/RSM, DCM (LNL 3975) *Discharged unfit*
Gore, Lt	Charles Leonard Hore, A/Capt., MC *W, sick*
Hartley, Cpl	James Hartley, Sgt, MM (LNL 1664 + 200346)
Harwood	John Harwood, L/Cpl (LNL 2272 + 200558) *KIA 31/7/1917*
Hautz, Lt	Reginald Hugh Tautz, A/Capt., MC *W*
Hunter-Weston, Gen. Sir A.	Aylmer Hunter-Weston, Lt-Gen. Sir, KCB, DSO
Ireland, RSM	John Ireland, CSM, DCM (LNL 2305 + 200575)
Jem	Jim Walker (LNL 1687) *Suicide 7/11/16*
Jenkins, Lt	Francis Crofts Jenkinson, 2nd Lt *W*
Jeudwine	Hugh Sandham Jeudwine, Lt-Gen. Sir, KCB, KBE
Lonsdale, Lt	Harry Lonsdale, Capt., MC and Bar
Lord, Oliver	Thomas Edward Lord (LNL 6680 + 203014) *KIA 1/6/17*
Murphy, Sgt, 'Spud'	James Murphy, private (deprived of the rank of Sgt), MM (LNL 6693) *W*
Old Swish	Thomas Horsfield, L/Sgt (LNL 3396) *KIA 28–29/9/16*
Orrell, Sgt	Thomas Orrell, Sgt (LNL 116 + 200051)
'Pass me, lad' (sgt, p. 51)	Thomas Wareing, CSM (LNL 1720) *KIA 9/9/16*
Peel	John Edward Maurice Peel (EL 4962 + LNL 6250 + CH 203201) *W*
Phillipson, Capt.	Arthur Lea Harris, Capt. *KIA 31/7/17*
Pringle, Col.	Ralph Hindle, Lt-Col., DSO *KIA 30/11/17*
Rimmer	Daniel Rimmer (LNL 2696 + 200689)
Rushton, Lt	Arthur Ashton, A/Capt
Snow, General	Thomas D'Oyly Snow, Lt-Gen. Sir, KCB, KCMG
Standing, Sniper	John Standing (LNL 3598 + 201223)
Stevens, Sgt, 'Stivvy'	Vincent Stephenson, Sgt (LNL 119 + 200052) *KIA 18/7/17*
Tilson	Arthur Wilson, L/Cpl (LNL 4705 + 201897)
Walker	James Harrison (LNL 16538) *DOW 2/8/17 from 31/7/17*
Whiteside, Sgt, 'Ginger'	Thomas Whiteside, Sgt (LNL 2 + 200001)
Wiles, Sgt-Maj.	Richard Isles, CSM (LNL 993 + 200195) *KIA 21/7/17*

GLOSSARY

adjutant: a staff officer who assists the CO of a regiment, battalion or garrison

Allemongs: Germans (from French *Allemands*)

APO: Army Post Office

Archies: anti-aircraft fire/shells

ASC: Army Service Corps

back sight: attachment on top of a rifle to determine whether the shot will fire to the right or left, low or high of the target

badinage: light playful talk and banter

bandolier: a shoulder belt with loops for cartridges

Bangalore torpedo: an explosive charge placed in a tube and used for clearing obstacles, developed in Bangalore, India, in 1912

barrage: a heavy barrier of artillery fire to protect one's troops or stop the advancing enemy

battalion: a military unit. In 1914 a standard infantry battalion was 1,000 men; this shrank in size with manpower shortages

battery: a unit of guns and missiles grouped together

bayonet-boss: a stud under the muzzle of a rifle used for attaching the bayonet crossguard

bearded: faced down

bee: presumably short for a mild obscenity

BEF: British Expeditionary Force

Bengal Lights: a bright blue flare used in signalling; also Indian troops

BF: bloody fool

BHQ: battalion/battle headquarters

bivouac/bivouack: shelter/to shelter

bivvies: shelter (from 'bivouac')

blancoed: whitened with a paste

Blighty: England/home (from the Urdu *bilayati*, foreign land)

Blighty wound: a wound serious enough for one to be sent home

blind to the wide: drunk

blues: a poor quality uniform worn by convalescing soldiers

bob: slang for a shilling, one twentieth of a pound sterling

Boche: a German (from the French *tête de boche*, blockhead)

bombardier: a non-commissioned officer in certain artillery regiments, equivalent to corporal

box barrage: artillery bombardment on a small area

Bradbury: a Treasury note

Brass Hats: high-ranking military officers

breastwork: a low temporary defence or parapet

breech cover: canvas wrap that keeps mud and dust from the action of a gun

buckshee: free of charge (from Urdu *bakhshish*, a tip)

Bull Ring: British Army training camp behind the lines; Étaples was an infamous example

bully beef: tinned corned or boiled beef

butts: rifle range

cannonade: continuous heavy gunfire

CB: Companion of the Most Honourable Order of the Bath

CCS: casualty clearing station

char: tea (from Hindustani)

chat: a louse; to de-louse

chit: a short note (from Hindustani)

clocking: hitting

CMG: Companion of the Most Distinguished Order of St Michael and St George

CO: commanding officer (of a battalion)

communication trench: trench providing protected passage between rear and front lines

conchy: conscientious objector

con. camp: convalescent camp

concentration trench: a forming-up area prior to an attack

conscript: a person enlisted compulsorily

cooked: falsified

cordite: an explosive smokeless powder

corps: an army unit consisting of at least 2 divisions

CQMS: company quartermaster sergeant

Crown and Anchor: an illegal popular gambling game played clandestinely in estaminets and billets, consisting of three special dice and a coloured cloth bearing the four aces and a crown and anchor

CSM: company sergeant major

CWGC: Commonwealth War Graves Commission

DCM: Distinguished Conduct Medal

demic: a useless person or thing (Lancashire slang)

Derby men: men recruited under a voluntary scheme instituted by Lord Derby

dixies: large oval metal pots with lid and carrying handle used for cooking

DOW: died of wounds

draft: a contingent of new men

dressing-station: a post or centre that gives first aid to the wounded

DSO: Companion of the Distinguished Service Order

duckboard: a path formed of wooden slats joined together, over muddy ground or in a trench

dugout: an underground shelter

dump: an uncovered spot where trench tools and supplies are placed

elephant dugout: a shelter constructed of corrugated iron sheeting (elephant iron)

Emma Gees: phonetic for MGs, machine gunners

enfilade: a volley of gunfire directed along a line from end to end

entrenching tool: a spade-like tool for digging hasty entrenchments

estaminet: an establishment found in villages and minor towns for eating, drinking and entertainment

FA: Fanny Adams (sweet) nothing (euphemism for an obscenity)

fatigues: labour of a non-military kind done by soldiers

firestep: a step in the base of a trench to enable occupants to fire over the parapet

fish-tail: German trench mortar shell

five-nine: German 5.9-inch artillery shell

flank: the right or left side of a body of people

Fred Karno: a music hall comedian

Fritz: slang for a German

Froggie: slang for a French person

funkhole: dugout or shelter for one or two men, usually in the front wall of a trench

gallery: a horizontal underground passage, especially in a mine

garrison: a body of troops stationed in a fortified place, originally to guard it

gaspers: cheap cigarettes

go west: to be killed

green envelope: the one uncensored letter that soldiers were allowed to send in a month

GS waggon: General Service waggon: a four-wheeled vehicle driven by an Army Service Corps driver, carrying general supplies

ha'porth: halfpenny worth (what you could buy for ½ d.)

HE: high explosive

hors de combat: out of action, out of the fight (French)

howitzer: large calibre artillery used for slow methodical destruction of fixed positions

HQ: headquarters

IBDs: infantry base depots: holding camps within easy distance of Channel ports

Jack Johnson: a heavy German artillery shell and the black smoke that ensued; from a popular African-American world heavyweight boxing champion

Jerry: slang for a German

jerry-built: built in a makeshift and insubstantial manner

jildy: quick (from Hindi)

jippo: watery juice or gravy, especially of bacon

Jock: slang for a Scotsman

John Bull: personification of the English/British character

KBE: Knight Commander of the Most Excellent Order of the British Empire

KCB: Knight Commander of the Order of the Bath

KCMG: Knight Commander of the Most Distinguished Order of St Michael and St George

KIA: killed in action

kip: sleep

Kitchener's Army: men recruited as a result of Lord Kitchener's appeal for volunteers

kowtow: to act in an excessively subservient manner

Koylies: men of the King's Own Yorkshire Light Infantry

lance-jack: lance-corporal, a junior NCO (one chevron); until 1961 an appointment, not a rank

landowner: a fatal injury

leadswinging: feigning illness or injury to avoid working

Lewis gun: a light machine gun

limber: a two-wheeled cart designed to support the trail of an artillery piece

Maconochie: tinned vegetable stew ration, named after the manufacturer

Magazine: a fortified place where large quantities of ammunition are stored for later distribution. In Ypres the town Magazine was used as a billet along with the Asylum and the Prison

malaga: sweet fortified wine

MC: Military Cross, awarded to officers for bravery

mentioned in dispatches: recommended for bravery or for outstanding work/s in an official report written by a superior officer and sent to high command

MG: machine gun

MID: mentioned in dispatches

Mills bomb: British No. 5 grenade

minenwerfer, Minnies: German trench mortar (from German)

MM: military medal

MO: medical officer

mon-gee: food (from French *manger*)

my eye and Peggy Martin: nonsense

nappoo: gone, finished, killed (from the French *il n'y a plus*)

nast: something repulsive

NCO: non-commissioned officer

No. 1 Field Punishment: British Army punishment for minor offences: soldier attached to a fixed object for up to two hours a day

nobbuts: nothings (Lancashire dialect)

No Man's Land: ground between two opposing front line trenches

nose-cap: part of a shell that unscrews and contains the device and scale for setting the time fuse

numerals: metal numbered badges

OC: Officer Commanding: commander of a company or platoon

Old Contemptibles: members of the BEF who took part in the retreat from Mons in 1914 (from the Kaiser's remark, 'That contemptible little army')

old soldier: (to play the) to shirk a duty

old stager: a person with experience
old sweat: an experienced soldier
on the wire: missing or killed in action
orderly: an officer's soldier-servant
Oros ('orrors): brand of cigarettes
ORs: Other Ranks

packet: (to cop a) to be wounded, often fatally
pan: magazine holding the ammunition of a Lewis gun
parados: a mound along the back of a trench
parapet: an earth defence on the top part of a front trench that faces the enemy
PBI: Poor Bloody Infantry
peg: (on the) having had one's name and number taken and reported to the CO as charged with some trivial military offence
PH gas helmet: a helmet gas mask (protected by phenate hexamine)
phosgene: a colourless poison gas
piling-swivel: bracket near the nose of a rifle, facilitating the making of a 'pile' of rifles to lean against each other
pill-box: reinforced concrete machine-gun post
pineapple: Mills bomb; also a type of German trench mortar shell
pineapple gas: chlorine gas, with a distinctive smell of pineapple mixed with pepper
pioneers: unskilled men, mainly used for digging, road building, etc. (but fought at times)
pip: shoulder insignia indicating the rank of certain officers
pip-squeak: small calibre shell (sometimes a gas shell) or rifle grenade
Pop: Poperinghe, a town in west Flanders
Pork and Beans: Portuguese
POW: prisoner of war
provost-marshal: a senior officer in the military police
provost-sergeant: an NCO in charge of the maintenance of good order and military discipline
pukka: genuine (from Hindi)
pulling through: a method of cleaning a rifle barrel
puttee: a long strip of cloth covering the lower leg from ankle to knee (from Hindustani)

quartermaster: an officer in a battalion or regiment responsible for supply

RAF: Royal Air Force (amalgamation of the Royal Flying Corps and Royal Naval Air Service in 1918). This is used in the text, but in 1916/17 it was still in fact the RFC, Royal Flying Corps

RAMC: Royal Army Medical Corps (known by the men as Rob All My Comrades)

ramparts: defensive wall of a castle or walled city with a broad top used as a walkway

RE: Royal Engineer

Red Cap: military policeman

Red Hussars: brand of cigarettes

Red Lamp: brothel

red letter day: a day that is pleasantly memorable

revetment: a barricade to provide shelter (as against strafing), or timber strutting to stop a trench wall collapsing

RFA: Royal Field Artillery

ROD: Railway Operating Division

RSM: regimental sergeant major

RTO: regimental training officer

runner: a soldier who carries messages by hand

SA: Salvation Army

salient: a battlefield feature that projects into enemy territory

sally: an outburst of fancy or wit

Sam Browne: a wide leather officer's belt with right shoulder strap

San Fairy Ann: it doesn't matter (from the French *ça ne fait rien*)

sap: a trench in no man's land connected at 90° to the fire trench

sap-head: a listening post in a sap

sapper: a private soldier who performs engineering duties

sausage: a barrage balloon

SB: stretcher-bearer

Schuler galleries: a series of trenches

scout: surveillance aircraft

scrimmage: a confused struggle or fight

Sedan: surrender (as the French Army did in 1870 at Sedan)

shrapnel: metal splinter from a shell (named after Gen. Henry Shrapnel who invented the shell)

skedaddled: departed quickly

SM: sergeant major

Soldiers' Friend: a brand of metal polish

SOS: distress signal, usually signalled by rockets to bring down supporting artillery fire on the enemy at a certain point

spiked: disabled

spout: rifle breech

square-head: a late nineteenth-century slur used against immigrants of Germanic and Scandinavian origin

square-pushing: seeking friendly female company

stager: see **old stager**

stand-down: order given in the trenches at dawn to let men know their night watch is over

stand-to: state of alert in the trenches, particularly at dawn or dusk

Stokes bomb/mortar: British trench mortar (invented by Sir William Stokes)

strafe: to attack repeatedly with machine gun fire, often from an aircraft (from the German *strafen*, to punish)

subaltern: an officer below the rank of captain

supports: trenches that held the back-up forces that could help repel an enemy attack or support a friendly attack

tater-masher: German stick grenade

Taube: a German aircraft

Terrier: a member of the Territorial Force (the Army Reserve, in operation from 1908)

TMB: trench mortar battery

traverse: an irregular adaption of a trench to reduce casualties

Trumpeters: brand of cigarettes

twitted: twiddled, tweaked

Very light: a flare or coloured light used for signalling at night, fired from a Very gun

W: wounded

Waac: Women's Army Auxiliary Corps

Waggers: signallers

wallah: person in charge of a particular object, duty or task (from Hindustani)

webbing: strong woven material used for belts, carrying straps, etc.

white smocks: camouflage uniform for snow

whizzbang: a small-calibre high-velocity shell